THE STEPNEY ALLIANCE

Carol Hellier

The Stepney Alliance - Text copyright © Carol Hellier 2024

All Rights Reserved

The Stepney Alliance is a work of fiction. All characters, places, and events are from the author's imagination. Any resemblance to persons, living or dead, events or places is purely coincidental.

The author respectfully recognises the use of any and all trademarks.

With the exception of quotes used in reviews, this book may not be reproduced or used in whole or in part by any means existing without written permission from the author.

Warning: The unauthorised reproduction or distribution of this copyrighted work is illegal. No part of this book may be scanned, uploaded, or distributed via the Internet or any other means, electronic or print, without the author's written permission.

DEDICATION

To my children and grandchildren, love you all to the moon and back.

And to each and every single one of you who have bought or downloaded and read my books, a big thank you. I hope you enjoyed them.

The story has references to abuse and suicide, which seems to be increasingly common in this society. If you feel in need of help you can contact these organisations:

SAMARITANS HELP LINE: 116 123
CAMPAIGN AGAINST LIVING MISERABLY (CALM): 0800585858
PAPYRUS – PREVENTION OF YOUNG SUICIDE: 0800 068 41 41
SOS SILENCE OF SUICIDE: 0300 1020 505

Secrecy is the enemy of intimacy.

I trust in you; do not let me be put to shame, nor let my enemies
triumph over me.
Psalm 31:14-15

PROLOGUE

September 1976

The woman crept around the Artichoke public house, making sure no one was awake. There were no signs of life. She didn't expect there to be at three a.m. He would be asleep. She smiled and grasped the petrol can, undoing the lid quickly. A sudden noise came from behind. She froze, her pulse racing. She glanced around in the dark. It had come from the bushes. She held her breath. A cat jumped out, stared at her, then ran off into the distance.

Releasing her breath, she carried on with her task. The liquid splashed against the walls. The fumes stung her eyes. Should she have brought more? It was too late now. Once she had emptied the can she stood back. Her hands trembled as she fumbled for the matches. Taking one, she stood ready to strike.

"All debts have to be paid," she whispered.

The match sparked to life, and she dropped it at the door. The heat hit her immediately. Turning, she ran back into the shadows while the flames licked at the walls.

CHAPTER 1

September 1976

Millie sat watching Finn as he lay in the hospital bed, her eyes sore from the continual crying. The smell from the fire hung in the air, a bleak reminder of the inferno he had escaped. He looked older than his fifty years and not the larger-than-life Irishman she had grown to love. Her thoughts returned to the fire. It didn't make sense. She wiped at her eyes. She needed to stay strong.

The door opened, and Paul entered the room, his face showing how weary he was. His eyes creased with worry.

"Mil, let me take you home, it's six a.m., babe. You'll be no good to Finn if you don't take care of yourself." Paul held out his hand to her.

Ignoring it, she returned her gaze to Finn.

"I don't want to leave him," she replied softly.

"I know, babe, but the nurse said he's stable... He'll need you when he wakes up, come on."

Millie took Paul's hand and allowed him to pull her up. She then leant over Finn and placed a kiss on his cheek. "You just get better. I need you." She then turned and left the room.

Paul's arm wrapped around her shoulders, he guided her along the corridor. A simple task, but her steps were clumsy. Her mind on Finn and the fire. The smell of disinfectant replaced the odour of smoke. She didn't know which was worse. Millie hated hospitals for that very reason.

"Do you think it was an accident, Paul?" she asked. It didn't make any sense; Finn was so safety-conscious when it came to locking up the pub. The fire was always covered securely with a guard. It even clipped onto the wall so it couldn't fall.

"I dunno, Mil, let's wait and see what the fire investigators say first before jumping to conclusions," he replied, hugging her tighter.

"I want to go and see it." She pulled back. "Now."

"What good is that gonna do? You're only gonna be more upset, babe. I don't want you seeing it. Plus it's early hours of the morning and pitch-black." Paul rubbed his face. "At least get some sleep first."

He sounded tired.

She knew she was being unreasonable, but the fire just didn't sit right with her. "Please, Paul. I need to see it."

"Fine." He sighed. "A quick stop then home to bed."

***

Millie gasped as she took in the fire damage. The walls were charcoaled, the door completely gone. The balcony over the main door had collapsed. She walked towards the building, stopping when Paul grabbed her arm.

"Don't go any closer, it doesn't appear safe," he warned.

"But we might miss something important," she begged. "Just a little bit closer, please."

"Mil, they put the tape round for a reason… For fuck's sake, don't look at me like that." He huffed. "You stay here, and do not follow me. Understand?"

She gave a short, curt nod. Her gaze followed him. He ducked under the tape that had cordoned off the pub.

"What can you see?" she called.

"Shh, we shouldn't be here," Paul replied.

"Sorry," she whispered back.

Instead of asking more questions, she switched her attention to the road. Everything was just the same as the last time she had been here. Only a couple of days ago, but now it all felt wrong. Finn was fighting for his life while everyone was tucked up in bed, sleeping soundly. Millie's lip quivered. She swallowed down the sob building in her throat. She turned to the flat opposite. That was where Rosie, her best friend, lived with her long-term boyfriend, Bobby. Was she asleep?

"Mil?" Paul placed his hand on her arm and pulled her around to face him. "I knew this would be too much for you. Come on, let's get you home."

"No. I want to know if you found anything," Millie said defiantly.

"Do you always have to be so stubborn?" He paused. "Look, I can't be one hundred percent sure, but—"

"I knew it," she cut in.

"Can you let me finish… I can't be one hundred percent sure, but there's definitely a faint smell of petrol at the front of the pub." He glanced up as rain fell. "Come on, let's get in the motor before we get soaked."

"So in your opinion was this arson?" she pressed. "I need to know."

"I'm not an expert, but it seems like the fire started at the door. The damage is mainly smoke inside. So in my opinion… yes, it's arson," he confirmed. "I'll phone the fire station later to see what's going on."

***

Paul threw his keys onto the telephone table after he closed the front door. He followed Millie to the lounge and towards the bar. He loved his home, felt safe here in the luxurious comfort. It had always been his dream to own a house like this. It was large, a nice area, secluded and detached. There were no prying eyes here, he could relax when that front door closed. He glanced at Millie. She was holding the brandy bottle. Paul collected two glasses. All this was done in silence, the same as the car journey home from the pub. He didn't know what to say. He didn't know how to make this better for her. It left a knot in the pit of his stomach.

After Millie had poured the drinks, they both stared at each other before downing the contents of their glasses.

"I needed that," she said, walking towards the sofa. She sat back and closed her eyes. She looked exhausted. "You know, I thought I had worked everything out... I was certain it was Jamie and Ronnie."

Paul refilled both glasses and then sat next to her. "Here, drink this." He sipped his brandy and then sighed. "You did work it out, Mil." He rubbed the back of his neck before continuing. "Ron would never work with an equal, so whoever has set fire to the Artichoke is an independent player."

"You don't think this is connected then?" Millie replied. "Because if it's not, the timing is pretty suss. It's been day's since Ronnie's death."

Paul shook his head. "No, I don't, but you're right, the timing is suspect. Listen, we should get some sleep; things may seem clearer after." He glanced at his watch. It was nearly seven-thirty a.m.

"You think I'm going to sleep after what's happened... Every time I close my eyes, all I see is Finn lying in that hospital bed with those machines beeping." Millie's voice quivered. "He will be okay, Paul, won't he?"

"Finn's a fighter, sweetheart. The doc said he's stable. We can go and see him later, after you've had some sleep." He stood over her while she downed the rest of her drink and then reached out for her hand, grateful when she took it.

Pulling her up into his arms, he held her tightly. He wasn't sure if it was an attempt to comfort her or himself. "Come on, Mrs Kelly, let's get you up to bed."

CHAPTER 2

Millie woke to the sound of rain pelting against the window. It was the end of September, and the heatwave that had remained all summer now seemed a distant memory. The standpipes had been taken down, and according to the weathermen, the reservoirs were filling nicely. She checked the bedside clock; it was already twelve-thirty p.m.

"Paul." Millie turned and glanced at the empty space next to her. She threw the cover back and reached for her dressing gown. She cursed under her breath while she traipsed down the stairs and into the kitchen.

Paul sat at the breakfast table staring into his cup of tea.

Millie could almost see the cogs of his brain turning. "You should have woken me," she snapped as she walked past him to the teapot.

"You needed your sleep, Mil." He stood and made his way to her. "Sit down, I'll pour your tea."

His face was etched with worry, like he had all the problems of the world on his shoulders.

Millie's slumped. "I'm sorry."

"You have nothing to be sorry for, well, other than not giving me a good morning kiss." Paul grinned.

Millie placed her arms around his neck and kissed him softly. "Is that better?" she asked when she pulled back.

"Hmm, could have been longer, but it's a start," Paul replied.

She smiled as she walked back to the table, that smile suddenly dropping when the image of Finn flashed through her mind. "Where do we even start with this, Paul? How do we find the person responsible?"

He placed the cup of tea down in front of Millie and sat next to her. "First we go and see Finn and then we start at the beginning and map it all out… There's always clues, Mil, we just need to find them."

"Do you think it's got something to do with the drugs?" she asked, thinking back to the kidnapping. She had set fire to all the boxes of drugs before she had escaped her kidnappers.

"No, babe, I don't. This seems more…personal." He swallowed the last of his tea and stood. "I need to phone the boys."

Millie waited for him to leave the kitchen then turned her thoughts back to his words. 'Personal'

But wouldn't that mean it was aimed at Finn?

She jumped when a crash came from the end of the garden. She rushed to the window, peered out, then sighed loudly. That was another problem to sort out, Duke and Connie Lee, her newly found parents. Millie had only known them a few months and found it difficult to forgive them. She knew deep down it wasn't their fault she had grown up in a children's home. It was Connie's mother who had taken Millie away after she had been born and abandoned her on the steps of the children's home. Connie was only a child herself. She'd been taken to her aunt's until after the birth.

Millie made a mental note to try harder. Even if Paul didn't like Romanies, she was, in fact, half Romani and half gorger. He would have to accept Duke and end the ridiculous feud once and for all.

She turned at Paul's approaching footsteps.

"Right, I'm meeting the boys later. I'll get a plan together and then we can get to the bottom of this." He stood next to Millie and gazed out over the garden. "What were you looking at?"

"I heard a crash coming from Duke's. Seems like they have company." Millie held her breath.

Paul's scar rose and went a deep red. It always did that when he got angry.

"Fucking pikeys. They need to go, Mil." Paul rubbed his scar as he continued to glare out of the window. "Is that another fucking caravan?"

Before Millie could answer, Paul was already making his way down the garden. A chrome-and-white trailer was being wheeled into place.

"Paul!" Millie yelled while running after him, then followed him over the fence. She stopped dead when she was greeted by her father, an elderly man and woman.

Millie knew straight away who they were. Her dad, Duke, was the image of his father, Nelson Lee. They both had dark-brown wavy hair, although Nelson's was greying. Their eyes were the same shape and colour, brown. Duke did, however, have his mother, Darkie's, full lips, and when she smiled, Millie could see the resemblance.

"Is this her, Duke?" his mother, Darkie Lee, said to her son.

"Here we go again. What's the problem this time?" Duke asked Paul, ignoring his mother.

"The problem is I've got a fucking pikey camp at the bottom of my garden," Paul snapped and balled his fists.

Darkie Lee grabbed her chest. She obviously wasn't a fighting woman. "Dordi," she exclaimed.

"What's that mean?" Millie asked Connie.

"It means 'oh dear' in Romani. You'd better stand back," Connie warned Millie.

Duke squared up to Paul and raised his fists. "Let's finish this once and for all then."

Millie ran between both of them, placing a hand on each man's chest. It was a feeble attempt to keep them apart. "*Stop!*" she shouted with more authority than she felt.

All eyes were on her, and in a moment of embarrassment, Millie remembered she was wearing a dressing gown with nothing on underneath. The belt slowly loosened, and the dressing gown slid open. Cold air whistled inside the robe. Millie grabbed the belt and wrapped it tightly around herself before she exposed herself further to her new family. She tied it in a double knot for good measure, her face heating, probably colouring up like a cherry.

"Don't you think you should go and get some clothes on?" Paul muttered.

"Well, that's one thing we agree on," Duke added.

She glared at both men. "I wouldn't have to be out here if you two could behave." Millie shook her head. "I can't deal with this right now. Finn needs me. I'm going to get dressed."

A firm hand rested on her shoulder before she could storm off.

"Your grandparents wanted to say hello, Millie, can you at least spare a few minutes?" Duke asked.

"Look, I don't mean to be rude, but I've got more pressing matters to deal with. This will have to wait. I'm sorry." She shrugged Duke's hand off and made her way towards the fence with Paul following.

"Wait," Duke called, jogging after them.

"I said not now, Duke!" Millie said firmly.

"What's going on?" Worry tinged Duke's voice. "I know I don't know you that well, but I can tell something's wrong."

Millie stopped and turned to face him. "Finn's in hospital fighting for his life. Now, I know your parents are important to you, just like Finn's important to me, but right now he needs me. He is like a father to me, Duke, I'm sure you understand that." She could see the hurt in Duke's eyes, but she didn't care. She was the one left to grow up in a children's home, and Finn had been the first person to show her any kindness.

"You know if I could change things, I would, Millie. You're more important to me than you will ever know." Duke sighed. "If you're hurting then I'm hurting, so what can I do to help?"

Paul grabbed Millie's hand and pulled her towards the fence. "You heard her, this is a family matter."

Once they had reached the fence, Paul scooped Millie up and lifted her over. Millie stole a quick glimpse at Duke before she headed in. His shoulders were slumped, and he turned to walk away. She had caused that.

***

Millie climbed into Paul's motor and fastened her seat belt while he did the same. "You can't keep arguing with Duke," she said, side-eyeing Paul. "I know how you feel about Romanis, but he is our neighbour, and let's not forget he is also my dad." She sighed.

"So you're happy with them living at the end of our garden?" Paul huffed. "Cos not so long ago it was you who wanted to move to get away from them, and by the way, they're gypsies."

"I don't know how I feel…it's confusing. All my life I had wished for a mum and dad. I even wished for them at Christmas and prayed for them in Sunday school. But now…"

"But now?" Paul pressed. At least he had the good grace to sound interested.

"But now it's complicated… I feel resentment towards them and my brothers. They had a normal life with parents who loved them while I grew up in a children's home." Millie shifted her gaze to the window. "Can we concentrate on Finn, he's all that matters at the moment."

"Of course, babe." Paul started the motor and eased away. "I think you should talk to Rosie. You know how nosey she is, she may have seen something out of place. Maybe a new face in the pub."

"Good idea, I'll arrange to meet her later while you're meeting the boys." A sudden surge of guilt swept through her. She hadn't seen much of Rosie lately and wondered if she was okay. Some friend she had turned out to be, and some daughter, too.

The houses flashed past the window with Millie barely noticing them. How could she please everyone? She was one person with a shedload of problems. How did other people manage? Face one problem at a time, she reasoned.

"Mil… Mil… Millie," Paul called, his voice growing louder.

"What? Oh, we're here." She unclipped her seat belt and grabbed the door handle.

"Whoa, not so fast." He reached for her cheek and pulled her around to face him.

His lips touched hers, and she closed her eyes, until he drew back.

"That was nice," she said.

"It was… Whatever happens, babe, we'll get through it together, okay?" he reassured her.

Millie smiled and reached up to stroke his cheek. "Does that include Duke?"

"To keep you happy, then yes," he confirmed with a small nod. "Although that's gonna be a tough one."

Millie returned his kiss. "I love you, Paul."

"I love you, too, now let's go and see how Finn is." He opened her door and helped her out.

He was a gentleman. Old school. He would always make her walk on the inside of the path. Hold her hand whenever they went out. Open doors and pull her chair out for her. She was lucky to have him. She led the way into the hospital and up to Finn's room.

Paul opened the door and waited for her to enter before he followed.

She sat next to Finn and held his hand. She thought some colour had returned to his cheeks but then decided it was wishful thinking.

"Look, there's a nurse outside. I'll go and see what I can find out." Paul stood and left the room without waiting for a reply.

Her gaze was fixed on Finn, so his voice barely resonated with her. Her mind was full of everything that had happened. The whole complete mess. Her parents, the caravans turning up on Duke's land. The Artichoke fire, Finn. Every thought and emotion crowded her mind, all fighting for dominance. She didn't think life would be this hard. After defeating Ronnie Taylor and finding her parents, Millie thought life would be better, but no. Here she sat, next to Finn's hospital bed, holding his hand and wishing he'd get up. Get up and tell her to get a grip, just like he always did when times were tough. The way he'd protected her when she'd first worked for him. He watched out for her, even when Paul was suspicious because of her. Looking back now, life was easier then. She had no one to worry about, except for herself. Now she had Paul and a new family.

Millie's mind flipped to Duke, the hurt on his face when she had told him Finn was like a dad to her. She would never admit it out loud, but it gave her a small sense of satisfaction. Seeing the hurt made her feel better. What type of person did that make her? She sighed. She knew deep down she needed to try harder; after all, how could she expect Paul to call a truce when she still felt bitter towards them?

Duke and Connie had been so kind to her. The love shone from Connie's eyes every time she looked at Millie. It was a bit like the warmth from a fire on a cold winter's day, it felt strangely comforting. She had to make more of an effort. At the very least she should get to know them and her two brothers.

Millie smiled vacantly. Despite her resentment towards them, she did like the boys. They were funny and protective, Aron more so than Jess.

She was pulled from her thoughts when Finn's hand moved. She peered closer. The movement was slight, but it was there, nonetheless. It was like Finn was trying to squeeze her hand.

"Nurse!" Millie yelled. The next thing she knew, Paul and a nurse came rushing in. "He moved his hand." She smiled up at Paul. "Finn moved his hand," she repeated, her voice laden with hope.

CHAPTER 3

"Where is he?" Millie asked, tapping her foot. "She said she would be right back with him."

"He has other patients, Mil, he may be in the middle of something. I'm sure the doc won't be long," Paul reassured her.

Before she could reply, the doctor strolled in with the nurse right behind him.

"Mrs Kelly, Mr Kelly." He nodded swiftly. "Right, Finn, let's have a look at you and see what's going on." The doctor started doing his checks and produced a tiny torch which he shone in each of Finn's eyes, lifting his eyelids.

Millie was immediately transported back to when she had been in hospital after the car crash that had killed Levi, her first husband. She had gone through the same checks.

Her body ached from head to toe. Even raising her head an inch from the pillow caused her to moan. Holding her left eye open, the doctor shone a tiny light into it and then did the same to the right one.

"Your reflex actions are good. Do you remember what happened to you?"

"I already told you, we were in the pub." Millie turned her head and stared at the window, the sky shadowy and stormy. "How long have I been here?"

"Three days, Millie."

Three days? Where is Levi?

Millie blinked away the flashback. It was like she was there once again, lying in the hospital bed. That hadn't been even a year ago. So much had happened since that dark time. She had moved in with Rosie, landed a job and eventually a home with Finn. Met Paul Kelly and murdered her ex-father-in-law. Millie went pale at the thought. It was Finn and Paul who had helped her through those pitch-black days, and of course, her best friend, Rosie.

The doctor coughed, bringing Millie out of her thoughts.

"Finn's reflexes are good, and he's making great progress, however, I'm not sure if it was a muscle spasm that you felt or an actual hand movement. It's difficult to tell, you see."

Millie's heart dropped. "No. He moved his hand."

The doctor then continued. "Give Finn another twenty-four to forty-eight hours and I'm certain he will have his eyes open, Mrs Kelly."

"Will he make a full recovery, Doc?" Paul asked.

"I'm expecting him to. You said he was reasonably fit before the fire. I can't tell if there will be any long-term effects from the smoke inhalation, I will know more when Finn retains full consciousness." With that, the doctor bid them farewell and left the room.

***

Duke drove to the Artichoke, surprised when he spotted the fire damage. He jumped out of his pickup truck and walked towards the side of the pub and the main entrance.

The fire had destroyed the entrance and bar area, however, the building looked pretty much intact. The smoke damage was evident from the upstairs windows where the glass had been blown out by the heat. Duke shook his head. Thank God Millie hadn't been in there. He knew the damage smoke could do; quite often it was the smoke that killed you long before the flames could.

He pulled out a cigarette from his packet and lit it. As he surveyed the pub, he thought of Finn lying in hospital. So Finn had managed to escape the fire, but how had the fire started? That was the main question. Could it be arson? Duke turned to walk away but stopped when he caught a young woman staring at him.

"All right, love, can I help you with something?" he called out.

The young woman shook her head and hurried away; she glanced back over her shoulder before disappearing from sight.

Duke continued to walk to his pickup. He flicked the cigarette away and climbed in. The smell of the fire had given him a thirst, along with the pissing rain. So his first stop would be the pub.

***

Duke gulped down half the pint straight off. He'd needed that more than he realised. He had laid off of the beer since his wife, Connie, had returned home. He didn't want to upset her or risk her leaving again. As it was, she still had the council house, for reasons unknown to him. They had spent the day she had returned home talking. Talking about the trauma she had gone through at the hands of her mother when she had taken Millie and told her she had died shortly after being born. Duke had realised in that instant what an arsehole he had been to her. Blaming her for Millie being brought up in a children's home because she had never told him she was pregnant. What could he have done if he had known? She'd thought she was dead. Connie had only buried the memory because it was too painful, which made sense.

Duke glanced up when one of his sons called.

"Dad, we've been looking all over for ya. What ya up to?" Aron asked as he eyed the pint.

Aron and Jess were Duke and Connie's twin boys, and at their ages of sixteen, Duke couldn't be prouder of them.

"What does it look like, you pair of dinlows?" Duke replied, a little annoyed his peace had been broken. "Did ya mother send ya?"

"No…we just wondered what you was doing." Jess grinned. "Can we have a pint?"

"No, I've got stuff to do." Duke drained his pint and stood. "Yous get off home, I'll be back in a while."

"Where are ya going, Dad, can't we come?" Jess asked.

He noticed the hopeful tone to his voice. He knew both boys loved working with him, and normally he loved having them, but he needed a clear head, without a hundred and one questions they would ask.

"Not today, I need to go see your sister, and don't tell ya mother, I'll talk to her when I get home." Duke snatched up his keys and left the pub.

***

Millie sat in the Wimpy bar, in Stepney High Street, waiting for Rosie. Despite the pain in the pit of her stomach, worrying for Finn, she was still looking forward to seeing her. She glanced up at the ping of the door. The door opened, and in she bounced, her black dreadlocks dancing on her shoulders with each step she took. She had a healthy glow to her Caribbean complexion. Her big brown eyes creased when she smiled.

"Hey, stranger," Rosie called out and made her way closer.

Millie stood and embraced her in a tight hug. "Hey yourself, and it hasn't been that long. How are you?"

"I'm fine. I'm guessing you're here about the fire," Rosie replied. Her smile fell.

"Firstly, I wanted to see you, but yes, the fire, too. So how have you been? Bobby okay?" she asked while sitting back in her seat.

"I'm all good. Bobby's okay, too, although he seems to be working all the time. God knows what he's spending all the extra money on cos we don't seem any richer."

"Maybe he's saving up for something… An engagement ring?" Millie grinned.

"I'm not getting my hopes up, however, fingers crossed." Rosie giggled.

"I'm glad you're both okay… With regards the fire, I need to know if you saw anything?" Millie replied with a little hope.

"Can you believe I slept through the whole thing? Poor Finn, how's he doing?"

"He looks terrible. Lying in that hospital bed, helpless. We think the fire was started deliberately. So you saw nothing at all?" Millie pressed. "Come on, Rosie, we both know you're nosey."

"No...but..." She trailed off.

"But what? Even if you think it's nothing, anything at all, please tell me," Millie pleaded.

"It is gonna sound silly." Rosie leant forward. "There was a car parked outside the pub, two nights on the trot, and since the fire I haven't seen it." She grinned. "And I'm not nosey."

"Can you describe the car? Colour, make? Did you see who was driving? Anything else you can think of. It's really important." Millie sat forward and leant on the table with her elbows.

"It was red. Mil, you know I'm not into cars... I think a man was driving, although it could have been a woman. He had long hair he looked butch. Oh, he had a big nose. There was someone in the passenger seat, but I couldn't see them, just their arms moving about. Is that helpful?" She shrugged. "I'm not very good at this kinda stuff."

"It's a start, Rosie, and definitely worth investigating. Do me a favour, though, if you see it again, can you let me know and try to get the number plate?" Millie asked.

Rosie puffed out her chest and smiled. "Private Eye Rosie reporting for duty. Now can we order? I'm starving."

CHAPTER 4

"So what do you think?" Millie asked Paul, her voice dripping with hope.

"Red car, man or woman, long hair, big nose," He repeated.

She nodded eagerly. "Yes."

"Well, it's a start, babe, but don't get your hopes up… I've got a couple of the boys keeping watch at the hospital and couple watching the pub. I'll let them know about the red car so they can keep an eye out," He replied.

"And the passenger, don't forget about that," She reminded him. "Hang on, why are you having Finn watched? Do you think he's in danger?"

Paul took hold of Millie and pulled her into his arms. "It's just a precaution, that's all." Before he could say anything else, there was a loud knock from the front door. "Now what!" He marched into the hall. "What the fuck do you want?"

"I need to see Millie," Duke answered. He was annoyed.

"She's busy." He went to shut the door, but Duke stuck his foot in, which angered Paul. "I'd move that if I were you or you'll end up losing it." Footsteps caught Paul's ear, and he turned.

Millie approached.

"What on earth is going on now?" she asked.

"Millie, I need to talk to you," Duke replied.

"And I told you she's busy," Paul snarled.

"Okay, just stop, both of you, please just stop." She walked up to Duke with her back to Paul. "What do you need to talk about, Duke?"

"Let's start with the Artichoke." Duke glanced between them both. Was he checking for a reaction?

"You'd better come in then." Millie disappeared in to the kitchen.

Paul closed the door and followed Duke in. First Millie made three cups of tea while he and Duke glared at each other across the table. She placed a cup down for each of them and then took a seat herself. Paul rubbed his scar. He needed to stay calm for Millie's sake.

"Okay, start talking," Paul ordered.

Duke took a sip of his tea before he switched his attention to Millie. Paul huffed. Typical fucking pikey.

"I went to the Artichoke this morning, it's burnt out."

Paul clapped slowly. "Well done, Sherlock."

"Paul!" Millie snapped. "That's not helping. Carry on, Duke."

"Looks like arson to me, and Finn's in hospital, so I'm guessing you're going after the culprit." Duke glanced between them both. "Don't you think you can trust me, Millie? Haven't I proved myself, or does murder not qualify?"

Paul focused on Millie's face; she was worried. Duke shouldn't be bringing that up. "That's in the past, we don't need to go over old ground. I will say, though, I'm grateful that you helped Millie, I don't know what I would have done if anything had happened to her." He grabbed her hand and squeezed it. "But this is a family matter."

"I agree with Paul, so what do you want, Duke?" She added.

"I am family and want to help my daughter. To make sure you're safe and to get to know you in the process. Also Connie's making a family dinner tonight, you know, as my parents, your grandparents, are here. I'd like you both to come." Duke was met by silence, so he continued. "They want to meet you, Millie... We've all missed out on twenty-four years of your life just like you've missed out on ours."

"Do you think the timing's right for a family reunion?" Millie said briskly.

"I think it's the perfect time. You need something else to focus on, too. If you get so wrapped up in the fire and Finn, you may miss something." He looked at Paul. "Don't you agree?"

Paul stared at his tea for a moment while he thought. "You'll have to meet them sooner or later, Mil, it may as well be sooner." Then he shifted his attention to Duke. "If we agree to dinner then I want your word that no more poxy caravans are going to turn up."

"You have my word. So that's settled, dinner will be about six. Now that's taken care of, what do you know about the fire?" Duke asked.

"Not much," Paul said, not wanting to share the information. He caught Millie frowning at him.

"There was a red car parked outside the pub for two nights. Since the fire, it hasn't been seen. We think the driver was a man, although he had long hair and apparently a big nose," she informed him.

"Could've been a punter. There'd be no reason for him to go there now if the pub's closed," Duke reasoned.

"No. This car has only been seen two nights before the fire. It's too much of a coincidence, and even if it turns out to be unrelated, we still need to check it out," Millie said firmly. "It's the only lead we've got."

Duke nodded. "What was the make?"

"We don't know. It was my friend, Rosie, who saw it. She lives opposite the pub... She also said there was someone in the passenger seat, but she couldn't see them properly," Millie explained.

"When I was at the pub earlier, I spotted a young woman watching me, about your age, quite tall for a woman, and she was dressed like one of those hippie types with long auburn-ginger hair... She was just staring at me while I studied the pub. When I asked her if I could help her, she shook her head and walked away. I say walk, it was more of a slow run. I didn't think much of it at the time, other than it was weird. If the driver had long hair, could it have been her?" Duke paused. "You know they say arsonists often return to the scene of the crime, or what if she was the passenger?"

"There's a lot of what-ifs and maybes." Paul looked over to Millie; hope shone in her eyes. "But it's definitely a start, and yeah, you're right, they do return to the scene of the crime, and the fact you felt something off with her, then you could well be right. I'll phone the boys, let them know what you saw. They can have a dig around."

"What about checking out hotels or bed and breakfasts? They must be staying somewhere," Millie added.

"Good idea, babe." Paul's chest swelled; she wasn't just a pretty face. "Right, I need to get on, I've another matter to deal with." He stood and motioned for Duke to leave.

"Right then, I'll see you both about six," Duke reminded them as he stood. He turned his attention to Millie. "Connie's gonna be over the moon."

Millie smiled. "I'm looking forward to it to."

Was she?

"I'll show you out," she said.

Paul listened to the front door close before calling Millie back into the kitchen.

"Now what?" She eyed him suspiciously. "What's going on?"

Paul cleared his throat. He knew what he was about to say would go down like a lead balloon. "It's Ronnie's funeral in a couple of days' time." He stopped dead when she cut in.

"You're not thinking of going, are you?" she asked.

"We both are," he said.

"I'm not, Paul... Do you even remember what he did or tried to do? There's no way I'm going other than to dance on his grave."

"Mil, calm down," He pleaded, placing his hands on her shoulders.

"Calm. I am calm, Paul Kelly. This is calm where that man's concerned." She shrugged his hands off and flopped onto the sofa.

He knew this was how she would react, not that he blamed her, but she needed to see the bigger picture.

"Just listen to me, please," he said softly. He would have to explain.

"Fine. Go ahead," she huffed.

"Me and Ron were friends, Mil."

"Ha, well, that's a lie," she added.

"Mil, shut up and listen to me. Everyone thought we were friends, no one is aware of what happened. His death looks like a burglary gone wrong, so we are off the hook, but if we don't go to the funeral, people are gonna ask questions, and that could cause problems." He watched her as she nodded in agreement.

"I guess you're right, but it doesn't mean I have to like it." She sighed.

"That's not all. I'm going to get his will and change it." He knew that bit would worry her most.

Millie's eyes widened, and she gasped. "Why, Paul, the docks are yours now?"

"Because I want the scrapyard." He had thought long and hard about it since Ronnie's death, and it made perfect sense. Who else would Ron leave it to anyway? His wife? All she would do would be to sell it to the highest bidder, and Paul couldn't have that. He didn't like competition, and besides, it was the perfect payback for Ronnie's betrayal.

Millie broke through Paul's thoughts. "What if you get caught?"

"I won't, babe, trust me," he said with an air of certainty. "The solicitor who has the dock paperwork also has Ronnie's will."

"So what are you going to do, break in and alter it? Don't you think they will know?" She replied sharply.

"No, babe, I'm meeting the solicitor, and he is going to change it... It's gonna cost, but the scrapyard will more than make the money back in a year, easily."

"What about Ronnie's signature, Paul, and the witness signature, have you even thought about those?" She shook her head. "His wife will know."

"Tony's coming with me," he said.

"Oh, that's great, Tony, the man who beats people up for fun. What's he gonna do, threaten to chop the solicitor's head off!" Millie jumped up and paced the floor. "This will all end in tears, Paul Kelly."

He burst out laughing and then grabbed her. "Tony can forge any signature out there, that's why he's coming. Now stop worrying, it's all sorted."

"I don't like it, but okay. When is this gonna happen?" she asked.

He grinned. "Tonight."

CHAPTER 5

Connie sat staring at Millie with a stupid smile on her face. She was finding it awkward. What with the questions from Duke's parents, her grandparents, she found the whole situation quite uncomfortable.

"Would you like some more dinner, Millie?" Connie asked.

"No thanks, I'm full." She smiled.

She was finding this whole family reunion tough. Too many people crowding her, asking questions and being overly friendly. Her thoughts were still on Finn and finding the culprits who'd nearly taken his life. It was now nearly nine o'clock, and Millie hoped she would be able to slip away soon. She glanced at Paul who looked like he was also having a tough time.

"So, Millie," Darkie, Duke's mother, started. "What do you do with yourself most days?"

"Housework and shopping, the normal things women do," she said, hoping that would be an end to it.

"Millie's modest," Duke chipped in. "She also has businesses to attend to, her and Paul own a club," he added proudly.

"A club!" Darkie repeated. "Now that must take up a lot of your time."

"Yes, it does, along with the docks and the brothel." Millie nearly laughed when Darkie's eyes bulged, but at least that was the end of the conversation.

"Nicely done," Paul whispered as he sat next to her. "I'm gonna have to go soon, Mil, to sort that other business."

"You ain't leaving me here." She gave him a stern look.

"I wouldn't dream of it. I can see it's hard for you, but I've got to give it to Duke and Connie, they are trying, babe."

"Would you like another beer, Paul?" Duke walked towards him with his hand stretched out, holding a can.

"No, no thanks… We've got to make tracks soon, work calls," he added.

"That's a shame, the evening's flown by. Still, we can do it again sometime." Duke looked at Millie.

"You'll have to come to us next time," Paul said quickly. "Let Millie show you what a good cook she is."

"That will be nice," Connie said with a smile that lit up her whole face.

"Right then, best get going. Ready, Mil?" He asked and pulled her to her feet.

She turned to the group and smiled. "Thanks for dinner, it was lovely. And thanks for making us both welcome. It was nice meeting you, Darkie and Nelson. Hopefully see you both soon."

Paul's hand wrapped around hers, and she was grateful for the comfort it gave her. They walked the long way round to the house and slowly sauntered along the road. It was strange walking from Duke's piece of land that was nestled behind all the large houses. It really didn't fit the area. Was she being a snob? Maybe. But what did she have to be a snob about? You should never regret what you have or where you came from. Would she prefer it if they weren't her parents? Honestly? No. If it wasn't for everything going on, then maybe, just maybe, the transition would have been smoother.

"How do you feel now that's over?" Paul asked and unlocked the front door.

"Relieved... They are trying, though; I should be more grateful, I guess. I could have ended up with parents who didn't want me." Then how would she have felt?

"I'll always want you." Paul turned around to face her. "I shouldn't be long, Mil, but just in case, don't wait up."

She stepped into the doorway then waved to him. He started the motor. She had an uneasy feeling. Paul had never been greedy, and this, to her, felt like greed. After all, wasn't Ronnie's punishment death?

***

Millie sat looking at the clock. It was now coming up to midnight. She had been pacing the floor for the last half hour, wondering where he was. She stopped when a car pulled up and ran to the window. After spotting him, she rushed to the door and threw it open. "Where have you been? You've been ages."

"Had to make sure it was done properly, Mil, and then we found out his missus has a copy," he said wearily.

"So you wasted your time and money. I told you not to go through with it," she snapped.

"Calm down, babe, it's sorted." He sidestepped her and walked to the cupboard; he clearly needed a scotch. "Do you wanna brandy?"

"No, Paul, I want an explanation. What do you mean it's sorted?"

"We did two wills, one for the solicitor and the other for Ronnie's wife." He took a gulp of his scotch before continuing. "The solicitor is going to swap it at the reading."

"How do you know you can trust him?" she asked, reaching for a glass. "Second thoughts, I think I do need a drink."

"Because if he doesn't, Tony, you know, the one who likes to beat people up for fun, is going to kill him." Paul smirked. "Now stop worrying and come and give us a kiss."

***

Duke sat in his pickup truck, down the road a little from the Artichoke. The thunderstorm was making it difficult to see. He was fed up with the rain. All month it had pissed down. The drought of 1976 was well and truly over. The twenty-ninth of August, the rain had started. It would be a date to remember, where life had got back to normal for folk. Not that he had ever had a tap. Being a traveller, he had grown up collecting water in buckets and milk churns. He smiled; Connie was grateful, though. She finally had all the mod cons in the mobile and at long last she could use the washing machine he had bought her. No more going to the launderette. It was nice seeing the excitement on her pretty face. The grass had returned to the lush green colour just in time for autumn to set in. Everywhere had sprung to life, almost like springtime, but he suspected it would soon turn colder.

Duke put the windscreen wipers on to clear the rain. The thunderstorm was pretty spectacular. He had been sitting here since nine-thirty p.m. and it was now coming up to one a.m. He had kept his eyes firmly on the pub and surrounding area for the whole three and a half hours. Apart from when he needed a parny. Then he nipped out of the pickup and peed against the tyre. Waiting and watching. That's what he was doing. He was determined to prove himself to Millie, prove he would do whatever he could for her.

Connie thought he was mad. "Why would they turn up at night?" she had asked.

"If you are up to no good, that's the ideal time to turn up," he had replied.

If the red car or girl were to show up, he would catch them. Looking at his watch, he noticed it was one-ten a.m. He decided to head off home. Maybe Connie was right. As he pulled off down the street, he had the weirdest feeling of being watched.

CHAPTER 6

It had pissed down all morning. Millie still felt damp, despite standing under an umbrella. The service had gone off without any hiccups, thank fuck, and they were soon back at the house, toasting Ronnie's life. Well, she suspected most people were. Personally, she was toasting his death and she suspected Paul was, too.

"Mil, will you stop smiling at everyone, it's a fucking funeral, for Christ's sake." Paul glanced around, obviously to make sure no one could hear. "Remember what I said, it's just an act."

"Sorry, it's hard...I feel happy." She almost smiled again. "Whoops."

Paul rolled his eyes. "I'll deal with you later... Look out, here comes his wife." He held out his arms and embraced Ronnie's widow, much to Millie's disgust. "Rita, love, how are you holding up?"

"I still can't believe it…my Ron was so good to me…I…"

"I know, love," he acknowledged. "It will get better with time, and don't forget, if you need anything, you let me know."

"Thanks, Paul, you always were a good boy." Rita placed her hand on his cheek. "I know my Ron loved you like a son."

Millie looked down at the floor, her temper building. Did he feel sorry for her? The memory of what Ronnie had tried to do burned in her chest. "Excuse me." She made her way outside. The rain was still lashing down, and everywhere had turned into mini rivers, even the pavements. She didn't care, though, she wanted to get away from this place. No, she *needed* to get away from this place.

"You okay, Mil?" Paul asked as he joined her. "You're getting soaked."

"I want to go home," she said firmly.

"Give it another half hour, babe, then we can slip out. Come on, let's get back inside, before you catch pneumonia." He grabbed her by the hand and led her back into the lounge.

"Oh, there you are, Paul." Rita approached him. She looked Millie up and down and gave a short, sharp nod. "Millie."

"Rita, my husband and I will be going shortly. I have a terrible headache, that's why we were getting some fresh air," Millie told her. *Fucking old hag.*

Rita ignored Millie and focused on Paul. "You will drop by and see me, Paul; in fact, we have the reading of the will on Tuesday. Perhaps we could have a spot of lunch after," she pressed. "You are like family, after all."

Paul glanced at Millie before he replied. She made sure he could see her disapproval.

"I'll have to see what we've got on, Rita, work's manic at the moment."

"I'm sure Millie is more that capable of holding the reins for a couple of hours." Rita looked at Millie and smiled. "Aren't you, Millie."

"I'm more than capable of a lot of things, Rita… You ready, Paul?" She turned and walked out without waiting for an answer.

"Mil," he called, jogging to catch her up. "Wait."

She stopped and spun around. "She was coming on to you, or are you that thick you can't see it?"

"Don't be ridiculous, she's fifty, and you heard what she said, I'm like family," Paul answered.

"But you're not, though, are you... And can I remind you her husband was going to do you over. I wouldn't be surprised if she was in on it." She sighed and carried on walking to the car.

"So I won't see her anymore once the will's read, okay?" He unlocked the motor and opened the door for her.

Millie turned back to look at the house, and there was Rita, staring back at her. "I don't trust her."

"After Tuesday we won't have to see her again, babe. Now let's go and see Finn." He started the car and pulled away.

Surely he didn't trust her, not after everything Ron had done. They were a partnership, so it really wouldn't have surprised her if Rita knew what Ronnie had planned. She pushed Rita to the back of her mind, there'd be time for that later. Finn needed her full attention.

***

The disinfectant seemed stronger today. The smell caught in her throat. The ward sister sat at her desk as Millie approached.

"Hi, how's Finn been?"

"He's had a little soup, but he's still very drowsy. Try not to wear him out, young lady," the sister said sternly.

"I wouldn't dream of it." She smiled. Although the sister was a bit scary, she ran the ward with an iron fist, and the patients benefitted, and that was all Millie cared about.

"He's sleeping, Mil," Paul whispered. "Maybe we should come back tomorrow."

"I just want to sit with him for a bit, he might wake up," she said hopefully. "You can go. Why don't you pick me up in an hour?"

"Right, I'll go and check on the house, make sure everything's okay with Gladys and the girls. Then I'll be back." He pecked her on the forehead and then left.

Millie returned her attention to Finn. He was definitely looking better, and the sister said he had eaten, so that was a good sign.

"Shannon?" Finn mumbled.

"It's me, Millie," she replied softly, wondering who Shannon was.

"Where's she gone?" He turned his head to the door. "She was here. I saw her."

"There's no one here but me, Finn. Do you want me to get the nurse?" She reached for his hand and held it.

"No." He closed his eyes. "I saw her."

"Who's Shannon?" Millie asked, now curious. Was he hallucinating? "Finn?"

But he had drifted off again.

CHAPTER 7

Paul sat in the solicitor's office. He adjusted his tie pin and sat up straight. The room seemed smaller today, or was that because he felt under pressure? He couldn't wait to get this over with. Once the scrapyard belonged to him he would be happy. He nodded to Rita, and she came and sat next to him.

"Paul. Lovely to see you again." She placed her hand on his leg and gave it a little squeeze.

"Rita," he said uncomfortably. Millie was right, she was coming on to him.

"Okay, Mrs Taylor and Mr Kelly, I shall now begin." The solicitor cleared his throat and started reading the will.

Paul watched the man's face as he read out all of Ronnie Taylor's assets. Not surprisingly, Rita was left the house, all of the bank accounts, and the holiday home in Mallorca. Paul kept his face neutral throughout the reading. At last the solicitor read that the scrapyard was to be left to him. Paul looked at Rita who stared right back at him. She did seem a little surprised, but she smiled and once again squeezed his leg.

Once the reading was over and all the paperwork had been signed, Paul made a hasty retreat to his motor. He was about to open the door when Rita's voice came from behind him.

"I think we need to talk, Paul," she said.

Was she demanding?

"I'm in a hurry, Rita, can we catch up later in the week?" He turned to face her.

"I don't think this can wait, Paul. I'd like to know how you did it?" Rita now stood in front of him with her hands on her hips.

"What are you talking about?" he asked, trying to hide the annoyance in his voice.

"Don't play dumb with me, Paul Kelly, I know my Ron never left you the scrapyard. Now you can come back to mine and discuss it, or I can go to the police. Your choice?"

There was a smugness to her voice that unsettled him. "You're wrong, Rita, but if you want to discuss it then fine, I'll follow you back." He climbed into his motor and cursed under his breath.

He drove back to Rita's, trying to form a plan. He'd thought the rewriting of the will had been foolproof. He decided the best thing to do was to bluff it out. Once he pulled up outside the house, Rita opened the door and ushered him in.

"I'll pour us both a drink, you look like you need it." She walked to the bar. "Scotch?"

Paul nodded but didn't speak.

"Cat got your tongue?" she asked.

"Cut the crap, Rita, what do you want?" He took the glass from her and downed the scotch in one.

"I want you, Paul Kelly, and you are going to give yourself to me." She grinned.

"You must be some kind of idiot if you think that will ever happen," he snarled back.

"Okay, let me spell it out for you. I had two copies of the will, both identical. You see, Ron never trusted anybody. He may have been a womanising old goat, but he was smart with things like this. So anyway, he got me to keep a copy that no one knew about. That, by the way, is how I know you tampered with the will." She refilled both glasses before she continued. "Do you know how long you'll get in prison? Five, ten years? I hear they come down hard on fraud, especially trying to con an older woman out of what's rightfully hers when she's mourning her dead husband. I reckon that would make the papers."

"I would never leave Millie; I'd rather serve time," Paul said defiantly. "And you certainly ain't mourning Ron."

"Firstly, why would I mourn a man who spent his entire life cheating on me? I was here for the money and the money only. And secondly, I don't want you to leave Millie. I'm sure we can come to some sort of arrangement. So, I suggest you follow me up to the bedroom."

***

Millie sat on the windowsill watching the rain. Rosie had phoned and was on her way round to see her. She hadn't sounded good on the phone; in fact, she'd sounded upset, almost hysterical. Millie wished she could drive; it was something she would definitely arrange once all this mess with Finn was sorted out. She spotted the taxi as it pulled onto the drive and ran to the door to open it.

"Hey, Rosie," Millie called, immediately spotting Rosie's tearstained face. "Whatever's the matter?"

Rosie ran in and crumpled into Millie's arms. "It's Bobby, he's been seeing another woman." She sobbed.

"What...are you sure?" She struggled to hold Rosie upright. "Come into the lounge, I'll make us a nice cup of tea."

"I don't want a nice cup of tea, I want Bobby." Rosie wailed.

"Err, excuse me, miss, where shall I put this?" At the door, an embarrassed taxi driver stood holding a suitcase.

"Just leave it in here, thanks," she said.

"I need paying, too," he added.

She helped Rosie into the lounge then returned to the taxi driver. "Here, keep the change." Before he could reply, she shut the door and went back in to Rosie. "Tell me what happened."

"Bobby's been going out a lot, and I mean a lot... He came home a few nights ago, and I could smell another woman's perfume on him. Oh, he lied, of course, said I was imagining it... Why didn't he just admit it in the first place?" Rosie blew her nose and wiped her tears. "I believed him, thought maybe he was right, you know, benefit of the doubt and all that, but then…"

"But then what?" Millie prompted.

"But then…I came home early from work today and caught him in bed with another woman. In *our* bed." Rosie's sobs became louder until she cried uncontrollably.

"Shh, it's going to be okay, Rosie, we'll get through this," she assured her.

"I p-packed my things and came h-here; I didn't h-have anywhere else t-to go." She sobbed.

Millie hugged her and stroked her hair. "You did the right thing. You can stay here for as long as you need to." She could feel Rosie's pain. She knew if Paul ever cheated she would feel the same. She would leave him, too, and there would be no going back.

CHAPTER 8

Millie glanced up as Paul walked into the kitchen. "Morning. What time did you get home last night?"

"Late, I had a few problems at work…"

"Anything I can help with?" She studied his face. He looked different.

"No, Mil, you've enough to worry about. Anyway, it's all sorted now." He poured himself a cup of tea and took it through to the lounge.

"Hey, are you not sitting with me in the kitchen?" she asked. "What's wrong, have I done something to upset you?"

"No, babe, you're the one thing in my life that's perfect, and just remember, whatever happens, I love you, I've always loved you," he replied.

Before Millie could answer, Rosie came into the lounge. "Sorry, am I interrupting?"

"No, not at all. Come in and take a seat, I'll make you a cuppa," Millie said, heading to the kitchen. Her thoughts were still on Paul; he was acting weird. She poured Rosie's tea, and his arms snaked around her waist.

"Shall we start again? Morning, babe," he whispered into her ear

She spun around and smiled. "I think that would be a good idea."

"What's Rosie doing here?" he asked.

"Bobby's cheated on her with another woman, so I said she can stay here until she finds a place. You don't mind, do you?"

"No, babe, I don't mind… Isn't there a way they can patch things up?" Paul asked.

He seemed a little too hopeful. Maybe he *did* mind Rosie staying.

"No, Paul, he slept with another woman. You don't patch infidelity up; you cut your losses and move on," Millie said defiantly. "So don't you go cheating on me!" she added.

***

Duke sat watching Connie as she loaded the washing machine. She had been a completely different person since Millie had been for dinner. She was like the old Connie, happy and content.

"You sure you know what you're doing?" he asked, laughing.

"I have been using the launderette for years, you know, or do you think the washing fairy cleans and irons your clothes?" Connie said with a grin.

Duke stood and pulled her in for a kiss, before easing apart when Aron walked in.

"Ain't you two a bit old for that?" Aron said, his voice ringing with disgust.

"Wait until you're our age and then ask again," Duke said. "Right, Con, I need to see Millie and Paul."

"Can I come?" she asked hopefully.

"It's business, Con, not a social call." He looked at her disappointed face, and his stomach dropped. "But I don't suppose it will hurt. Get ya coat, it's still pissing it down."

"We're coming, too, Dad," Jess informed him. "After all, we have been going around all the bed and breakfasts for them."

"Fine, get ready and hurry up." Duke sighed. He wasn't sure how well this would go down, tuning up mob handed. "We'll drive round, I ain't getting completely soaked."

They all crowded into the van and drove around the corner to Millie and Paul's.

***

"Can you get the door, Paul?" Millie shouted down the stairs. She had just showered and was in the middle of getting dressed.

"What the fuck is this?" Paul bellowed and opened the door.

"Morning, Paul," Duke said. "Millie about?"

Millie came running down the stairs and stopped abruptly when she spotted the group of visitors. "You'd better come in." She looked at Paul's cross face and wanted to laugh. "Come through to the lounge."

"Take your shoes off first," Paul ordered.

"Of course, Your Lordship," Duke replied with a bow.

"Rosie," Millie called. "Can you put the kettle on, we have visitors."

Paul led the tribe into the lounge and then stood guard with his arms crossed. What he was guarding, Millie didn't know.

"So, to what do we owe the honour of this visit?" Paul asked.

Duke swallowed before answering. He sounded annoyed when he said, "I thought we should catch up and see if there's any more information about the fire. You are still wanting to catch the culprit, I presume?"

"Of course," Millie said. "Have you any news on the hotels or BnB's?"

"We've been to every single one in the area; no luck, though," Duke answered. "Even Connie's been helping."

"They could have family or friends in the area," Connie added. "Or they could be sleeping in their car. Duke said the girl who he saw looked like a hippie, they could even have a tent."

"Could it be possible that they might be staying with travellers?" Millie asked Duke.

Duke shook his head. "No, we've asked about. No one's seen her... Is there anything else that's been found out?"

Paul looked at Millie. "What about this Shannon?"

"Finn reckons he saw this Shannon at the hospital, but we can't be sure because he's on so much medication he could have been hallucinating."

"Who is Shannon?" Connie asked.

"That's his daughter," Rosie announced and entered with a tray full of teas.

"How do you know that?" Millie asked, a little jealous. Finn had never disclosed that bit of information to her.

"One night in the pub, Finn had a lock-in. Everyone was drunk, including Finn. He just mentioned her; he was telling everyone about her beautiful auburn hair and how she was the image of her mother. I don't think he's ever mentioned her since," Rosie told them. "Anyway, tea's ready."

"Thanks, Rosie." Millie grabbed a cup and stood at the window while she thought. "The girl you saw, Duke, had auburn hair. What if she has been up the hospital... But then wouldn't the men who you put up there have seen her, Paul?"

"I doubt it. They can't stay on the ward, they have been watching from outside looking for the red car." Paul took a sip of his tea. "Maybe they are sleeping in their car. I'll get the boys to drive around tonight, see if they can find it."

"Oh, they won't be sleeping in the car," Rosie interrupted. "It's way too small."

"What do you mean it's too small?" Millie asked.

"Do you see that car parked over there, the green one?" Rosie pointed out of the window.

"The Mini," Duke said. "It's a red Mini."

"Red Mini, girl with auburn hair, and a man with long hair. That's certainly more to go on," Paul added. "Right, I've got stuff to do. I'll put the word out. Mil, I need to make tracks, I'll see you later." He pecked her on the cheek and then left.

Millie walked to the door with Paul and watched him leave. Something was going on that he wasn't telling her. She had a sinking feeling that when she found out she wouldn't like it.

CHAPTER 9

Paul sat perched on the edge of his desk at the club. He counted the pills and then looked at Tony. "Are you sure there's enough to do the job?"

"That's what the doc said, there's enough here to kill a horse. All you've got to do is grind them up and put them in the drink, make sure they dissolve, get the victim to drink it, and it will look like suicide." Tony smiled. "Job done."

"Good, I've got to go and take Mil up to see Finn at the hospital, so let all the boys know what we're looking for and tomorrow we'll go to the scrapyard. I'll want six men with me." Paul scooped up the bag of pills and placed them in his pocket. "See ya tomorrow, six a.m. Make sure everyone's there, we'll meet outside."

With that, he left and made his way home.

THE STEPNEY ALLIANCE

***

Millie picked up the phone, annoyed about the interruption. "Hello."

"Hello, is this Millie?"

"Yes, who is this is?" she asked cautiously.

"Rita. I just wanted to let Paul know he left his watch here last night. I didn't want him searching for it, and can you thank him for me? It was so nice to have male company, and let him know I really enjoyed it," she told her. "I'll look forward to next time."

"What do you mean, male company?" Millie asked, but Rita had already placed the phone down.

Millie paced the floor, waiting for Paul to return home. She checked the clock on the mantelpiece every few minutes and then continued pacing again.

"Mil, you need to stay calm," Rosie said. "You don't know what's happened, and like you said, this Rita sounds like a right bitch."

"And you'd stay calm, would you?" Millie snapped. "Because the Rosie who turned up here last night wasn't calm."

"I caught Bobby in my bed shagging another woman, there is no explanation for that. At least hear Paul out," Rosie replied with a tinge of sadness in her voice. "There's no going back for me, but you don't wanna throw your marriage away until you know what's happened."

Millie looked out of the window when Paul's car rumbled down the street. "Can you leave us, Rosie; I need to speak with him." She took a deep breath and sat on the edge of the armchair, waiting. Her heart was both thumping and breaking at the same time. She needed to scream, cry, smash the place up, but more than anything she wanted to hurt him, just like she was hurting.

"Okay, but don't jump the gun, let him explain. If he's cheated, then I'll even help you hide his body." Rosie darted up the stairs.

"Mil. You ready?" Paul called, his voice drifting in from the hallway. "Mil?" He entered the lounge. "What's wrong?"

She kept her face neutral. "What's wrong?" Millie repeated. "Now let me see, what's wrong… Let me ask you a question, Paul. How would you feel if a man phoned here telling you I had left a piece of my jewellery in his house? Would you think it's okay or would you have questions?"

"I'm sure there would be a logical, reasonable answer," Paul said. "What's this about?"

"Hang on, I have another question. What would you say if a man phoned here and told you to thank me for spending the evening with him and how much he enjoyed the female company. What would you say to that, Paul?" Millie fought back the urge to scream and remained calm.

"What the fuck is going on?" Paul snapped.

Was he sweating? He certainly looked uncomfortable.

"I'll tell you what's going on. Rita phoned me to let me know you had left your watch at hers last night, and she wanted me to thank you for the male company… This is last night while I was sitting here on my own, alone, and you were apparently working. Now I've never been naive, and I can pretty much guess what you and her got up to, but I'd like to hear it from you. I want to see if you are man enough to admit it."

"There's nothing to admit to. I went there after the will reading and did a couple of jobs for her. I took my watch off, so I didn't damage it, and then I rushed out before she got me to do anything else. Then I went to the club and was there until late. Do you actually think I'd cheat on you?"

Millie remained silent.

"Rita is causing trouble, Mil, and I won't be seeing her again, so when she phones up, you tell her to fuck off."

"I don't know if I believe you. You were acting strange this morning." She thought back to the kitchen; he had poured his tea and then walked into the lounge. No kiss, no affection, no nothing.

"It's not what you think, babe, I promise you… Look, just give me until tomorrow night to sort things out and I'll tell you everything, I promise," he pleaded.

"I don't know." Millie looked up at him and slowly shook her head. "I don't know if I'll ever trust you again."

CHAPTER 10

Paul drove up to the tall metal gates of the scrapyard and smiled. "This is ours from today," he told Millie who sat beside him with a face like a slapped arse. "Smile, Mil, for fuck's sake. I've already told you tonight I'll tell you everything." He blew out slowly, containing his temper. She had been like this since he had got home yesterday. Barely speaking to him.

"It's hard to get excited when you don't know what's going on." Millie paused. "Or maybe I do."

Paul turned and grabbed her cheeks, pulling her around to face him. He then planted his lips on hers and kissed her, annoyed when she didn't kiss him back. "I would rather go to prison than cheat on you."

"What?" Millie asked.

"Just wait until tonight. Right, shall we go and see our new business?" Paul waited for the gates to open and then he drove through with his men following behind in another car. He jumped out and marched around to Millie, opening the door and helping her out.

"It stinks of cars." She waved her hand in front of her nose. "I can almost taste the engine oil," she added.

He laughed. "That's the smell of our fortune, Mil. My old man always said there's money in shit."

"Well, I'm glad I can't smell shit," she said flatly.

He grabbed her hand and walked to the Portakabin. "Ladies first." He motioned to her after opening the door. He followed her in and studied the room. It was exactly the same as it was the last time he had been here. The desk was full of paperwork, and a dirty glass stood next to a half-empty whiskey bottle. "I need to go through all this paperwork, dya fancy giving me a hand?"

"I don't know anything about scrapyards. What help can I be?" she asked as she ran a finger over the top of a dusty filing cabinet.

He took a seat at the desk and placed his hands behind his head. "Well, you like cleaning." He ducked before the magazine hit his head. "That was a joke, Mil." He laughed.

Tony opened the door and came in with five men following. "Everything looks okay, Paul. The men want to know if you are keeping them on. What shall I tell them?"

"I'll come out and see them. Who have we got who can oversee the place?" Paul asked, standing.

"Why don't you ask Duke and the boys?" Millie interrupted. "Didn't he say his brother collected scrap?"

"That's not a bad idea. Right, let's go give them the good news. I won't be long, babe." Paul left, followed by his men.

Millie walked to the window just as the men gathered around Paul. Worry was etched on their faces with the possibility of losing their livelihoods. She eyed a man at the back of the crowd. He was dressed in dirty overalls the same as the others, but his hands were spotlessly clean. Frowning, she studied him for a few seconds before stepping outside.

"Paul. Can I have a word?" She waved over.

He walked towards her with an air of authority she didn't think she liked.

"Mil, I'm busy..." he started.

"I wouldn't have called you over if it wasn't important. Don't look, but the man at the back, he's out of place," she whispered.

Paul sighed. "Okay. Is that it?"

"I thought you would have learnt not to dismiss my gut instincts, Paul Kelly. If you can be bothered to check him out, he is wearing dirty overalls but has spotlessly clean hands. Look at the rest of the men, they have dirt ingrained into their skin. That bloke hasn't done a day's graft in his life." Millie turned and went back inside, slamming the door for good measure. Before she had reached the desk, Paul was standing behind her.

"I wasn't dismissing what you had to say. You told me not to turn around, Miss Snotty. I'll go and check him out now, without him knowing." Paul pecked her on the check.

"I'm not snotty." Millie folded her arms; she was sure Paul laughed as he left.

She refocused on her surroundings. It was dingy and smelly. Not the type of place she expected the great Ronnie Taylor to dwell. No, she imagined him in a castle. Millie took a seat behind the desk. It made her feel sick, knowing she was sitting in the same seat the treacherous bastard had sat in. Then again, how would he feel knowing she was here, sitting in his tin castle? Taking over. A sly smile crept onto her lips. Maybe Paul was right, it was a fitting punishment. But then her mind returned to Paul. She had trouble shaking the comment he had made.

"I would rather go to prison than cheat on you."

Why would he say that? Why would he have to choose? Millie picked up the whiskey bottle and swirled it around. It mimicked her thoughts. Swirling around her head.

"I would rather go to prison than cheat on you."

She dropped the bottle and stood. "Blackmail." Paul was being blackmailed.

CHAPTER 11

Millie lay back on the bed. She had a lot of thinking to do. She started laying everything out in her mind. The first thing was, who set fire to the pub? She reminded herself to check with the fire brigade to see when it could be fixed up. They had said the investigation had finished. The fire officer also admitted that the perpetrator would probably never be caught. The police thought it was more than likely kids.

Fucking police are useless.

The second, who would blackmail Paul and why? She knew he had enemies, all businessmen had. But cheating? It had to be a woman, surely. Then there was Rosie, poor broken-hearted Rosie. What could she do for her? "Break Bobby's kneecaps."

"What?" Paul entered the bedroom.

"Nothing. Where are you going now?" She eyed him suspiciously.

"I've gotta go to the docks. The new office is going up today, I want to see how they're getting on. Then I'll be going straight to the club," Paul replied. "Get a taxi to the hospital, I'll phone you later to see how Finn is."

"Whatever happened to: whatever happens we'll get through it together?" Millie reminded him. "Because that's what you said, and now you're off doing fuck knows what, with fuck knows who, while I'm dealing with it on my own."

"Babe, Finn's on the mend. Here's the money for the taxi." Paul held out his hand with a wad of notes.

"I don't need your money, Paul, I'm more than capable of paying for a taxi." She pushed his hand away. "Oh, and give Rita my love." She was pleased to see the effect her words had on him. He looked like he had been punched in the gut. "Shouldn't you be going?"

"You are gonna look pretty silly later, Mil, just remember that." He stormed out of the bedroom.

The sound of Paul's footsteps rang in her ears as he descended the stairs. Had she been too hard on him? Maybe. It was true, though; she was left to deal with everything on her own.

"*Mil,*" Rosie shouted up the stairs.

"I'm in the bedroom." Millie stared at the door until Rosie's face appeared.

"Is everything okay? Paul didn't look happy when he left," Rosie asked.

"Everything's fine. Do you fancy a trip to the hospital? I'm sure Finn would love to see you." Millie plastered on a smile. That was one thing she was good at. Pretending.

***

The taxi stopped when the light turned red. The High Street was busy with shoppers. Millie wished they would all get out of the way. She wanted to be with Finn. She glanced out of the window and sighed, doing a double-take. Paul was leaving the off licence, a large bouquet in one hand and a bottle of bubbly in the other.

"What the fuck?"

"Mil?" Rosie followed her eyeline and grinned. "Looks like Paul's gonna surprise you."

Millie doubted that very much. They had every type of booze you could think of at home. There was no reason for him to be buying more. Not for home anyway. The taxi pulled away.

She smiled at Rosie. "We'd best play dumb then."

"I loved being bought flowers...that's not gonna happen anymore." Rosie reached for her hanky and dabbed at her eyes.

"You deserve better, and one day you'll meet someone who will treat you like a queen." She placed her arm around her shoulders. *We both do*, she thought. "Look. We're here."

Millie paid the taxi, and both women made their way into the hospital.

"Good afternoon." Millie greeted the nurse who walked towards them.

"Good afternoon. Finn's popular today, you're the second visitor he's had," the nurse replied as she passed.

"He's a popular man," Millie called over her shoulder then entered Finn's room.

Millie stopped dead; her gaze rested on a woman with long auburn hair. "Oh, hello."

The woman met Millie's eyes and smiled. "Hello." She had a soft Southern Irish accent.

"I'm Millie, and this is Rosie. And you are?" Millie asked, although she already knew.

"I'm Shannon, Finn's daughter." The woman returned her gaze to Finn. "He looks different to how I remembered him."

"I guess being almost burnt alive will do that to a person," Millie snapped.

"Mil!" Rosie whispered.

Millie took a deep breath at Rosie's warning and blew out slowly. "It must be a shock for you, seeing him like this." She walked to the other side of the bed and placed a gentle kiss on Finn's forehead before turning her attention back to Shannon. "How long have you been here?"

"About an hour. Dad's been asleep the whole time. The nurse said he needs his rest... Maybe you should come back later," Shannon suggested.

"I meant how long have you been in Stepney?" Millie pressed. She had already decided she wasn't going anywhere.

"A couple of days. If you don't mind, I think you should leave. My dad needs rest." Shannon stood and walked to the door. "Nurse," she called.

"What are you doing?" Millie asked.

The nurse entered the room.

"Can you ask these women to leave? My dad needs rest, and they won't stop talking." Shannon pointed to Millie and Rosie.

"I'm here to look after Finn, I've been here sitting at his bedside every day." Millie glanced at the nurse for support, however, the nurse remained neutral.

"Well, I'm here now, and as his daughter I will be looking after him." Shannon took a seat next to Finn and placed her hand on his. "Come back in a couple of days, I'm sure he'll be pleased to see you."

"I think we should leave, Mil." Rosie sighed.

Millie turned and walked to the door, pausing briefly. "I will be back, and he had better be okay." She marched from the room and down the corridor. "What the hell just happened?"

"Calm down, Mil. Shannon's obviously upset at finding her dad in that state. You need a bit of compassion for her." Rosie stopped dead as Millie spun around.

"Calm down? A stranger turns up out of the blue, kicks us out of the hospital, and you tell me to calm down? Jesus, Rosie, my whole life is falling to bits, and you want me to calm down." She pointed back towards Finn's room. "That little episode made no sense whatsoever. I mean, you said one word, and that was a whisper, but she accused you of keeping talking, too, or did you not hear that bit?"

"I know it seems a bit strange, but people act differently when they're upset. She's just found her dad and discovered he's lying in a hospital bed," Rosie argued.

"Why are you sticking up for her?" Millie snapped.

"Because I think you're being unreasonable. You have everything, Mil. A husband who adores you, parents who love you, a big house, businesses, and even my brother, Scott. Who I rarely see these days." Rosie fumed.

"Scott works for Paul; I had nothing to do with that," Millie reasoned.

"You are one and the same, two peas in a pod. Scott is my brother, Finn is her dad, and neither are yours." Rosie turned and stormed off down the corridor.

Millie leant back against the wall in an attempt to keep upright. The knot in her stomach tightened. She closed her eyes. Why did Rosie feel like this? Scott had worked for Paul before Millie had even known of Paul's existence. Rosie knew that. Hadn't she pointed it out in the pub that first night? And as for Finn, he was like a father to her, so why was it wrong to care for him? Yes, she did have a husband. Who was more than likely cheating on her.

CHAPTER 12

Millie climbed out of the taxi just as Rosie came out of the house carrying her suitcase. Fumbling with her purse, Millie handed the driver the fare and headed towards her.

"Rosie. What are you doing?"

"I can't stay here." She sidestepped Millie and continued towards the road.

"Rosie, wait," Millie called. "You can't leave. Where will you go?"

Rosie stopped and placed her case down. "I don't feel welcome here. I need a place where I can get my head straight... Look, I'm sorry for blurting out all that stuff in the hospital. I know you're worried about Finn, we both are. Sometimes you have to step back and let family deal with their own stuff. Anyway, I best get going. I'll be in touch."

She stood on the path until Rosie disappeared from sight. Was that the end of their friendship? They had been friends forever. She couldn't remember a time without Rosie and Scott in her life. The fun they'd had growing up in the children's home at such a young age left Millie with so many fond memories. They had become family. Wiping her eyes, she headed into the house. She closed the door behind her and glanced around at the emptiness. The quiet was deafening. The loneliness crushing. She couldn't be on her own. She needed her family.

***

Paul climbed out of his motor and stared at the house. He turned and grabbed the bouquet and champagne, then made his way up the path. His heart beat faster than normal at just the thought of what would happen when he walked through the door. Placing the bottle under his arm, he tapped his pocket, just to make sure he had what he needed, and then knocked. The door opened immediately.

"Paul, I thought you were going to come up with another excuse tonight. I'm pleased to see you have come to your senses." Rita stepped back and ushered him in.

"I told you last night, I'm not a man to rush. Millie isn't expecting me home until tomorrow, so we can take our time." He smiled and handed Rita the flowers.

"How thoughtful of you. You know, I think we would make a powerful couple. You should think about it. We would own half of London between us." She beamed.

"I have a wife, Rita. I'm up for a bit of fun, which is what you wanted. I'm not up for hurting Millie either, so no more phone calls," he replied. "Let me crack open this bottle. Where are the glasses?"

"Here." Rita handed him two champagne flutes. "Bring them up to the bedroom. I'll pop these in a vase and go and make myself comfortable."

Paul popped the cork and then moved to the doorway. Rita had disappeared up the stairs, leaving him alone to pour the drinks. He pulled the small plastic bag from his pocket and tipped the powdery contents into one of the glasses. When he poured the champagne in, the powder fizzed over the side of the glass.

"Shit," Paul muttered. He took a couple of deep breaths and then tried again. Content that both glasses looked the same, he carried them up to Rita's bedroom.

"About time. I thought I would need to send out a search party." She huffed. "Now come and make yourself comfortable." She patted the bed beside her.

He climbed onto the bed, handing Rita her glass. "Cheers." He smiled when she took a sip.

"Hmm, I love champagne." Her gaze rested on him. "I think you're a little overdressed for my bed, Paul. Why don't you strip."

He swallowed down the bile that had just shot up his throat and into his mouth. He needed to compose himself. "Why don't you enjoy your drink while I get ready."

"Oh, I think I'll be enjoying more than my drink," she said smugly.

He slowly undid his jacket. He wasn't sure how much time he needed to play for. Tony had said the drugs were fast-working, but she was taking her fucking time drinking it. He placed his jacket neatly on the back of a chair and unclipped his tie pin.

Rita lay there looking like the desperate piece of shit she was. Christ, no wonder Ron had played away. She was embarrassing.

"Can we speed things up a bit, Paul? I'm getting a bit lonely here on my own." She downed her drink and pulled the cover down, exposing her naked breasts.

Paul didn't know whether to laugh or cry when he glanced over. If that was supposed to entice him into her bed, he wondered what she would do to kick him back out. She had rested her head back. She appeared tired. Thank fuck for that.

"Are you okay, Rita?" He asked.

"I think the champagne has gone to my head. I…" she slurred.

Paul replaced his tie pin and slipped on his jacket. "You know, Rita, it's a dangerous game, blackmail."

"What…are you…doing?" She closed her eyes. "What…?"

"I would never cheat on Millie. For one, I don't think I could live with myself, and two, she'd fucking kill me. Just like she did Ronnie." Paul grinned. That wasn't completely true, however, she had planned it and she had been there. He just wanted Rita to know Millie wasn't to be messed with.

Rita's eyes flicked open.

"That's right, Rita. Millie helped kill Ronnie. You see, my wife is full of surprises, and I for one would never want to be on the receiving end of her temper, so think yourself lucky that I dealt with you and not her."

"What…have you done…to me?" Rita's arms flopped to her sides, her speech slowed.

"You, my darling, are about to overdose. You missed Ronnie so much that you couldn't go on any longer without him." Paul tipped the remainder of the powder onto the side with a few pills for good measure. "Now where did you hide that other will?"

Paul shoved his hand into his jacket pocket and pulled out his gloves. Putting them on, he proceeded to clean the crime scene. Finishing with knocking the bottle over along with the glass. His last job was to find the will.

"Where would a woman keep something so precious?" he wondered. "Millie keeps everything in her handbag." He rooted through the wardrobe and cupboards, making sure not to disturb anything. Finally, he looked under the bed.

"Bingo!" he called, dragging the bag out.

There, in a zipped compartment, was the will. It wasn't even a good place to hide it. In fact, it was a fucking stupid place. He tucked the will in his jacket pocket, picked up his glass, and left the room.

After washing up the glass, Paul returned it to the cupboard. Wiped the cork and threw it into the bin. Wiped the bouquet wrapping. Job done.

CHAPTER 13

Millie checked her watch. It was twelve-thirty a.m. The streetlamps highlighted the rain, which was still bucketing it down. She checked the address once more and made her way up the road. She wished she had taken more notice on the day of the funeral.

This was definitely an affluent area. She hadn't expected Ronnie Taylor to live anywhere else. A man who thought he owned everything, and everyone, would hardly live in a two up, two down. A small smile crept across Millie's face at the thought of Ronnie having an outside loo.

She stopped at the address she had jotted down. She was going to get answers, even if she didn't like what she heard. Knocking loudly on the door, she stood and waited. When no answer came, she snuck around the back, peering through the windows as she went. Reaching the back door, she twisted the handle. Pleased when it opened, she let herself in. The house was in complete silence despite the lights being on.

Millie walked through the kitchen; her gaze darted around the room. It was big and flash, but then so was hers. Next she entered a large entrance hall and glanced up the stairs. She tiptoed up slowly, wondering what would greet her at the top. Silence.

She swallowed down her nerves and called out, "Rita?"

No reply came.

She continued along the landing until she came to a half-open door, pushing it open further. Her attention fell on Rita. Her naked upper half slumped back in the bed.

"Rita?" Millie called again and approached the bed. She pulled the covers up over Rita's body then checked for a pulse. "Shit." She clocked the spilt bottle of champagne next to the bed. Had Paul been here?

Millie jumped when a noise came from behind her. Startled, she turned.

"What are you doing, miss?" the police officer asked.

"I…" Shit. What was she supposed to say?

"Step away from bed, miss," he replied.

"I think she's dead," Millie managed when she had composed herself.

"You are going to have to wait downstairs. The WPC will take you." He nodded to a policewoman.

Millie followed the WPC down to the lounge and perched on the edge of the sofa. Her gaze landed on the large bouquet that was placed on the side, next to the French dresser. So Paul *had* been here.

She listened to the footsteps charging up the stairs and guessed the forensic mob had turned up. Who had phoned the police? Rita, before she'd fallen asleep? Or had Paul done it anonymously?

"Miss, I need to ask you some questions down at the station," the police officer informed her.

"Am I in trouble, Officer?" Millie asked, her eyes going wide.

"I don't know. Are you?" he said coldly.

Millie followed him out to a police car, the WPC holding her arm. She ducked down as she climbed in, feeling like a criminal. The neighbours had gathered outside the house, most of them glaring at her. She put her head down. What the fuck had Paul done, and was she about to pay the price?

***

Paul leant against the mantel and downed his scotch. Where the fuck were Millie and Rosie? Everywhere was closed at this time of night, or rather, morning. The lights were all off over at Duke's. The Artichoke was still burnt out. There were no other options. Finn, Paul decided. They must be with him. Had something happened?

"Fuck." He had meant to phone Millie earlier to find out.

He picked up his keys and grabbed the door handle. At the same time the phone rang. Paul snatched it up.

"Mil?" He hoped by saying her name it would be her.

"Mr Kelly?" the male voice enquired.

"Speaking. Who is this?" Paul demanded, although he had a rough idea. He didn't have time for coppers or Rita.

"I'm Police Constable Whitmarsh. I'm phoning to inform you I have your wife here; she is helping us with our enquiries."

"Where is here, and enquiries for what?" Paul growled.

"Islington Police station. I'm afraid I can't say at this point what it relates to. Your wife is distressed, so I said I would phone you to let you know where she is," Whitmarsh concluded.

"Tell my wife I'm on my way, with our solicitor, and —"

The line went dead before Paul could protest. Placing the phone down, he picked it back up and dialled the number he knew off by heart. "Meet me outside Islington nick. Millie's in trouble." He slammed the phone down.

***

Millie blew her nose. The policewoman kept watching her. She wasn't sure how long she could keep the hysterics up for, but she knew she needed to play for time. Why wasn't Paul here yet? Would he leave her here to fend for herself? Millie let out a loud sob. She dabbed her eyes and took a few deep breaths. She turned when the door opened.

"Mrs Kelly's brief is here," Whitmarsh informed the woman police officer.

Mr Barrett entered the room with an air of authority. Millie smiled when he informed all that he would talk to his client alone.

"Mr Barrett, I'm so pleased to see you," Millie began, but he held his hand up.

"I don't appreciate being pulled from a good night's sleep, especially when you haven't done anything wrong. They have no grounds to hold you. Just tell them the truth. Paul asked you to check on Mrs Taylor because earlier, when Paul went to check on her, she was acting strange. Understand?" Mr Barrett stood and walked to the door. "Okay. You can come in now."

Two plainclothes Old Bill walked in and sat opposite Millie and Mr Barrett. One hit a button on a tape recorder, then the two coppers introduced themselves.

"My name is Detective Inspector Swain, and my colleague is Detective Inspector Peters. Can you please confirm your name, miss?" Swain prompted.

"My name's Mrs Millie Kelly."

"And can you walk me through the events of tonight, Mrs Kelly?"

"Rita, erm, Mrs Taylor, lost her husband recently and he was buried only a couple of days ago My husband and I have been keeping an eye on her. She hasn't been too good lately. Drinking quite a bit, I guess to blot out the pain. Anyway, my husband called in earlier and was worried about her. He said she was acting strange." Millie stopped as Swain cut in.

"Strange in what way?"

"Strange as in distant. Reminiscing, and when he left, she thanked him for all he had done and that he mustn't blame himself." Millie dabbed at her eyes. "Is she dead?"

Swain sighed. "I'm sorry to say, yes she is. There's one thing I don't understand. Why did you go so late?"

"I had been up the hospital in the afternoon. A very close friend nearly lost his life in a fire, and then I had an argument with my best friend. I came home, fell asleep, and when I woke up I remembered what Paul had asked. I went straight over," Millie replied tearfully. "Oh no." She placed a hand on her chest. "Is she dead because I turned up too late?"

"Okay, Mrs Kelly. This is not your fault. It sounds like you've had a very upsetting day. You can go home now." Swain gestured to the door.

Millie walked out to find Paul waiting in the reception. He wrapped his arms around her and kissed the top of her head.

"Let's get you home."

She fastened the seat belt and waited for Paul to climb in.

"What the fuck where you doing at Rita's?" he asked.

Millie turned to him, her face neutral. "Did you sleep with her?"

CHAPTER 14

Millie stormed into the house and headed straight for the brandy. Pouring herself a large measure, she knocked it back in one, then refilled her glass and sat on the sofa, glass and bottle in hand. She could feel Paul's eyes on her. "I'm still waiting for a fucking answer, Paul."

"Look at me," He demanded. "No. I didn't sleep with her."

"You bought her flowers and expensive champagne." Millie took a large swig before she continued. "She was naked, in bed, and you had been there. In the fucking bedroom, you piece of shit."

"Do you want to know what happened or are you just going to jump to conclusions?" he asked.

She glanced up, he poured himself a large scotch. "You'd better start talking then."

"I told you last night, or rather the night before, seeing as it's now morning, I would explain everything, but when I got home you were on the missing list." He necked his scotch and poured another. "Rita had a third will. She knew Ronnie didn't leave me the scrapyard."

"So she blackmailed you for sex." Millie sighed. "Great."

"No, Mil, she tried. I told you I would rather go to prison than cheat on you and I meant it. She tried it on with me the other night. I made out I had a big deal going down and I would see her last night so we could spend the night together. I told her you thought I was away on business."

The sofa moved as Paul sat next to her. She didn't want to look at him.

"I had to make it seem convincing, so I bought the flowers and booze. Tony gave me a load of pills; I crushed them up and put them in her drink before she had a chance to touch me. I let her drink while I took my jacket off. Thank fuck they kicked in before I had to undo my shirt." Paul blew out a breath. "It's been a fucking shit day, but d'ya know the worst bit?"

Millie shook her head. "No."

"The worst bit was knowing you were banged up and I couldn't get to you." Paul sat forward and placed his glass on the table.

"What are you doing?" She gripped her glass when he reached for it.

"I'm taking my wife up to bed. I'm going to show her how much I love her." He yanked the glass from her hand.

"Why didn't you tell me sooner, Paul?"

"Because you've enough on your plate with Finn."

"You don't ever put yourself in that situation again and you definitely don't buy another woman flowers. Understand?" Millie ordered. "Unless it's your nan or mum."

"I understand, babe. Now come on, tomorrow's gonna be a better day." He smiled.

Millie doubted that. There was something odd about Shannon. She may have pulled the wool over Rosie's eyes, but she wasn't so easily fooled.

***

Paul slumped down and drew Millie towards him. "I love you," he mumbled in her ear.

"I love you, too," she replied. "Do you think there will be any comeback regarding Rita?"

"No... Can you stop worrying, please... Just focus on Finn," he added.

"About that..." Millie trailed off.

Paul opened his eyes. "Now what?" The bed moved, and the light flicked on. "Jesus, you could have warned me." He blinked, the light blinding him for a few seconds. Sighing, he turned to her who now rested against the headboard. "What's happened?"

"Yesterday at the hospital a woman was sitting with Finn. Apparently she's his daughter, Shannon." Millie paused. "She got me and Rosie kicked out."

"Why?" Paul asked, hoisting himself up to sit next to her.

"She said Finn needed rest and we were talking too much," Millie explained. "And then me and Rosie had a row. She reckons I should keep out of it as Finn is Shannon's dad and Scott is her brother."

"What the fuck has Scott got to do with it?" he asked. He rubbed at his scar, annoyed.

"She thinks I interfere... I've had nothing to do with Scott working for you," she said.

"Technically, Scott works for you, too, babe." He was quick to continue when he saw the glare from Millie. "But he worked for me before we were together... Look, I'm sure Rosie will regret what she's said. Snuggle back down, I can feel round two coming on." He leant over and turned the light off, drawing Millie back down.

CHAPTER 15

Millie showered and dressed then descended the stairs and headed to the kitchen. Paul sat with a cup of tea, waiting for her. She bent down and pecked him on the lips before sliding onto his lap.

"What have you got planned for today?" she asked him.

"Off to the scrapyard. You coming?" he offered.

"No, the house needs cleaning, and I need to see Connie. Did you find out who that man was?" She was annoyed she hadn't asked sooner, but with everything that had happened, he had gone out of her mind.

"What man?" Paul frowned.

"The man with the clean hands," She reminded him.

He had obviously forgotten, too.

"When I checked, there wasn't a man there with clean hands. Are you sure you saw him? Could he have had gloves on?" Paul asked.

"What, flesh-coloured gloves, in a scrapyard? He was there. Maybe he spotted me staring." Millie smiled as Paul kissed the back of her neck.

"Well, he wasn't there when I went back to check, but I'll keep my eyes peeled. Now give us a kiss, I need to make tracks." He stood, tugging her up in his arms. "And please don't go to the hospital. I don't want you being upset."

After she watched him leave, Millie picked up the phone and dialled for a cab. As if Paul thought she wouldn't go and check on Finn. Someone had to.

***

Millie stood at the door of Finn's room. He was sitting up. That was a good sign. She pushed open the door and greeted him with a smile. Sitting next to him was the delightful Shannon; she didn't look so happy to see her.

"Good morning, Finn." Millie bent and pecked him on the cheek. "Morning, Shannon."

"Morning, Millie," he replied. His voice was hoarse. Was that from the smoke damage?

"Good morning," Shannon said.

Well, that was short and sweet. Millie kept her focus on Finn. "How are you feeling today?"

Before he could answer, Shannon cut in. "He is to rest, so you shouldn't stay long."

"It's okay, Shannon. I want to see her," Finn mumbled, his voice raspy.

"Excuse me." Shannon stood, then left the room. She didn't appear happy.

Millie smiled at Finn and held his hand. "You do need to rest, but I need to ask you something. Did you see anything weird that night, a strange face in the pub, anything that you might think out of place?"

"What the feck are you doing? I told you he needs to rest," Shannon's voice bellowed over Millie's shoulder. "I want her removed."

Millie turned and came face to face with Shannon.

A nurse stood by her side. "I'm sorry, miss, I need you to leave."

Millie stood, her eyes on Shannon. "Someone did this to him, and I'm not gonna stop until I find them." As she got to the door, she stopped and faced her. "You seem more worried about yourself than Finn."

***

Duke sat across the road from the Artichoke. He had his motor running to warm himself up. He was even wishing for the drought to come back.

"Fucking rain," he mumbled.

Everywhere looked grey, grey and wet. He glanced at his watch. Was he wasting his time here? A taxi pulled up outside, and Millie climbed out. Was she angry? The way she slammed the door shut would say yes. Why was she standing in the pissing rain staring at the pub?

Duke sighed then left the dry, warm motor to see what his daughter was up to.

"Millie."

She spun around; she looked guilty. Guilty and angry.

"What's up?" Duke asked.

"I've messed up," she replied blankly.

"We're both getting soaked. Let's go to the café. I'll buy us a cuppa." He took her arm and led her to his motor. After guiding her in, he trudged around to the driver's side and jumped in.

The journey, although short, was made in silence. Once he had stopped outside, he helped her out, and they entered the café together.

"Two teas, please." Duke refocused on Millie. "Do you wanna start at the beginning?"

Millie shrugged. "Paul told me not to go."

"Not to go where? You need to start at the beginning, Millie."

"I went to see Finn yesterday. Shannon, who has long auburn hair, actually it's more ginger, was sitting with him. She's Finn's daughter and she got me and Rosie kicked out. Said we were talking too much and Finn needed to rest."

"And you're angry because…?" Duke jumped when Millie banged the table.

"Because she has no right kicking me out." She paused as two cups of tea were placed in front of them. "Thank you… I'm the one who's been there for Finn. Sitting with him, wishing him to get well. Where did she come from?" Millie glanced at Duke then continued. "Something isn't right, but I can't put my finger on it."

Duke sipped his tea and thought for a few seconds. "So what has Paul said?"

"He said I was not to go up there today. He's gonna be mad." She shrugged.

Tears filled her eyes, which made him angry. "Paul will be fine, if not, I'll talk to him… You know you've gone about this all wrong. You should make friends with her…"

"What!" Millie's eyes widened in disbelief.

Duke held his hands up. "Whoa. Let me finish… If you make friends with her, you can watch her. She's more likely to slip up if she's up to no good."

Millie went quiet. Duke knew she was thinking it over.

"You're a genius. Can you drop me at the hospital?" Millie smiled.

"No. You're not going back up there today. Clear your head and leave it a couple of days. She's less likely to suspect anything then." He grabbed the menu and studied it; he knew she was watching him. He had to keep her busy. At least until he saw Paul. "I'm starving. Shall we order something to eat?"

"I'll have something to eat if you come back to the pub with me. I want to search the area. There's got to be some clue as to what happened," she replied.

"Don't you think the fire brigade would have checked the place out?" Duke was met with a determined stare. "Very well, but you eat first."

CHAPTER 16

Paul stood at the window of the Portakabin, looking out over the yard. The men went about their business, stripping back the cars of their batteries or anything else of value. He watched the grab as the claws crunched into a car. It picked it up and swung it in the air. It reminded Paul of the arcades at Southend. He had spent many summers there as a child, trying to win a lolly.

Then the car dropped into the crusher. The noise of splintering glass and screeching metal rang in his ears. How could Ron stand this place, the dirt, the noise? It was all too much to take day after day. Tony entered and coughed, pulling him from his thoughts.

"Everything's all in order, Paul. The men know what they're doing. Who are you getting in to run the place?"

"I'm gonna have a word with Duke, I just haven't had time yet." Paul motioned to the filing cabinet. "Pour the drinks, Tone." He then took a seat behind the desk. All morning he had been thinking about this mystery man. Millie's senses where always spot-on. If she'd noticed something was wrong then it was wrong. But where had he gone? And more to the point, who was he?

"Here ya go, boss." Tony placed the drink down in front of him. "With all these businesses, we're getting spread a bit thin on the ground. We could do with more manpower."

"Yeah, I've thought about that, too." Paul sighed. "Nothing on the mystery man then?"

"If he was here, no one's admitting he was. Do you think he could be someone checking the yard out, maybe wanting to take over? This isn't our patch after all," Tony asked while sitting on the sofa.

Paul sighed again. He had thought about that, but then why hadn't the men spotted him? No, he had to be someone they knew, someone who could blend in. "First things first. I'll go and see Duke, get someone here I can trust."

Tony laughed. "What, a gypsy?"

"I know what he is, Tone, but he is also Millie's dad. He wouldn't turn her over, I'd bet my life on it." He swallowed the remainder of his drink. "Pour us another." He riffled through the paperwork on the desk. Most of it was old receipts.

Tony handed Paul his drink and perched on the edge of the desk. "You're lucky, ya know. Beautiful wife, nice house, money and power. People get jealous when they see a man like you, a good-looking geezer who has everything. You need to watch your back."

"Fucking hell, Tone, I thought you were gonna tell me ya love me for a minute there." Paul laughed.

"No, mate, I'm telling you you're at the top of your game and that you ain't invincible. The wannabes are gonna be gunning for you. We need to sort out the extra muscle first," Tony replied and then necked his drink.

"Well, on that cheery note, I'm gonna head home and see my beautiful wife." Paul stood and took one last peek out of the window. If this mystery man was after something, he would show himself soon enough.

***

Millie flopped back on the sofa and kicked her shoes off. She dug her toes into the plush carpet. Heaven.

Duke had made her promise not to go up the hospital for a couple of days. He'd said he would drive her and make sure she was okay. It annoyed her. Another man giving her orders.

She glanced around the lounge. Connie had Crown Derby china and cut-glass vases and fruit bowls everywhere. It seemed a bit minimalistic in here. Maybe she could go shopping tomorrow and buy a few bits.

"With everything you've got going on, you want to go shopping?" Millie asked herself.

She was sure Duke would accompany her there, too, like he had today at the pub. Nothing was found, though. Duke wouldn't let her go inside and look around, she had to stand back and wait for him to do it. Was this what having a dad was like? Being dictated to? Christ, she had enough with Paul, now she had it in stereo.

Rosie slipped into her mind. Where was she staying? Scott's maybe? There was no one else, unless a work friend. That was possible. Millie needed to find her and make everything right. Rosie had been so good to her when she had left hospital after the car accident. She had taken her in and helped rebuild her confidence after the years of abuse from Levi.

How strange, Millie rarely thought about Levi. All those black eyes, cigarette burns, and fractures, the verbal abuse, which was just as bad, had gone from her thoughts. No more flashbacks. Just a distant memory, almost like it had happened to someone else.

Millie jumped when the letter box rattled. Odd. The postman had delivered hours ago.

Dragging herself up, she walked to the front door. There on the mat was a piece of paper. Millie bent down and swooped it up. She returned to the lounge and unfolded it. She froze. Letters had been cut out and glued to the piece of paper.

I know what you did.

Millie's hands shook. Was this for her? Was it about Ronnie Taylor? "Shit!" She placed the note down and reached for the brandy bottle. Her hands still shaking, she poured a large measure. The burn hit the back of her throat as soon as she swallowed it. It didn't warm her, though. When she glanced down at the note, a cold chill swept over her.

***

Duke placed his arms around Connie's waist and breathed in her scent while he nuzzled into her neck. He loved her. No other woman had ever caught his eye and no other woman ever would. Those big blue eyes made him go weak at the knees. Her petite figure and pretty face had him mesmerized at the age of fifteen, and he made sure she was his and always would be. He nuzzled in a bit deeper.

"Duke Lee, will you let me sort this dinner?" Connie laughed. "The boys will be back soon, and they'll be starving."

"Can't a man show his wife how much she means to him?" He grinned. "Come to bed. The boys can wait."

"Wait for what?" Jess asked while walking in.

"Impeccable timing, boy," he called to Jess. "We'll pick this up later, Con." Duke sat at the table. He still wasn't used to living in the static trailer. Too much room for him, but Connie was loving it, and if she loved it, he would, too.

"I thought we could pop round and see Millie after dinner," Connie said over her shoulder. "Maybe invite her and Paul for dinner again?"

Was that a question? "We can do, if that's what you want." Duke paused to get his words right. "We don't want to crowd her, Con, or make her feel under pressure. We were supposed to be having dinner at theirs next time."

"But...I suppose you're right," she replied.

"We can pop around and see her, she is our daughter after all," Duke added quickly. Millie may be their daughter, but Connie was still his wife, and her feelings counted, too.

"Dad." Aron popped his head into the trailer. "Paul's here, he wants a word."

Duke nodded to Paul and led him into the sitting area, closing the door firmly behind him. "I take it this isn't a social call?"

"No. It's business. I need someone to run the scrapyard. Someone trustworthy," Paul replied. "I know your lot deal in scrap."

"My lot? Oh, you mean us pikeys?" Duke wanted to laugh. Paul was clearly uncomfortable. He must be desperate, though, if he was asking him.

"I'll pay well…" Paul said.

Jess and Aron burst through the door, both smiling.

"We'll do it, Dad."

"I don't want a couple of kids running it," Paul blurted out in surprise.

"These couple of kids are better fighters than most men, Paul. They're my sons, and they have a gift for the bare-knuckle boxing." Duke turned to Jess and Aron. "Although to be fair, boys, I would rather yous didn't."

"He wants someone he can trust, Dad, so who better than family?" Aron asked.

Duke ran a hand over his face. "They have a point. I can check in on them from time to time, make sure everything is running smoothly."

"Okay, you can have a month's trial. If you boys cut it, the job's yours." Paul held his hand out.

Duke shook. "Deal. I'll drop them over in the morning."

Duke stood at the door and closed it behind Paul. Would Millie tell Paul what had happened today? He hoped so, because there was no place for secrets in a marriage.

CHAPTER 17

The rattle of Paul's keys drew Millie's attention. The door opened then closed, then came a clatter as the keys hit the side. His footsteps grew louder. Shit. She had been practising this conversation all afternoon, along with downing a quarter bottle of brandy, and still she didn't know what to say. Should she wait and see if he'd had a good day?

"Mil, you okay?" Paul asked before he had reached her.

"Paul, I..." *Don't stop there, say something.* Ignoring the voice in her head, she poured him a large whiskey and herself yet another brandy. She could feel him watching her. "Here, drink this."

"Are you drunk?" he asked.

"No. Maybe..." *Shit.*

"What have you done?" Paul asked. He didn't look angry, yet.

"I'm sorry, I went to the hospital." Millie sank onto the sofa and waited for the bollocking that was sure to follow.

"And?" Paul knelt in front of her.

Why was he being nice?

"And I have made things worse." She waited, but still Paul didn't shout. Instead, he took her hand and kissed it.

"Why aren't you shouting?" She studied him. He wasn't angry. If anything, he looked hurt.

"I didn't want you to go the hospital because I didn't want you getting upset. You need to let the dust settle before reacting, babe." Paul swallowed his drink then sat next to her.

Millie leant into him when he threw his arm around her shoulders. "There's something else."

"Okay," he replied.

Millie reached for the bit of paper and handed it to him. He unfolded it and read the contents, his scar raising immediately. Well, if he wasn't angry before, he was now.

"Where did you get this from?" Paul folded the paper back in half and placed it on the coffee table.

"It came through the letter box a couple of hours ago." She sighed.

"Was there an envelope?" he added.

Millie shook her head. "Someone knows I killed Ron."

"No. This isn't about you. Technically you didn't kill Ron. I know you planned it, and you were there, however, it was Duke who killed him… This is about the scrapyard." Paul stood and refilled their drinks. "I don't want you worrying about this, but I don't want you left on your own. I'll get Duke to come over."

"Don't worry, but you want me to have a babysitter? Why can't you get rid of the scrapyard? Sell it, it's brought nothing but trouble. Please, Paul," she urged.

"Babe, I think it's too late for that," he explained. "If some nut has done this, then they think they have a grievance… When I find out who's responsible I'll cut them up into pieces and glue them to the fucking paper."

"What are you doing now?" she asked, following him around all the windows. He was checking them one by one.

"I'll make sure everything is secure then I'll get Duke to come over." He ran upstairs.

Millie chewed at her nails. Paul was worried. If he was worried, she needed to be, too.

"Okay, babe, everything's locked up; I'll only be a minute." He left by the kitchen.

She followed him to the door. He marched down the garden then hopped the fence and disappeared from view. She turned her attention to the front window. Were they being watched? Why didn't Paul call his men? Couldn't they guard the house? She pulled the curtain back a touch and scanned the front. She couldn't see, it was pitch-black outside.

"Mil," Paul called.

She jumped.

Duke came into view, followed by Connie and Millie's brothers.

"Okay, so I'll go to the scrapyard with Jess and Aron," Duke started, but Paul stopped him.

"I need someone with Millie," Paul demanded.

"Do you think they would hurt her?" Connie asked, her voice laced with concern.

"No one is touching our daughter," Duke reassured her while he slipped his arm around her shoulders.

"Do I get a say in any of this?" Millie turned back to the window. "Because I'm not gonna be a prisoner in my own home."

"Mil, we don't know who we are dealing with, it could be some idiot trying his luck or it could be a total nutter. I for one am not willing to take a chance." Paul sighed. "Okay, so you three go to the scrapyard. Mil, you'll have to come with me."

"What about your men, why can't one of them watch the house?" She studied Paul's face.

He shook his head. "The men are spread too far with the club, brothel, docks, and now the scrapyard."

"But if Duke and the boys are taking care of the yard, couldn't you spare one, say Scott?" Millie thought of Rosie. If Scott were here, would Rosie come back? "Connie could keep me company, and it's only while you're out," she added.

Paul rubbed his neck. "I'll phone Scott and let him know. Duke, are you happy for Connie to be here?"

"I can speak for myself, Paul," Connie replied. "I would be more than happy to be here."

Millie witnessed a small smile of affection pass between Duke and Connie. It warmed her to see.

"What about night-time, though, surely you'll need someone on guard through the night?" Duke reasoned.

"I'll figure that out in the morning. Don't think I'm gonna sleep tonight anyway. Right, I'll phone Scott and I'll see yous tomorrow." Paul nodded then left the room.

Millie showed Duke, Connie, and the boys out and then waited for Paul in the lounge. She massaged her forehead. A headache was beginning, or was that a hangover? She cursed the scrapyard. It had brought all this trouble into their lives. Why did Paul have to have it? Just why?

CHAPTER 18

Millie rolled over and stretched her arms above her head. She glanced next to her, but Paul was already up. Wrapping her dressing gown around herself, she slipped her feet into her slippers and descended the stairs. Voices came from the kitchen.

"Morning, Mil." Scott smiled. He jumped up and pecked her cheek.

"Morning, Scott," she replied. "I think I've just had the worst night's sleep ever," she added, sinking onto a chair.

Paul handed her a cup of tea and placed a kiss on the top of her head. "Right, I'm off to the scrapyard. You do not go out. Understand?"

"Paul—" She was cut off before she managed two words.

"I said, understand?" he demanded.

THE STEPNEY ALLIANCE

"Yes, I understand. You will be careful?" She stood and laced her fingers around his neck. "Maybe I should come with you, safety in numbers and all that."

"Not today. Today I want you here. Connie should be over soon. Just think of it as a mother-daughter day." He grinned before kissing her. "I'll phone in a little while, babe. Love you."

"And I love you, Mr Kelly."

Millie waved goodbye at the door and then headed back to the kitchen. As Connie wasn't there yet, she wanted to talk to Scott about Rosie. "Have you seen Rosie lately?"

"No, not lately, why?" Scott asked.

"She split up from Bobby. I thought she would have told you." Millie kept eye contact. Was Scott telling the truth? "You have seen her, I can see it in your face."

"Listen, Mil, she's my sister. She wants a bit of time to herself. She will see you when she's ready," he reasoned.

"She's gonna love you being here. As I'm the cause of you not seeing her." Millie sighed.

"Where did you get that idea from? I see her every week." Scott sipped his tea before he continued. "Look, I don't know what's going on with you two, but it's got nothing to do with me. I'm here to do a job and I intend to do it well or my boss will nail my bollocks to the fence post... I'll go and watch the front." He stood and left the room.

Millie jumped when a knock came from the back door. Before she reached it, Scott had barged past her and opened it.

"Scott! This is still my house, I take it... Connie, come in." Millie locked the door behind her. "Maybe you should watch from the upstairs bedroom, Scott, you'll have a better view." She motioned to the ceiling, then waited for him to leave.

"Is everything okay, Millie?" Connie asked. Could she sense the atmosphere?

"Apart from a nutter out there wanting to hurt me and Paul, yes, everything's wonderful... I'll pop the kettle on." She wondered why Rosie was so angry with her. If she saw Scott every week, what was the problem? Maybe Millie should back off from everyone. Let them all deal with their own problems.

Rosie never backed off from helping you. "I know."

"Pardon?" Connie stared at her.

Great, another look of sympathy. "Nothing, I was thinking out loud. Here, sugar's on the table."

***

Paul paced the Portakabin. "It doesn't make sense. If Millie spotted this bloke, then he was here."

Tony stared out of the window with his back to Paul. "We could question the men, one at a time."

"No. Duke will keep an eye out. He's got the bit between his teeth now Millie's in danger. Talking of Duke, how's he getting on?" Paul joined Tony at the window and did a double-take. "What the fuck?" He turned and stormed out of the cabin and approached the grab, motioning to Duke. "*Oi!*"

Duke lowered the grab slowly, and Jess and Aron climbed off the huge claws.

"*What the fuck are you playing at? That's not a toy,*" Paul roared.

"Don't you ever have fun, Paul?" Duke laughed. "Cos when you have kids you'll be doing crazy things to keep them entertained, too."

"I don't call swinging from a bloody great machine fun. What if they had fallen? And I have plenty of fun… With your daughter," he added. He could see in Duke's eyes that he didn't like that comment. He walked back to the Portakabin with a smile on his face. He sat behind the desk and sighed when Duke followed him.

"For your information, we were letting that lot see how mad we are. Do you think they are gonna take the piss if they think we are loopy?" Duke held his finger up and spun it next to his temple. "You have your way of doing things and I have mine, and we're both doing it for the same reason. Millie."

He had a point. It was mainly for Millie.

"Fine, but be careful, I don't need the Old Bill here if one of your boys has an accident."

"Nice of ya to care." Duke huffed.

Tony entered the cabin and took a seat on the sofa. "So what's the plan?"

Grateful for the distraction, Paul sat forward and placed his elbows on the desk. This stranger had to be the answer. "This bloke, we need to find him. I reckon he's something to do with it."

"Could he have been scouting for another firm?" Tony asked.

Duke leant against the wall and shook his head. "What if he's something to do with Ronnie?"

"What, like an employee?" Tony frowned.

"Or a relative?" Duke added.

"No," Paul said assertively. "He had no relatives. His parents were dead, he had no siblings or kids."

"What about his wife?" Duke paused. "Ya know, if Ron had no one, then wouldn't her side stand to inherit?"

Paul's gaze rested on Duke. He wasn't as thick as he looked. "Well, if she had, they will be at her funeral." Millie popped into Paul's mind. She was gonna have a fit at having to go to Rita's funeral. She would have to, though, she was the only one who could identify this mystery man. "I'll see when the funeral is. It's as good a place to start as any."

"Right, on that note, I'll get back out there, see if I hear anything. Someone's bound to slip up sooner or later." Duke left.

Paul glanced at Tony. "Pour the drinks, Tone. I'm gonna need a bit of Dutch courage." Picking up the phone, he dialled the number. "Mil?"

***

"Calm down, Millie." Connie grabbed Millie by the arms and pulled her to a chair.

"Calm down? How can I calm down when I've got to go to that old tart's funeral?" Millie slumped forward and leant on the table. So now this mystery man was important, and Paul wanted her to identify him. Great.

"You won't be in any danger, Paul will be with you, and I'm sure Duke will be nearby, watching," Connie called over her shoulder while she stirred the tea.

"I'm not scared. It's because I don't bloody like her; in fact, I despise her." Millie blew out slowly. The phone rang, and she rolled her eyes. "That'll be Paul again."

"Well, you did slam the phone down on him," Connie reasoned.

Millie walked out to the hall. As much as she hated Rita, she knew Paul was right, she was the only one who could spot him. She grabbed the handset and placed it to her ear. "Hello."

"You calmed down yet, babe?" Paul mumbled from the other end of the line.

"I am calm. I'll go to the poxy funeral, and I'll look for the creep who was at the scrapyard if you take me to see Finn." Millie smiled. Why shouldn't she get something in return?

"Blackmail?" Paul replied.

"No, it's a favour for a favour. Take it or leave it." Millie listened to his breathing. Was he getting angry?

"Fine." He huffed. "I'll see you later." The connection went dead.

Had she done the right thing? After all, this nutter had put a note through the door. Millie replaced the receiver and turned to walk away. The phone rang again. She snatched up.

"Now what, Paul?"

She could faintly hear his breath.

"Paul, stop messing about." Still no sound came. Millie stood glued to the spot. "Paul?" she whispered, a cold sweat covering her body.

A deep laugh came from the other end, and then it went dead.

"Shit." Millie glanced up the stairs. "*Scott!*"

"What's up?" he asked while taking two steps at a time and landing at the bottom in front of her.

Millie stared at the receiver in her hand. "I think the nutter just phoned."

CHAPTER 19

F inn opened his eyes. The nurse smiled down at him.
"How are you feeling today, Finn?" she asked.
Finn swallowed. His throat was still sore from the breathing tube. "I need to get home." He lifted his head and then flopped back down. He barely recognised his own voice. It was raspy, like he had smoked a hundred fags a day since leaving the womb.

"We need to get you better first." She smiled. "Your daughter will be in soon, then you'll have some company."

"Shannon?" Finn returned her smile. How had she found him? It didn't matter, he was just glad she had.

"The doctor will be round later. In the meantime, I'll get you a nice cup of tea." The nurse left the room, closing the door behind her.

Why hadn't Millie been in? All he had done for her, and she couldn't be bothered to come and see him. Or had she been and he was too out of it to remember? At least he had Shannon, his beautiful daughter. He never thought in a thousand years he would ever see her again.

The door clicked open, and Shannon came into view. "Dad, you're looking so much better," she greeted. A soft kiss was placed on his forehead.

He stared at her. She looked different to what he could remember. She'd been a child the last time he had seen her, he reasoned. "It's good to see you."

There was a little niggle in the back of his mind, but he pushed it away. His daughter was here, and that was all that mattered.

***

Paul pulled up on the drive and ran towards the house. The door opened before he reached it. Scott stood back, allowing him to run straight in.

"Millie?"

"I'm in here, Paul."

He headed to the kitchen. Millie sat at the table with her arms wrapped around herself. She was scared.

"Babe, come here." He reached for her hand and pulled her into his arms. "I am going to kill this prick when I catch him."

"If you catch him," she added.

"No. There's no *if* about it, babe. He's crossed the line." He pushed Millie back and studied her. She wasn't going to like what he had to say. "Mil, you can't stay here."

"What?" Her face was filled with confusion. "I live here, Paul, this is my home, our home."

"Just for now. I want you to stay with Duke and Connie…"

Before he had finished, Millie cut in.

"That's ridiculous. Don't you think they would know where I am? I mean, it's at the end of our garden, for Christ's sake." She paced the kitchen floor.

He kept his eyes on her. He knew she wouldn't like it, but it was for her own protection.

She stopped pacing and stared at him. "A caravan's not going to be very secure either, and what about Connie and Duke? It's their home, there's no room in there. I don't think you've thought this one out."

Paul held on to Millie's arms and led her back to the chair. "Sit." He pointed. Once she had done as he had said, he continued. "I've spoken to Duke, and he agrees." He glanced at Connie who sat next to Millie. "Connie, what do you think?"

"Of course you can stay, Millie, I will do whatever I have to do to help keep you safe, and if Duke thinks it's a good idea then so do I."

Paul knelt next to Millie. Her eyes had misted up. "Mil, please listen to me. My first priority is you, so Duke is going to be with you at all times..."

"If I was your first priority, *you* would be with me at all times and not dumping me on someone else." She huffed.

"Will you let me finish... Duke is the only other person I trust to look after you, other than myself, but I need to find whoever is doing this, stop them and kill them." Paul took a deep breath. "I can't do that if I'm worried about you."

"Why can't we tell the police?" Millie pleaded.

"Tell them what? 'Officer, someone put a note through my door saying: I know what you did.' And when the copper asks, 'What did you do?' we will say what, exactly?" He rubbed at his scar. She was making it increasingly difficult to remain calm. He needed a bit of bribery. "If you agree to stay with Duke, I'll get him to take you to see Finn. Once and once only."

She was thinking, he could see it in her face. Had this tipped the scales?

"Okay, but..." Millie began.

"Why does there always have to be a *but* with you? That's the deal, take it or leave it." He held firm; he was banking on her wanting to see Finn.

"I said okay, didn't I? I wanted to know when will I see you," she snapped. "I'll go and pack a bag."

Paul followed her up to the bedroom. He sat on the edge of the bed and watched her open and slam the wardrobe doors. "Mil, it's not going to be for long."

"You don't know that." She placed her things into her overnight bag and then went to get her toothbrush.

"I'll come and see you as much as I can. We still need to be careful, I don't want anyone following me," Paul called through to her.

"And what about the scrapyard? How's Duke gonna look after that?" she called back.

"Duke's bringing in his brothers for now, they will keep an eye on that, along with Tony. Duke and his boys can watch you. I'll go there when I can. I'll need to put a couple of the men at the docks, too. Scott can keep an eye out with the girls, Gladys is an old hand. She'll spot anything off." He glanced up as Millie entered the room with a handful of bottles. "What's that lot for?"

"Shampoo, conditioner, soap, you know, the things you need to keep yourself clean. Where's the toothpaste?" Millie asked and headed into the en suite.

"I'm sure they've got everything you need, babe…" He stopped when she glared at him.

"I want my own stuff, Paul, or is that also not allowed?"

He stood and walked towards her. Placing his arms around her waist, he pulled her body against his. "Do you think I want this? It nearly killed me the last time we were apart." He brushed his lips over hers and mumbled, "It's what we need to do, just for now." He pushed his tongue in deeper, pleased she responded.

Millie pushed him back a few seconds later. "We haven't got time for this, I need to finish packing."

"You won't go until it's dark, we've got plenty of time." Paul closed the bedroom door then faced her. "Are you gonna take those clothes off or shall I?"

CHAPTER 20

Shannon entered Finn's room with a fresh water jug. "I'll pour you a glass now." She took the glass over to the windowsill and fumbled around.

"What are you doing?" Finn couldn't see, but she certainly wasn't pouring water.

"The glass has a mark on it, I'm just cleaning it," Shannon replied. Was she annoyed?

She placed the jug and glass on the bedside cabinet. "I will be back later for visiting, Dad. Now you make sure you do as the nurses tell you," she told him.

Finn gave a small nod. "I'll do my best."

She gave him a peck on the cheek and then left the room.

He moved in the bed; he was stiff. That damn nurse had propped him up in the bed, and it was uncomfortable. He looked for the call button. Where the feck had that gone? His thoughts turned to Millie. Shannon said she hadn't been in for a couple of days. Did he really mean so little to her?

The door opened, and in came the dinner trolley. A cup of tea was all he wanted. It was too painful to eat. "Can you call a nurse for me?"

The dinner lady nodded. "Of course. Is it urgent?"

"I need these pillows sorting, my back's fecking killing." Finn huffed.

"Where's your call button?" the woman asked. She glanced up over Finn's bed. "What's it doing up there? Here, let me get it for you." She headed to the wall and pulled the call button down. "Whoever put it up there needs a telling-off. It should be where you can reach it." After she plumped his pillows up and made sure he was comfortable, she placed the cord on the edge of the bed.

She attended to the food and placed a hot cup of steaming tea on the table. "This should have you built up in no time." She grinned. "A big strapping man like you needs good food, Finn. Now make sure you eat it all. I'll be back in a little while."

Finn ignored her. *I don't want fecking food, I want to go home.*

Shannon had said the pub had been destroyed, so where would he go? Millie's?

He was finding it hard to believe Millie had abandoned him. Shannon's face had changed when he had mentioned Millie. Was it in anger or jealousy?

***

Duke pulled onto his piece of ground and stopped. He climbed out of the pickup truck and checked that Aron had closed the gate.

"Why didn't we just drive round to Millie's?" Jess asked.

"Because we don't want anyone knowing she's here," Duke replied with a roll of the eyes. "Why d'ya think we were checking to see if we were being followed? No one must know, and it's up to us to keep my daughter, that's your sister, safe," he added.

"We know, Dad. So what's the plan?" Aron scanned the ground. "Do we need to keep a lookout here?"

"We need to keep a lookout everywhere, boy. Right, let's get something to eat, Millie won't be over till after midnight." Duke walked into the mobile and switched on the light. It was a stark reminder of when Connie had left him. The place felt empty. Grabbing the kettle, he filled it with fresh water and then lit the gas. He could see why Connie loved it in here. All the mod cons of a house, but at least they were still in a trailer, even if it was the size of a small bungalow.

Duke sat at the table. It would be strange having his daughter here. Strange but good. They would all need to have a discussion, put their heads together and come up with a proper plan. From what he had learnt of Millie so far, there was no way she would stay here for long.

***

"Ready?" Paul asked.

Millie glanced at the clock. It was twelve-thirty on the dot. "I guess so." She picked up the two bags.

Paul immediately took them from her. "I'll carry them."

He stood close to her. She could smell his cologne. This would be harder than she thought.

"Are you sure this is the only way?" Millie blinked; she wouldn't cry.

His face was creased with worry; she wouldn't make it harder for him.

"I promise I will sort this as fast as possible, Mil, and when I do, we'll take a trip away, maybe Ireland. You can meet the rest of the Kelly clan." He smiled. He was trying to make it easier for her.

"I'll look forward to that. Come on then, we'd better go." Millie followed Paul out, stopping abruptly at the kitchen door when he stopped. "Paul?"

"Shh, I just wanna make sure no one's watching." He walked outside. "It's okay."

Millie stepped out into the cold fresh air, her gaze darting around the darkness. She could feel Connie behind her. Was she frightened, too?

They continued down the garden. Paul motioned to Duke. Had he been there all night?

"Anything?" Paul asked him.

"All clear. Me and my boys have checked everywhere. There's no one here, Paul." Duke vaulted the fence and landed on two feet in front of Connie. He swooped her up and placed her on the other side of the fence, then jumped back over himself.

Millie turned to Paul. "This is harder than I thought it would be." She raised her hand and placed it on his cheek. "I love you, Paul." She blinked away the already dripping tears.

His arms wrapped around her, and she felt safe in his embrace.

"Babe, don't cry. I love you more than life. I'll see you as soon as possible." Paul's lips smashed against hers.

The kiss ended too quickly. She wanted it to last longer. "How will I know you're okay?" she whispered. Millie looked over to Duke when he coughed.

"I've got these. One for Paul and one for you." Duke handed Paul a walkie-talkie.

"Do they actually work?" Millie asked. They were scratched and dented.

"They work fine. You can speak to Paul whenever he's home. They won't work any further than that. Now shall we go? The longer you're out here, the more chance of you being spotted," Duke added.

He sounded a bit put out. Had she upset him?

"Thanks, Duke, that's something to look forward to." She did her best to smile, even though her heart was hurting.

Paul lifted Millie and placed her over the fence. "I'll try to see you tomorrow, babe. If not, we'll try out these things." Paul held the walkie-talkie up. "Now go and get some sleep."

She followed Duke and Connie. When she reached the mobile, she spun back towards Paul. He stood there watching her. She waved and then turned the corner.

"I've put your bags in the end bedroom, you can sleep with Connie," Duke informed her.

"I would rather sleep on my own," Millie replied. "I'm an adult."

"The two small rooms have the beds under the window, so you can't sleep in them. Connie will hear if anyone tries to get in the end bedroom. It's for your safety, Millie, and not up for discussion," Duke snapped. "Do you want a cup of tea before bed?"

Millie shook her head. She didn't want tea, she wanted Paul.

"Fine, Connie will show you where to put your stuff." He reached for the kettle. "Goodnight."

Millie marched to the end bedroom. Christ, it was small. The bed looked tiny compared to the king-size she shared with Paul. There were two small cabinets either side of the bed and a row of wardrobes on the opposite wall. Again, the bedroom was all lace.

What is it with these travellers and their bloody lace?

"I need to get changed, so can you close the door, please?" she asked Connie. "I'll let you know when I'm done." She waited for Connie to leave and then reached into her bag. She pulled out a glass and a bottle of brandy. A nightcap was in order if she stood any chance of sleeping. Pouring herself a large measure, Millie knocked it back in one. The burn was welcome. It felt comforting. She poured another then undressed.

"Okay, I'm ready," Millie called through the closed door while slipping into the bed.

The door opened, and Connie appeared. "Are you comfortable, Millie, is there anything I can get you?"

"I'm fine, thanks, I just want to go to sleep." She felt the bed move when Connie climbed in. She picked up on footsteps. Duke must be pacing the floor. "Why isn't he going to bed?"

"I doubt he'll sleep much tonight, Millie, he will be worried about you." Connie said. "Now you rest, and don't worry, let the men sort this out."

Millie pulled the blankets up over her ears; the dogs were barking. "I'm not gonna sleep with that racket. What are they barking at?"

"I don't know, let me go and ask Duke." Connie climbed out of bed and peeked out of the window, then, without saying anything, she left the bedroom, closing the door behind her.

Minutes later she returned. "Duke's let the dogs off. If anyone comes near they will have them. Now sleep."

Millie closed her eyes. If she wasn't worried before, she certainly was now.

CHAPTER 21

Millie woke to the sound of shouting. She fumbled for the light cord over the bed and pulled it, illuminating the room. She blinked and rubbed her eyes. The bed next to her was empty. Where had Connie gone? She pushed the covers back and swung her legs around, her feet firmly hitting the floor. Grabbing a cardigan, she opened the door and walked through the little hallway to the kitchen. Connie stood at the window, her head almost pressed against the glass.

"What's going on?" Millie asked. She glanced at the clock; it was four-thirty a.m. "Where's Duke and the boys?"

The door opened, and Duke appeared. He didn't look happy. "Will you two go to bed," he snapped.

"No," Millie replied defiantly. "What's going on?"

"Nothing for you to worry about."

Millie cut in. "Do not tell me not to worry, it's those exact words that will make me worry more… Why were you outside?"

Duke sighed. He sounded like he'd had all the wind punched out of him.

"The dogs were barking, it's probably just a cat, but I wanted to check it out anyway. Now can you please go back to bed." He motioned to the bedroom.

Was he dismissing her? She looked at Connie who appeared worried.

"Where are the boys?" Millie asked. If there was nothing to worry about, then why weren't they here?

Duke ran his hand over his face, stressed. "They are tying the dogs up, one each corner of the trailer. Now please, Millie, go to bed."

"Millie, come on, let Duke and the boys get their heads down, it'll soon be morning," Connie coaxed.

She allowed Connie to guide her back towards the bedroom. Once in she'd flopped onto the bed, she wondered what Paul was doing. Would he be asleep? No, he was probably in the bedroom watching the grounds for signs of life.

***

Finn lay staring at the ceiling. The nurses' footsteps tapped outside his door. They sounded like a herd of fecking elephants. His head was still fuzzy from yesterday.

"Good morning, Finn," a nurse called as she entered the room. "How are you feeling today?"

"Can you keep the fecking noise down? I've the headache from hell." Finn huffed.

"I need to take some blood so we can work out why you had that turn last night. Now lie still and you won't feel a thing." The nurse was done in seconds and left the room.

Finn couldn't remember exactly what had happened. One minute he was sitting chatting to Shannon, the next he was doubled over in pain. Then the sickness had come. The nurses had come and cleaned him up, changed his bedding, and given him more pain relief. He thought he was on the mend, but maybe the fire had done more damage to him than he realised.

Millie, where was she? Why hadn't she been in? They said people showed their true colours in times of need. Well, she had certainly shown hers.

***

Duke kept his attention on Millie as she sipped her tea. She was still upset after speaking to Paul this morning on the walkie-talkies. Duke wouldn't admit it, but it hurt him to see her hurting.

"What time do you want to go to the hospital?" he asked her.

"After visiting, I don't want to bump into Shannon," Millie replied.

She didn't even look up. He glanced at Connie who was firmly focused on Millie. She was worried, too.

Jess came through the doorway and nodded. "What's for breakfast, Mum?"

"I think a fry-up's in order. We could all do with a good meal to start the day. What do ya say, Millie?" Duke could feel the tension in the room, and it was leaving a nasty taste in his mouth. Paul had said to keep her busy. "Maybe you could help Connie prepare it while we go and check outside," he added.

"I'm not hungry," she answered.

"Well, if you don't eat, you don't go to the hospital." Duke folded his arms. That was his final word on the matter.

"The deal was I stay here so I could go and see Finn," she shot back.

"That was the deal you had with Paul, not me. Now if you want to go up the hospital, you eat first," he ordered.

"You can't do that." She sighed. Was she going to cry?

"I can and I have... Listen, Millie, you need to keep your strength up, you need to eat, and you need to sleep... I'm telling you this as your dad." Duke stood and slid onto the chair next to her. "Keeping you safe means looking after all of you. Now please, help Connie with the breakfast, you have three hungry men to feed." He smiled when Millie stared at him. She resembled Connie so much when she had been that age. Baby-faced and innocent, only he knew his daughter wasn't innocent. She had masterminded Ronnie Taylor's death. She might have the same features as Connie, but she certainly had his cunning and brain.

"Fine, but you can't keep blackmailing me, Duke. Where's the frying pan?" She asked.

"Cupboard next to the…" Before Duke had finished, Aron poked his head into the trailer.

"Dad," he called.

"Right, give us a shout when the breakfast if ready. Come on, Jess." Duke jumped out of the trailer and followed Aron to the gate. "What's up, boy?"

"There's footprints in the mud, and they ain't ours. They stop just up the track. That could have been why the dogs went mad." Aron pointed. "Come and see."

Duke followed with Jess in tow, stopping when Aron stopped. He glanced down at the muddy mess. "Someone was here all right, but it could have been anyone having a nose." He scratched his head. "Don't say anything to ya mother or Millie, not until we know for sure. Tonight we can take it in turns watching the lane from the motor… Right, boys, let's go get some grub." He marched back to the trailer. If some arsehole thought they could harm his daughter, he would show them otherwise.

***

Millie stood in the stairwell of the hospital, waiting for visiting time to be over. She glanced at Duke who leaned back against the wall with his arms crossed. He seemed in deep thought.

"Shouldn't be much longer," she told him, only to receive a nod. He obviously had other things on his mind. Was it the nutter? He had been quiet since breakfast.

She stood back as a few people passed her and then they descended the stairs. "Five more minutes and it should be clear."

She poked her head through the doorway and scanned the corridor. It appeared empty.

"How about I go and check the room, make sure she's gone?" Duke asked.

"Okay, she's got long—" Mille started.

"Auburn hair. I know," Duke finished.

"I was gonna say ginger… It's the second door on the right, you can see it from here," Millie continued, ignoring Duke. "And don't get caught."

"She doesn't know who I am, I'll just say wrong room." Duke pulled the door open then strolled towards Finn's room.

Millie held her breath and silently prayed Shannon was gone. She grinned when Duke turned and motioned for her to follow him.

She entered the room and smiled at Finn. "How are you feeling?" She placed a kiss on his cheek and stared down at him.

"Well, I must say I'm surprised to see you," Finn snapped. "Did you have something better to do, more important maybe?"

"Finn, I was up here every day, then when Shannon turned up she didn't want me here. In fact, she got me thrown out," Millie replied. She tried to keep the shock and anger out of her voice. Had Shannon told him she hadn't been to see him? Why? It didn't make any sense. If she was as worried as she made out, then she would have told Finn she had been here.

"Don't go accusing my Shannon. The Millie I knew would never have been told she couldn't do something if she really wanted to. Now you need to go. Visiting is over." Finn closed his eyes.

"Millie, we should go." Duke grabbed her arm to lead her away.

"No." Millie stared at Finn. "I did want to see you, and if you don't believe me, ask the nurse, Susan. She had to tell me to leave, you know, when your daughter got me kicked out. Why do you think I'm up here after visiting?" Millie waited for Finn to answer, but he remained silent. "Fine, I'll go, but don't think for one minute I didn't want to be here." She followed Duke out. As she approached the lift, a voice called from behind. She turned.

It was Susan, the nurse she had been friendly with.

"Millie, you shouldn't be here," Susan whispered. "You'll get into trouble."

"Why will I?" Mille asked. "Is it an arrestable offence to come and see someone in hospital?"

"Finn's daughter has asked for no other visitors until Finn is stronger. Please don't come back without asking," Susan replied while checking behind her.

"But surely Finn's on the mend now, he looks so much better than the last time I saw him." Millie studied Susan's face. Was something wrong with Finn? "What's going on?"

"Nothing. Please, you need to go." Susan made to walk away.

Millie grabbed her arm. "I know there's something you're not telling me. Please," she pleaded.

Susan opened her mouth, but before she spoke, the sister bellowed from the other end of the corridor.

"Please, you need to go," Susan urged.

Millie pulled a pen and paper from her bag. She scribbled a phone number down and handed it to the nurse. "If Finn takes a turn for the worse or there's something wrong, please phone. You can leave a message here. Ask for Gladys. Okay?" Millie smiled when Susan nodded. "Thank you."

Before the sister had reached them, Millie followed Duke to the lift and stared back at Finn's door. There was something in Susan's expression that didn't sit right with her. It left a niggling feeling in the pit of Millie's stomach.

CHAPTER 22

Paul sat in the Black Bear public house, staring at Duke. "And you're absolutely sure?"

"As sure as I can be. Someone was up the lane, the dogs went mad, but they were gone by the time we got out. It could be nothing, but with everything that's gone on, I wouldn't want to chance it," Duke replied.

"Fuck!" Paul downed his scotch. *Now* what was he supposed to do? How could he find this prick and keep her safe? He glanced around the pub. You couldn't tell it had been in an arson attack a few months previous. Everything was back to normal; in fact, it looked better with the fresh paintwork and a refurbished bar.

"There is one other option," Duke mumbled, pulling him from his thoughts. "I take her away, to a camp."

"A gypsy camp?" Paul shook his head. "No."

"Think about it, forty-odd travellers to protect her. No gorger in his right mind would dare come there," Duke said. "You won't get no safer than that."

"This fucker isn't in his right mind, though, is he." Paul sighed. "She is not gonna like this—fuck, *I* don't even like it."

"From what you've said, this nutter is trying to get to Millie to hurt you, so if we take Millie out of the equation he will have to focus on you... I'm not having my daughter put in harm's way."

Paul rubbed his scar, his temper rising. "Do you think I want my wife caught up in this shit?" he snapped.

Maybe Duke was right, if Millie was somewhere safe he could focus on finding the prick and get rid of him. Was he acting alone, though? Could it be a firm trying to muscle in? Paul's judgement was clouded. He'd been so determined to get the scrapyard that he'd never given a second thought to the consequences. Millie was all that really mattered, and even if he didn't like it, if going away was best for her, then that's what would happen.

"We've got the funeral in two days' time. She needs to be there to identify the bloke from the scrapyard, so you can go after that."

"Do you think it's him?" Duke asked.

"I've made a lot of enemies in my time, but this is personal. I'm certain it's got something to do with the scrapyard." Paul glanced at his watch. "We'd better get back and give her the good news."

***

Millie stared out of the window. Her head was still full of Finn. The way he had shut her out. The look he had given her. Like she didn't care. She was broken from her thoughts when the door opened, and Paul walked in behind Duke.

"Paul!" She jumped up and threw her arms around him. "Does this mean I can come home?"

Paul's arms slipped around her; she felt safe, loved, even needed. His lips met hers, and her body shuddered. She had missed him more that she'd realised.

Paul leant back. "Babe, we need to talk."

She wasn't going to like this, she could see it in his face. "Now what?"

"We have no leads on who sent the message, and as someone was poking about up the lane last night—"

"What…? Is that why those bloody dogs were going mad?" Millie turned to Duke.

He nodded but didn't answer.

"Can you let me finish… Duke's gonna take you away—"

"No." Millie folded her arms in defiance.

"Mil, will you just listen? Please?" Paul's voice was soft. Why wasn't he shouting?

"Fine. But I'm not going anywhere." Millie stared at the floor, she didn't have to look at him.

"After the funeral, Duke and Connie will take you to one of their camps. It's only gonna be a few days, at most a week," Paul reasoned.

"It's for your own safety, Millie. Paul can concentrate on sorting the problem and then you can come home," Duke added.

Millie glanced between Paul and Duke. "So when was this little alliance set up?"

"We both want what's best for you, and your safety is our number one priority." Paul rubbed his scar.

Was he angry at her?

She walked to the sofa, her stomach dropping further with each step. She plonked herself down. It was no good to argue. If Paul had made up his mind then he was unlikely to change it, but who was going to watch his back while he hunted this man?

"Okay, but I want to come home until I leave, or I don't go." That was her final word.

CHAPTER 23

Paul listened to the sound of Millie crashing around in the bedroom. He knew she was pissed off. Christ, he was, too. Just the thought of her being away, God knows where and for how long, gave him a sinking feeling deep in the pit of his stomach. He had to sort this out, and fast. She needed to be here, where she belonged, with him.

He took the stairs two at a time and entered the bedroom. Millie looked up; she had been crying. Paul closed the gap between them and took her in his arms. She almost fell against him. His throat constricted.

"It's gonna be okay, babe, you'll be back here before you know it." He closed his eyes and held her tighter. Her grip seemed to tighten, too. Could she hear the doubt in his voice?

Paul swallowed down his own sadness.

"We need to get going soon, funeral starts at eleven a.m. I'll take your case and give it to Duke." Placing a soft kiss on Millie's forehead, he grabbed the case and left the room.

She didn't answer him. Why? She always had something to say. Had this broken her? Paul sighed as he handed the case to Duke.

"We'll meet you at the green about two-ish. If we get held up, you'll have to wait," Paul confirmed.

"How's Millie?" Duke asked. His voice was etched with a mix of worry and concern.

"Quiet. She's hardly said two words the last couple of days." Paul ran his hand over his face.

"She will be fine, Paul. Once she's away you can get business sorted and she can return. We are doing this for her safety, that's all that matters. Right, I'll get the trailer hitched up and ready. Me mum and dad will be staying here while we're gone. They can keep an eye out and feed the dogs." Duke turned and headed off with Millie's case.

Paul watched him disappear around the side of the mobile. He was right, this was best for Millie. He just hoped she wouldn't hold it against him. She had the unnerving knack of recalling every cross word, argument, or fuck-up he had ever made with her. Paul smiled. Even when he was in the wrong, and that was most of the time, she always forgave him. He guessed that was what true love was all about. Accepting each other's faults.

He marched back up the garden and found Millie in the kitchen, coat on and leaning against the side. "Ready, babe?"

"I guess," Millie said, her voice a whisper.

Paul's chest grew taut. "If there was any other way…" Her eyes met his, the pain evident on her face. "Come on, we best go, and remember, just nod if you spot him. Do *not* go anywhere near him on your own."

***

Millie stood by Paul's side, her hand gripping his. She watched the sombre procession of mourners file past the coffin. The church was packed, so it was making it difficult to see the faces. Millie hadn't realised Rita was that well-liked, or was it because of her wealth?

She shook that thought from her mind and focused on the vicar. They always said the same old claptrap. Will be sorely missed... Was a wonderful person...blah, blah, blah. Millie was glad when the service had finished. Having been seated at the back of the congregation, she waited for everyone to leave before following at the rear.

"Anything?" Paul whispered.

"No, it was difficult to see in there. How did she have so many people like her? She was a nasty vindictive bitch," Millie said.

"Shh, see if you can spot him here." He pulled Millie in front of him as they stood at the graveside.

Rain drizzled down from the grey sky, adding to the already heavy atmosphere of the funeral. Paul's grip on Millie's hand was tense. Millie could tell he was on edge, his mind undoubtedly preoccupied with thoughts of the man from the scrapyard.

Millie scanned the crowd, her gaze darting from face to face in search of anyone who seemed out of place. But try as she might, she couldn't spot anyone she thought suspicious. The mourners all seemed to blend together in a sea of black umbrellas and solemn expressions. Frustration gnawed at Millie's insides, and she struggled to keep her composure. She hated feeling so vulnerable, so exposed. Some arsehole was trying to take the scrapyard and destroy them in the process. Not that it was really theirs, but here they were, fighting for something they didn't need. They had enough, the club, brothel, protection racket, and now the docks. Why did Paul have to go after the scrapyard? Greed.

In one way she could see how he felt. After discovering Ronnie Taylor had fitted him up for murder and fraud, taking the scrapyard seemed poetic justice. It was Ronnie's pride and joy. Maybe if it had been Paul who had killed Ronnie, he may have felt differently, but it was too late for ifs.

"Babe, I need a quick word with Tony. Stay here and don't move," Paul ordered.

She continued to stare at the faces around the grave. It was no good, she couldn't spot the man. Just as she was about to give up hope, a voice whispered in her ear, sending a chill down her spine.

"You must be Millie."

She turned. A woman stood beside her, her dark eyes gleaming with an intensity that sent alarm bells ringing in Millie's mind. She had never seen this woman before.

"Who are you?" she asked, trying to keep her voice steady despite the fear bubbling up inside her.

The woman smiled, a cold, calculating smile that made Millie's blood run cold.

"Let's just say I'm a friend of a friend," she replied.

Millie took the time to study her. Her light-brown hair wrapped up in a tight bun. Her features pinched. Was this woman ill? She was pale and thin. Millie placed her at around sixty, but she could well be less.

"Who are you, and what do you want?" Millie demanded, her voice rising with anger and frustration.

A few heads swivelled their way. Millie had to compose herself.

The woman's smile widened, and she leaned in close, her breath hot against Millie's ear. "We want what's rightfully ours," she whispered. Her voice dripped with malice.

Paul's voice wafted over the crowd. He was calling over to her. She snapped her head around towards him. She spun back to the woman just in time to see her disappear into the crowd. Shaking with anger, she balled her fists. "Fuck," she muttered.

Millie dived into the crowd, following. Where had that bitch gone? She scanned the mourners who were now dispersing. Her attention was drawn to the road. A man held a door open while the woman got into a car. Their eyes met briefly, and Millie glared at her. Before she could give chase, a firm hand wrapped around her arm.

"I thought I told you to stay over there," Paul growled.

"Did you see that woman talking to me?" Millie asked, her gaze still firmly on the disappearing motor.

"What woman?" Paul replied.

Was he annoyed?

Of course he hadn't noticed the woman, he'd been looking for a man. She realised this was gonna be a bigger problem than Paul had first thought.

CHAPTER 24

"I don't want Duke with me, I want him to stay here, with you. Please," Millie begged.

"I want Duke with you, I don't trust anyone else to look after you," Paul replied. "We now know what we're dealing with, babe, it's going to be okay."

She suspected he was trying to make her feel better, but it wasn't working. "You will be careful?" she asked. "Because this woman was pure poison." Millie was more annoyed with herself. Why hadn't she grabbed the bitch? But then what, would she have got arrested for attacking an old woman, an old, frail woman?

"I'll be careful, you make sure you are, too. You stay with Duke at all times. Understand?" Paul leaned into her, his lips brushing against hers.

Her eyes watered, and she did her best not to cry. It was as hard for him as it was for her. Savouring the kiss, she then climbed out of the motor.

Duke stood in front of his Transit, with the chrome trailer hitched behind. Connie stood at his side, concern etched on her face.

She turned to Paul. "I love you."

His arms wrapped around her; warmth and safety embraced her. How long would it be before she felt this again?

"I love you, Mil, more that you will ever realise. Now you need to get going. I'm gonna check out Rita's family and put names to faces. Once I know who we are dealing with, I can sort this shit out and get you back where you belong."

After one last kiss, she was climbing into the middle seat of the Transit, nestled between Connie and Duke. Although it was old, the interior was spotless, just like the trailer. "Where's Aron and Jess?"

"They're behind us, keeping a lookout for anyone following," Duke said.

Millie spun around and peered in the back of the van. "Where?"

"In the pickup truck," Duke answered.

"But they're sixteen, that's not old enough to drive," Millie exclaimed.

"I taught them to drive when they were fourteen and they'll be seventeen in a couple of weeks. Now can we concentrate on the journey?" Duke snapped.

Millie sighed. This wasn't gonna be a pleasant trip. "It's illegal," she muttered. She caught Duke's glare and rolled her eyes. If he thought for one minute she was gonna be a good little gypsy girl he could think again. She had been brought up as a gorger, in a children's home. They had never been a part of her life. Okay, so they didn't know she had existed, but even so, she would not be dictated to by any man. Plus she had Paul. One bossy man was more than enough.

***

Paul swallowed hard when he watched them pull away. He already missed her as they drove into the distance. Still, he had a job to do, find this mob and neutralise them. First stop, the solicitor's. Find out who was in Rita's will. That's where the answers lay. He jumped into his motor and headed off.

The journey was slow, but it gave him time to think about Millie. Was that a good or bad thing? He needed to clear his mind and concentrate on the situation. But try as he might, she kept creeping into his head.

Will she be all right in a gypsy camp?

He stopped outside the club and took a deep breath. "It's the safest place for her, you know that," he told himself, but was that true? He climbed out of the motor, heart thudding. Why was he so on edge? No man had ever scared him, but this time it was different. He had never worried about his own life. What will be, will be. Now, though, he had a wife to think of. Millie.

Is she hurting over Finn?

He unlocked the front door and marched to the office. Passing through the bar area, he glanced up at the glitter ball, which hung over the dance floor. Millie loved that. The first time she'd seen it her eyes had lit up. Continuing through to the office, he listened to Tony talking to the boys.

Will she really be safe?

Paul opened the office door and studied the men who sat dotted around the office. They were the best, personally hand-picked team he had. Each one had proved themselves to be trusted. He took a seat behind his desk and motioned to Tony. "Get the scotch, and I'll fill everyone in."

Is Duke really the best person to look after her?

Paul shook Millie from his mind. He wanted her here with him, and to do that he needed to concentrate.

***

Sitting between Duke and Connie in the middle of the beat-up Transit was the most uncomfortable journey she had ever taken. Not just because the seat was uncomfortable — she was sure a spring was poking her arse — but also because the atmosphere seemed strained. To be fair, it was her doing. She sighed as Duke's leg brushed against hers. Just how much room did he need to drive?

She stared directly out of the front window, trying to avoid Connie's glances. It was a shitty October day. The rain hammered against the windscreen, turning the world outside into a blurry mess of mud and darkness. She hugged her coat tightly around herself; the damp chill seeped into her bones. What was Paul doing now? She would bet a pound to a penny he wasn't cold. She should be in her house. Her lovely, big, warm house. Making a cup of tea in her nice kitchen. Sitting in the lounge with her feet up on the plush four-seater sofa.

Duke wound the window down an inch. She shivered. He wound it back up without looking at her.

They are leaving their home, too, you ungrateful cow!

It had only been a few months since Millie had learned the truth about her heritage. The half-gypsy revelation had been a shock to say the least. She had spent her whole life believing she was just a regular, unwanted kid in a children's home. Did they really expect her to embrace this whole other part of herself that she had never even known existed? She hadn't taken the news well, to put it mildly, but then Paul had taken it a lot worse.

And now, here she was, being taken to a gypsy camp by Duke Lee, her dad, of all people. Bare-knuckle boxing champion of the gypsies. Duke was a rough, no-nonsense kind of man, the kind who didn't take no for an answer. Did she get her stubbornness from him? More than likely.

"Why do I have to go to this stupid camp?" Millie finally broke the silence, her voice laced with frustration. She felt Duke's stare so turned to meet it head-on.

His weathered face was unreadable. "Because it ain't safe for you at home, Millie, not with that nutter after your husband."

Millie's heart sank at the mention of Paul, even though Duke was right. Paul now had a new enemy, one he couldn't see. That's what made this situation different. You couldn't fight what you couldn't see. She knew they wouldn't hesitate to come after her to get to him. Cowards.

"But a gypsy camp?" Millie huffed.

Duke sighed. "Because it's the safest place for you right now. Can you just trust me on this?"

He sounded hurt, and a pang of guilt prodded her. She was ungrateful and taking Paul's stupid decision out on Duke. She focused back on the window and the rain-soaked countryside. Just where were they going?

She hated feeling so powerless, at the mercy of forces beyond her control. But what choices did she have? She glanced at Duke; his knuckles had turned white. He was angry. Had she insulted him with the gypsy camp comment?

She had to concede that she was just a pawn in a dangerous game, caught between her husband's enemy and her own identity crisis.

What a fuck-up!

Millie's heart sank as they approached the camp. It was nestled in a clearing surrounded by dense forest. Smoke curled lazily from a central fire. It reminded her of the time she had gone to see Duke, asking him to call off the feud with Paul, and look at them now, working together to keep her safe. The Stepney alliance. Millie allowed herself a small smile. Never in a hundred years did she think these two men would agree on anything.

Duke pulled the Transit to a stop, and he and Connie climbed out. Was she supposed to join them? Reluctantly, she got out, the mud sucking at her shoes. She had trouble keeping them on her feet. She glanced around, unease creeping over her. Was this to be her new home for the time being? A firm hand rested on her shoulder. She turned and looked up at Duke.

"Welcome to the camp, Millie," Duke said proudly. "You'll be safe here, I promise."

He walked over to Jess and Aron as the pickup truck came to a halt. Millie couldn't hear what he was saying, but as soon as he stopped, the boys jumped out of the motor and sprang to life, unhooking the trailer and pushing it into place. They were joined by a couple of other men, all helping Duke set up quickly. Duke spoke to them in hushed tones. They glanced at her. Both nodded then turned away. Was he talking about her?

Millie stood next to Connie. The rain had eased off slightly, but she could still feel it soaking into her bones. It was a pity Duke didn't get the heater fixed in the Transit. He had to open the window every so often to demist the windscreen.

"Get inside, both of you, you'll catch a chill," Duke ordered to Connie and Millie.

She climbed into the trailer. It was spotless. All chrome, lace, and cut glass. She slipped her muddy shoes off and stood in the middle, wringing her hands together. Tears dripped down her cheeks.

Duke approached her. Could he see she was anxious?

Before she could speak, he pulled her into his arms and held her tight. "I won't let anyone hurt you," he whispered into her ear.

"I'm scared, Dad," she sobbed back.

CHAPTER 25

Paul stormed into his solicitor's office, his eyes surely blazing with a mixture of anger and determination. He slammed his fist down on the desk. Papers scattered across it and fluttered off the edge with the sudden gust of air.

"Paul!" Mr Barrett's eyes widened.

"I have a problem, and in turn, you have a problem," Paul growled, his voice low and dangerous. "Who has Rita put in her will? I need names and addresses."

The solicitor looked up from his desk, his expression a mixture of surprise and shock. "Calm down—"

Paul interrupted, his patience at breaking point. "This is calm. I want to know who's in Rita Taylor's will. Names, addresses, everything."

Mr Thompson hesitated, his gaze darting nervously around the room. "If you give me a minute—"

Before he could finish his sentence, Paul lunged across the desk, grabbing him by the collar, pulling him close.

"You listen to me, I haven't got a minute. You're up to your neck in dodgy dealings, I've got the proof," Paul snarled. "I didn't come here to play games. I came here for answers. Just do as you're fucking told."

Barrett's eyes widened. Paul grinned—*that* was the effect he wanted.

With a trembling hand, Barrett reached for a file on his desk, flipping it open to reveal the contents. "Here," he stammered, his voice as shaky as his hands. "Here are the names and addresses you asked for. Please, Mr Kelly, just leave me be."

Paul snatched the file from his hand, his lips curling into a satisfied smirk.

"Good boy," he sneered, placing the file inside his jacket. "Remember, I own you."

With that, Paul turned on his heels and marched out of the office, leaving a quivering Mr Barrett in his chair. Paul knew he wouldn't talk, he couldn't. He had done too many dodgy deals over the years, and Paul had him exactly where he wanted him.

***

Millie sat staring out of the window. It was pitch-black outside, the only light coming from the bonfire and a few of the trailer windows that had their curtains open. Jess and Aron had gone to the chippy, wherever that was. They seemed to know where they were, but she didn't. She had never heard of Halstead. She knew Essex, of course, but this place was in the back of beyond.

She glanced at Connie who was busy setting up a table with plates, knives, and forks. It seemed more spacious in here than the last time she'd visited. Although she was so scared last time she could barely remember.

The door opened, and in came Duke. He smiled, but Millie sensed he was worried about her.

"Boys are back, Con. They're at the gate," Duke called to Connie before sitting next to Millie. "Are you okay now?"

Millie gave him a short, curt nod. She didn't want to speak in case she started crying again. She refocused out of the window. She hadn't forgotten she had called him Dad. She'd been upset, it didn't mean anything. Did it? Her attention was drawn to headlights; the boys pulled up outside.

"You'll be sleeping with Connie, I'll sleep on the bunk," Duke announced.

"Where's Jess and Aron gonna sleep?" Millie asked, a little surprised. She hadn't given a thought to the sleeping arrangements.

"In the tourer they were towing," Duke replied as the door opened.

Millie immediately got the whiff of fish and chips. Her stomach grumbled loudly, but could she eat? Her guts twisted with worry. "Where's the toilet...I don't feel so good?" She stood, waiting for an answer.

"We haven't got a toilet. We—"

Before Duke had finished, Millie jumped up, flung open the door, and ran barefoot to the trees. She let out a gasp when pain surged through her foot, it felt like she had stepped on a razor blade. She didn't have time to worry about that; instead, she bent forward, bracing one hand on her knee, the other holding on to a tree for fear of collapsing. Her mouth was watering, so she spat out saliva. Without warning, the contents of her stomach landed at her feet. She stood, knees trembling. Wiping her mouth on the back of her hand, she leaned closer to the tree, clinging to it.

"Millie?" Duke called.

Shit, he was behind her.

"I'm okay." She gasped. "Go away." Of all the times to get a sick bug, she had to get one when there was no bleedin' bathroom.

***

Finn rested in his hospital bed, the sterile smell of antiseptic hanging heavy in the air around him. The events of the past few weeks felt like a blur. A fire, the flames licking at his skin, the agonizing pain as he'd fought to escape the inferno that had engulfed his pub and his life.

Now, as he lay here recovering, Finn couldn't shake the feeling of unease that settled over him like a heavy fog. He had been making progress, the doctors had assured him of that, but lately, something felt off, as if his body was betraying him, as if his strength slipped away with each passing hour.

And then there was Shannon, his long-lost daughter, the one bright spot in an otherwise dark and uncertain world. She had come to visit him, her presence a ray of sunshine in his dreary existence.

"Shannon?"

"I'm here now. You rest while I go and get you fresh water," she said.

Finn gripped his stomach again; the pain was retuning. "Nurse?"

"Finn, I'll get you something for the pain." The nurse rushed out.

Finn nodded weakly, his strength fading with each passing moment. The darkness that lurked at the edges of his consciousness threatened to consume him whole. He closed his eyes. He saw Millie's face. Where was she?

CHAPTER 26

Millie sat up and rubbed her eyes. She glanced at the bucket that had been placed next to the bed, just in case she was sick again.

How fucking embarrassing.

Of all the times to be ill, she had to chuck up in front of Duke. After he had helped her inside, he had then sat with her while Connie heated water for her to wash. The boys, however, tucked into their fish and chips like nothing had happened.

Millie threw the covers back and padded to the other end of the trailer. Duke looked up, his face showing a mix of concern and worry.

"How are you feeling, Millie?" he asked, wrapping his arm around her and leading her to a bunk. "Sit down and rest."

"I'm fine. Actually, I'm also hungry," Millie said.

"Did you eat or drink anything at the funeral?" Duke had a suspicious tone to his voice.

"No, I didn't touch anything, I was to het up looking for the scrapman, and then that woman who spoke to me finished off any appetite I might have had." Millie glanced out of the window. "Where's Connie?"

"Your mother has gone to get shopping with the boys." Duke informed her. He seemed to linger on the word mother.

Shit, are they expecting happy families?

She knew it was dumb calling Duke Dad, but she'd been upset. It was no more than a slip of the tongue.

"So what have you planned for today?" Millie asked, swiftly changing the subject.

"I'm with you all day, remember. I'm to keep you safe," Duke reminded her. "I would like you to rest today, after last night. How is the cut on your foot?"

"Sore, but I feel fine, and I need the toilet. Where am I supposed to go?" Millie looked out of the window. Where did they all go?

"You can go in the woods. I've got a shovel." Duke grinned.

Millie stared at him, her face heating up. "I am not going in the woods. Christ almighty! You're gonna have to take me home."

"Relax Millie, there's a toilet block just over there." Duke pointed. "And before you say anything, it's clean."

***

Paul drove along the upmarket street, pulling up opposite the house. No one could tell it was a brothel. It had a large driveway, and the house itself was set back and surrounded by trees. It was the perfect place for the business. He knew Gladys had a fair few upmarket clients, too, ranging from local politicians to judges. She had told him something about some bloke off the radio. Paul wasn't a prude, however, the thought of paying for sex disgusted him. Paying to fuck a woman who had been fucked a hundred times before by fuck knows how many men turned his stomach. It was something he would never do.

Gladys appeared at the door. She had an air of urgency about her. "Mr Kelly, I've had an urgent phone call for Millie. From the hospital, a nurse called Susan. She said something's wrong with

Finn. He was doing well, but now something else is wrong with him. He's going downhill for no apparent reason."

Paul blew out slowly while entering the house. "Why is the hospital phoning here?" He opened the door of the office with Gladys behind him.

"She said Millie gave her this number and if anything were to happen, she was to phone here and leave a message. Millie is supposed to be phoning me and checking," Gladys replied.

"If Millie rings here, do not, and I repeat, do not tell her that. Fuck's sake, she's in hiding for a reason. If she finds out Finn's taken a bad turn she'll be straight back." He paced the floor. Why couldn't things be simple? Something always had to happen and fuck everything up.

"And while we're at it, Tony will be here shortly. I'll need the office and I don't want any disturbances."

Gladys nodded and left the room, returning minutes later with a bottle of scotch and two glasses. "I thought you could do with a drink." She placed them on the desk and left, closing the door behind her.

Paul sat behind the desk and picked up the bottle. A drink was needed, but he doubted it would help. A knock came from the door.

"Yes," he called without looking up. He filled the two glasses and sat back.

Tony grabbed a chair and sat facing him.

"So what we got?" he asked, reaching for a glass.

Paul placed the file on the desk. "I've had a quick look through. Everything goes to Rita's sister, who happens to have one son."

"The bloke from the scrapyard?" Tony scanned the paperwork.

"I'd say so. They couldn't act on their own, I reckon a few of Ronnie's disgruntled men are helping them." Paul knocked back his drink, the burn hitting his throat immediately. "I've got patrols at the scrapyard, day and night, Duke's family's taking care of that. I want the same at the club, here, and the docks."

"We could do with some more men, Paul, we can't expect them to work day and night," Tony reasoned.

"Already taken care of. I've got my cousins coming over from Cork. There's four of them; they won't be able to stay indefinitely so we'll need to work fast. Put the men on shifts; you, me, and the

Irish will stake out these addresses. We need to know who they're working with, and more importantly, who is pulling the strings."

The phone ringing interrupted Paul, and he snatched it up. "What!" After a minute, he slammed it down. "Shit."

CHAPTER 27

Paul stood in the arrivals hall of Heathrow Airport, his arms folded across his chest, a scowl etched on his face. He tapped his foot impatiently as he scanned the crowd for any sign of his four Irish cousins, who were supposed to be arriving on a flight from Cork. The airport was busy, people everywhere. Millie popped into his mind. Her beautiful face, the way she flicked her hair when she was annoyed. Paul smiled. What was she doing? Did she miss him as much as he missed her?

A loud noise broke Paul's thoughts. He looked over to the security barrier and spotted the drunken four, stumbling through the crowd, their loud laughter and boisterous antics drawing the attention of everyone around them. Paul sighed deeply.

"Fucking Irish," he mumbled.

They weren't *supposed* to draw any attention to themselves.

"Oi, Paulie," his cousin, Aiden, called out.

They were flanked by airport security. Aiden approached and slapped Paul on the back with enough force to nearly knock him off balance.

"Long time no see, eh?" Aiden added.

Paul gritted his teeth, resisting the urge to throttle his rowdy cousin. "Cut the crap, lads," he muttered. "This is a business trip, remember?"

Paul glanced at the six security officers and gave them a curt nod. "I'll take them from here, fellas, they'll be no more trouble."

He turned his attention back to his cousins who exchanged confused glances. Paul rolled his eyes; he needed to sober them up. There would be no work done while they were in this state. He knew they were all big drinkers, but to get that pissed and rowdy on such a short flight was beyond him.

"Follow me and keep your mouths shut," he demanded. Content when they all nodded, he turned and led them out of the airport and to his motor.

They all piled in to the Range Rover, and Paul allowed himself a small smile. His other cousins, Conor, Sean, and Liam, all six-foot lumps, sat squashed in the back like sardines.

"Move ya fecking elbow," Conor groaned to Liam.

"Where the feck am I supposed to put it, it's attached to me fecking arm," Liam replied curtly.

"Fellas," Paul called over his shoulder. "It's a short journey. Now shut up and listen." He started the motor and pulled away. "I told you this was a business trip. You don't get fucking pissed when you are doing business."

"Calm down, Paulie," Aiden said. "You didn't tell us anything on the phone about this business, so what's the craic?"

"And for good fucking reason." Paul blew out slowly, doing his best to contain his temper. He didn't want to upset them too much, he needed them. They were his best shot at getting to the bottom of this situation, and he also trusted them as much as he did Tony. They were blood, and as the old saying goes, blood is thicker than water.

"Someone's after my livelihood. They have been messing with Millie, who is now in hiding with her old man, Duke—" Paul stopped when Aiden abruptly cut in.

"The gypsy?"

"Yes, he—" Paul began.

"I tought you didn't like him?" Aiden continued.

"Will you let me fucking finish?" Paul growled. Content when he was met with silence, he started again. "Millie is in hiding with Duke, who is also her dad."

"Fecking hell, I did not see that one coming!" Aiden blurted out. "Sorry Paulie, continue."

"Are you sure that's okay, Your Majesty? There isn't anything else you'd like to add?" Paul rubbed his scar; he was more than a little annoyed. "Duke's all right, he loves Millie, and I trust him more than anyone to keep her safe. He's also roped his family in to watch the scrapyard. My boys are taking care of the other businesses, so this brings me on to you four. I need you lot to help find the prick who's causing the problem."

"And how do we do that?" Conor called from the back.

"I've got the addresses of the people who stand to inherit from Rita, we'll start there. Yous boys need to sober up first, so we'll go tonight and watch their gaffs. Any questions?" Paul asked.

"Can't we just kill them?" Aiden replied with a shrug.

"And what if they aren't the real threat? Then there'll still be someone out there and I'd have no leads. No, we watch and wait, see where they go and who they talk to." Paul came to a stop on his drive, his heart sinking at the thought of Millie not being there waiting for him. When he got his hands on the person responsible, he would make sure they paid in the most painful way possible.

CHAPTER 28

Millie sat on the edge of the bed, resting her hands on her knees. The latest wave of sickness was subsiding. Connie came in and sat next to her, the bed moving. She swallowed down the bile that threatened once more.

Connie placed her arm around her shoulders. "I think we should take you to see a doctor. It's been three days now, Millie, and you look a bit pasty."

"I just need to rest, it's probably a bug or stress. With everything that's going on, I'm just run-down." In truth, she wanted to go home, to see Paul and lie in her own bed. "Has Duke spoken to Paul?"

"Did I hear my name mentioned?" Duke asked as he entered the already cramped bedroom.

"Millie was just asking if you had spoken to Paul," Connie said.

"No, but me and ya mother have been speaking, and we both think you should see a doctor." Duke knelt in front of her.

"I don't need a doctor, I need my husband," she snapped.

"Okay." He held his hands up in surrender. "Here's the deal. You see a doctor, and I'll arrange for you to speak to Paul."

"That's blackmail." Millie sighed.

"That's the deal. Take it or leave it," Duke reaffirmed.

Why should I have to make a deal to see my own husband? "I want to make a phone call, too."

"Who are you phoning?" Duke's eyes narrowed.

Christ, he's so suspicious, the nosey bastard. "I do have friends, you know… Phone call and see Paul, then I'll go to the doctor. *You* take it or leave it." Millie folded her arms in defiance.

Duke gave a curt nod. "I'll get a doctor's appointment today and see if I can sort something for tomorrow."

***

Paul sat in the kitchen nursing a cup of tea. His cousins, who were in the lounge, laughed and joked. They were giving him a headache. He had already hidden all the booze in the house. They didn't need tempting. The phone rang, and Paul went to answer it.

"Hello."

"Paul, it's Duke."

"What's happened, is Millie all right?" Paul's heart beat rapidly.

"She's been sick. Now don't worry, I'm gonna take her to the doctor, but—"

"But what?" Paul snapped, cutting Duke off.

"Calm down, Paul… But she wants to see you, or she won't go. I told her I would see what I can arrange. I'm taking her to the doctor in an hour."

Paul sighed. "I can't see her, we're staking out the addresses tonight. What about a phone call once she's been to the doc? I'll be here till about eight?"

"Okay. But she also wants to make a phone call."

Paul cursed under his breath. "I know who she wants to phone. Let her, and make sure you find out what's wrong." He slammed the phone down and then picked it back up and dialled the number for Gladys. He would remind her to keep her mouth shut.

***

Millie closed the door behind her and stared at the doctor.

"Please take a seat." He motioned.

She smiled and did as he'd said.

"How can I help you today, Miss…?"

"Mrs Kelly," she replied. Why was she sweating? "I've been sick the last couple of days. It comes on suddenly and then goes just as suddenly."

"I see… Any other symptoms?"

"I feel tired but I'm not sleeping well." Millie watched as the doctor scribbled on a piece of paper. "I've got a lot of stress in my life at the moment, I was wondering if it was that?"

"Can you lie on the examining couch, Mrs Kelly, and I'll have a feel of your tummy."

"Please, call me Millie."

"Okay, Millie, up here." The doctor tapped the couch.

She kicked her shoes off and jumped on, swinging her legs around, then lay flat. The doctor prodded her tummy; at times it was painful, and Millie let out a short gasp.

"Does that hurt Millie?"

"A little. What's wrong with me, is it serious?" She swallowed down the worry. *Please let it be a bug.*

"Let's do some tests first, shall we? Now, can you provide me with a urine specimen? The toilet is just opposite as you go out, and I will arrange a blood test for you. You will need to go to the local hospital for that, just turn up, no need to book."

Millie took the small tube he held out and blushed. How on earth was she supposed to pee in that?

She left the doctor's room and felt Connie's and Duke's eyes on her. Without glancing at them, she rushed into the toilet. It was hard enough stopping them both from coming in to see the doctor with her, never mind telling them she had to pee in a tiny tube. Would Connie have wanted to assist her with that, too?

She flushed the chain and washed her hands before returning to the doctor.

"I will send this off. In the meantime, can you get the blood tests done and then I will see you in a week's time?"

"Can't you tell me what's wrong now?" Millie asked, her heart sinking.

"I won't know until the tests come back and I'm not going to guess. I'm certain it isn't life-threatening, so try not to worry. That will only make things worse."

How the fuck can I not worry? She nodded and joined Duke and Connie in the waiting room. "I need to have a blood test tomorrow and then come back next week. He did say it wasn't serious, so I guess that's good."

"So why have you got to have blood tests then?" Duke queried. "Cos you don't have blood tests if it's nothing." He turned towards the doctor's room.

Before he had chance to move, Millie stepped in front of him, blocking the way. "Don't you dare show me up. Now I've held up my end of the bargain. You owe me a visit with Paul and a phone call."

CHAPTER 29

Finn looked at the sky. It was pure brilliant blue. The birds sang, and the sun shimmered on the water. He was home in the Emerald Isle. Kinsale. The brightly coloured cottages lined the way along the harbour wall. He glanced at the end cottage. His mammy was hanging out the washing.

"Finn. His pulse is weak, get the doctor. Finn, come on, love, open your eyes."

"What…where am I?" Finn mumbled. He slowly opened his eyes. The light was blinding.

"You're in hospital, remember?" the nurse asked. "The doctor's coming to check you over."

Finn groaned. His mouth tasted funny. "Water."

"Let's wait for the doctor first. Ah, here he is," the nurse replied.

He looked at her—Susan, was it? She was nice, caring. "Where's Shannon?"

"You can't have any visitors today, you've been poorly. Maybe tomorrow," Susan offered.

He closed his eyes, his head aching.

Millie?

"Nurse, there's a phone call for you. Can I remind you this is not a place to take personal calls. Get rid of them, and quickly," the matron ordered.

Susan rushed to the desk and snatched up the phone. "Hello?"

"Susan, it's Millie, how's Finn?"

"Millie, I can't talk right now. I phoned that number you gave me. Finn's not—"

"*Nurse!*" the matron bellowed.

"I'm sorry, Millie, I've got to go."

***

Millie sat on the bunk, staring out of the window. Paul's angry words rang through her head.

"Stop worrying about Finn and worry about yourself," he had ordered. Just like the sodding dictator that he was.

Hadn't she done everything he had asked? She was living in a gypsy site, for Christ's sake. All he had to do was check on Finn or let her do it.

"I hope you're gonna eat something, Millie. You won't be able to eat or drink until after your blood test tomorrow," Connie reminded her.

"I'm not hungry," Millie barked. She felt like a prisoner—she *was* a prisoner.

"Here, drink your tea." Connie pushed a cup in front of her. "You need to keep your strength up. That might be why you're so tired."

"Doesn't explain the sickness, though, does it?" She picked up the cup and took a small sip. It was hot. Turning her attention to the window, she watched the chavvies playing outside. It was nearly dark, and she suspected they would be called in before long.

She glanced at the trailer opposite. A young woman stood on the step talking to a man, her arms moving around in anger. Was she gonna hit him?

"Who's that?" she asked Connie.

"Gypsy Ward. The man she's talking to is her husband, John Jo. He's an Irish traveller. Apparently, he won her in a poker game. Not sure if that's true, though. No one's brave enough to ask him. He's a fighting man, like Duke, but with the temper of the Devil," Connie said glancing out of the window.

Millie turned away when John Jo swivelled towards Gypsy.

Shit! "Poor woman. What idiot would bet a person on a poker game?"

"It was supposedly her grandfather. Will you please drink your tea, Millie, and stop nosing."

"I'm not nosing."

She glanced around to where the couple had been standing. They had both disappeared inside. She flicked her head towards the campfire. Duke stood there with some other travelling men, drinking beer. Was that why he liked this life so much? It did seem more of a man's world.

He had spent the afternoon telling her about the Romani way of life. "It's your heritage," he had said. Only she wasn't sure she wanted it to be, especially after he had told her about his nan, her great-nan. "She would wear a long skirt and no underwear, Millie. She'd go and sell her lucky heather up the races, and if she needed to pee she just squatted on the grass. No one would know what she was doing."

Did all the women do that? Did Connie?

Millie shook the thought from her head.

"Connie, why did you buy that bit of land?" she asked without looking at her.

"I wanted to be in Stepney, near you. I didn't realise it would be at the end of your garden, but I'm glad it is," Connie replied with a smile.

"But Duke looks more at home here, he must get lonely there," Millie surmised.

"No!" Connie's voice was firm. "He wouldn't want to be anywhere else now he knows you're his daughter."

She turned. Connie sat beside her, her expression serious.

"Are you sure he's not going to resent me, for taking away this?" Millie jerked her head towards the group of men at the bonfire.

A small laugh escaped Connie's lips. "No, Millie. You don't realise what family means to us, what you mean to us… Duke can go and see his people whenever the fancy takes him. We will still go to the horse fairs, races, and get-togethers, but if he had to choose between them and you, you would win every time."

"His people?" Millie questioned.

"He's Romani, I'm a gorger. As much as they have welcomed me into the family, and they have, I'm still a gorger. His mum, your gran, is a lovely woman, hard-faced but would fight for you." Connie laughed. "And I mean fight, fisticuffs and all… You need to get to know them, stop putting a barrier up."

"I'm not!" Millie huffed.

"You are, I can feel it as though it's an actual brick wall… Now I'm going to prepare dinner, and you will eat, even if it's only a small plate." Connie stood and paused. "I love you, Millie, so does Duke and your brothers. Maybe it's time you allowed yourself to love us back."

***

Paul sat in the cramped confines of the old Ford motor he had rescued from the scrapyard. It was smaller than his Range Rover, but it was untraceable to him and just the job for the stakeout.

His gaze remained fixed on the house across the street. It was dark, the only light coming from the occasional flicker of a television screen or the dim glow of a streetlamp. He shifted uncomfortably in his seat, his muscles tense.

Beside him sat Sean, and Liam sat behind. They had been staking out the place for hours now, waiting for any sign of movement from Rita's nephew, the one he suspected of being involved in the threats against his wife, himself, and his livelihood.

But as the hours dragged on, the tension in the car grew thicker and thicker, until it felt like they were suffocating in the stifling silence.

Without warning, Sean let out a loud, raucous fart that echoed through the car like a gunshot. Paul recoiled in horror, his nostrils assaulted by the noxious odour that filled the air. He gagged and coughed, frantically rolling down the window in a desperate bid for fresh air.

"Jesus, Sean!" he exclaimed. Turning his head towards him, his voice choked with disgust, he said, "What the bloody hell did you eat?"

Sean didn't even look embarrassed. Instead, he just shrugged. "Must've been something from the airport."

Paul whipped his head around when Liam snorted, his shoulders shaking.

Paul fixed him with a solid glare. "Can we please focus. We're on a fucking stakeout, not a lads' night out at the pub." He returned his attention to the house, waving his hand in front of his face to dispel the lingering smell.

He wasn't sure at what point he had decided it was a good idea to bring the Irish lads over. He just hoped Tony was having better luck with Aiden and Conor.

CHAPTER 30

Millie woke to the sound of snoring. It was filling the whole trailer. She turned towards Connie who was still sound asleep. The noise wasn't coming from her. She pushed the covers back slowly and slid out of the bed, making sure not to wake her. Goosebumps covered her skin from the cold winter air.

It was normally toasty when she got up, but then she was always the last one up, and Connie always sorted the fire out.

She tiptoed out of the bedroom and almost laughed when she spotted Duke, lying flat on his back with his mouth open. That was the source of the disturbing noise. Christ, how could Connie sleep through that?

She grabbed her coat and slipped on her shoes, then unlocked the door and went outside. The darkness was subsiding as daylight seemed to loom over the horizon. Millie peered around. She hadn't been out other than to use the toilet, and she hadn't allowed herself to explore. She walked slowly towards the other end of the camp. Passing by Gypsy and John Jo's trailer. It was similar to Duke and Connie's. Thick chrome bands wrapped around it, making it gleam even in the darkness.

Her thoughts turned to Gypsy. No wonder she was angry. Being given away to pay a debt. She looked young. Millie reckoned seventeen, maybe eighteen at a push.

Still older than me when I married Levi. Yeah, but I wasn't forced into it. No, you bleedin' jumped in headfirst like an idiot and paid the price.

Millie closed her eyes. She promised herself she wouldn't think about those dark days. Continuing on her way, she glanced around. Everyone was still tucked up in their beds. Even the dogs slept.

She passed the firepit, the branches that had danced with flames the previous night now nothing but ash. She continued along the bumpy track, glancing at all the trailers that were in total darkness, until she spotted a gypsy wagon.

It had a soft glow coming from the tiny window, and smoke billowed from a small chimney. She couldn't remember seeing it before, but then it was tucked away, partly hidden by trees. Millie marvelled at the bright paintwork. It was like a piece of art; the intricate painting involved greens, reds, and golds. The woodwork looked like it had been created by a master. She stood and stared in awe. Was this her heritage?

"You better come in, girl, you'll catch a chill if you stay there much longer."

Millie blinked and spun her head to an old woman who leaned out of the door at the end of the wagon.

"I..." Millie started.

"Now, girl, before all the warm airs let out," the old woman snapped.

Millie walked towards the door, her pulse racing. "I didn't mean to disturb you," she began as she climbed the wooden steps. "I've just never seen anything so beautiful," she finished. She stepped into the wagon and stared around in amazement.

There was a double bed at one end, neatly made with brightly coloured blankets. A fire was in the centre of one wall and seating the other side. Above the fire, a stove-like thing with a pot of boiling water on top.

The old woman took two cups and poured the boiled water into them. "Sugar?"

"Oh, I can't have anything to eat or drink, I need to have a blood test today," Millie informed her.

The old woman's face snapped towards Millie. "Why?"

"Because I've been under the weather," Millie replied, a little put out. This was her private business, it had bugger all to do with anyone else. She averted her gaze; the old woman was studying her. It made her nervous. Why?

"Rubbish. You're not ill."

"And you know that because you're a doctor?" Millie glared. Everyone had an opinion on her life.

"I'm a healer. I've been around a long time. You are not ill. You're 'aving a chavvie."

Millie took a sharp breath. "Don't be ridiculous. Don't you think I would know if I were pregnant?"

"No, obviously not." She cackled, which set off a cough.

Millie sighed. "I've been sick in the evenings, so it's not morning sickness."

"It doesn't have to be in the mornings, girl. You're pregnant, I can see it in your face. Now I can't read your tea leaves if you don't drink your tea. Do you want sugar?"

"I don't believe in that stuff." Millie turned to leave, but the old woman's voice drifted over her shoulder.

"You're troubled, child. I can sense your unhappiness. What are you afraid of?"

Millie spun around and studied the old woman. Her face was weathered, like she had lived a hundred years. Could she really sense her unhappiness, her pain? Millie sat onto the bunk next to her, the warmth welcoming. She held her hands out towards the fire and rubbed them together. "One sugar."

***

Duke stretched his arms over his head and yawned. He glanced at the end of the trailer. Connie was still asleep. He stood and headed towards the fire. It was a bit nippy this morning so, deciding to get the fire going, he began to clean out the ash and debris.

"Morning," Connie called as she joined him.

Duke stood and wrapped his arms around her waist, pulling her towards him. "Morning, Con." His lips met hers, and his blood rushed to his cock. He needed some alone time. Maybe he could get the boys to watch Millie while he took Connie in the tourer for an hour. Millie?

Duke drew back and leant over to look at the bed. It was empty. "Where is she?" he said, his voice laced with panic.

"Toilet?" Connie guessed. "I didn't hear her get up."

"That fucking child will be the death of me." Duke slipped on his dealer boots and coat. "I'll go find her." He stormed out of the trailer, smashing the door shut behind him.

He marched to the toilet block and stuck his head in. "*Millie?*" he yelled. When no answer came, he scanned the site. Most of the trailers were still in darkness. He took his keys from his coat pocket. Should he drive around and look for her?

"Duke," Connie called. "She hasn't got dressed, her clothes are still here."

Could someone have taken her? No. No one would have got into the trailer without being heard. Had she been abducted going to the toilet? Unlikely, the dogs would have gone mad if a stranger was on the site.

"Get the fire going and kettle on, she must be here somewhere. I'll search for her." Duke trudged along the rows of trailers, stopping at those with lights on and asking if they had seen his daughter.

He knocked on John Jo's door and stood back.

"Morning, Duke. What can I do for you?" he asked while rubbing his eyes.

"You ain't seen me daughter, Millie, have ya?" he asked, doing his best to remain calm.

"No, me and Gypsy just got up. Do you want me to search with you?"

"Na, she'll be here somewhere." Duke turned and headed further along the track. He stopped at the old witch's wagon. Without knocking, he yanked open the door to find Millie sitting next to Patience.

"Millie, get out, go back to Connie," he ordered.

Millie's eyes had gone wide. Had he scared her?

"Duke... I—" Millie stuttered.

"Now, Millie." He waited for her to leave and then turned to his great-aunt, Patience. "If you've filled her head with that shit, I'll torch the fucking wagon with you in it. Now stay away from my daughter." Duke walked away, and Patience's strained voice caught his ear.

"I didn't tell her all I saw."

***

Millie slumped down onto the bunk. Damn Duke Lee, interrupting just as she was pressing the old woman for more information. Millie could see it in her eyes; she looked sad. Just what had those sodding tea leaves shown her?

Hang on, you don't believe in that mumbo-jumbo.

The door opened, and Duke stormed in. His face contorted with anger. "You do not just disappear like that, and you do not go anywhere near Patience again. Understood?"

"Don't bring the old woman into this, you're angry at me," Millie replied with a sigh.

"Yes, I'm angry at you. You can't just disappear like that. Fucking hell, Millie. Someone's after you and Paul. You," Duke stabbed a finger at her, "are here for me to protect you, keep you safe."

"I wouldn't worry, if anyone came here they'd die from boredom long before they got to me," Millie snapped.

"We were worried." Connie's quiet voice hit her like a punch to the gut.

Millie turned away and fought back the tears that threatened. "I'm sorry. You were both asleep… I didn't think."

"Look at me." Duke's voice was softer. Like the fight had left him.

Millie glanced at him.

He knelt in front of her. "What did she tell you?"

"Nothing really, same old crap they always say, kids, long life, blah, blah, blah." She shrugged. She wouldn't tell him. It was private.

"Take whatever she tells you with a pinch of salt." Duke stood and walked to the door.

"You're not much of an advert for fortune telling, just because you don't believe," Millie called.

"She fills people's heads with rubbish and then they have to carry that around all their lives, waiting for it to come true. No one should know the future, especially when it's made up."

Millie swallowed the lump in her throat. It sounded to her that Duke was one of those people. What had Patience told him?

CHAPTER 31

Paul rubbed his eyes. He'd been thinking about Millie. Had she had the blood tests done? He wished he could wrap her in his arms and breathe in her scent. He smiled; he would never tire of that soft, sweet smell.

Movement caught his eye. He flicked his head to the front door of Rita's nephew's house.

About fucking time. Doesn't this lazy bastard work for a living? No, he's too busy trying to con me out of what I've worked for.

"He's on the move, boys, keep an eye out." Paul started the engine and followed Rita's nephew who pulled out of the driveway and headed towards the High Street. Paul kept a safe distance, his gaze darting around for signs of being followed.

"Where the fuck is he going?" Liam asked.

"Looks like he's heading to Whitechapel," Paul replied. "We might just find out who's behind this shit, with any luck."

The car ground to a halt outside the Blind Begger public house. Paul stopped across the road and watched. Rita's nephew entered the pub.

"He's meeting someone," Paul thought out loud.

"I'll go in and see who it is." Liam unclipped his seat belt and reached for the handle.

Paul grabbed his arm before he could get out. "Sean you go, too. Yous boys see if you can overhear any names and get a good look at who he's with." He let go once Liam gave him a nod.

Paul sat back and sighed. He needed to be in there but knew he couldn't. If whoever the nephew was saw him, they would know he was onto them, and then who knew what they would do. At least Millie was safe.

Paul sat forward when he spotted a man walk towards the pub. He seemed familiar, but Paul couldn't place where he had seen him before. He wore a trilby hat, just like Ronnie Taylor had. In fact, he looked a bit like Ronnie, same build, same mannerisms. Did Ronnie have a brother? If he did, he'd never mentioned him.

Strange.

Paul flicked through the photos he had taken of Rita's sister and her nephew. He needed to show Millie these, she was the only one who could identify them. Was this the woman at the funeral? Was Rita's nephew the man from the scrapyard?

Paul rubbed his hand over his face. He was tired. There were to many unanswered questions.

The door of the pub opened, and Rita's nephew marched out. He didn't appear happy. A few minutes later, the Ronnie doppelganger came out. He walked off in the opposite direction. Paul kept his attention on the pub door. Where were Liam and Sean

After waiting another ten minutes, Paul marched over to the pub. There at the bar, the two lads were necking a pint of Guinness.

"What the fuck are you doing?"

"Paulie, you gonna join us for a drink?" Sean asked. His eyes creased with joy.

"We have business to attend," Paul said through gritted teeth. "Let's go."

"Jaysus, Paulie, it's a little lunchtime bevvy. We deserve a lunch break," Liam added.

"You've been sat on ya arses all night, you can 'ave a break when you've earned one." Paul pointed to the door. "Out."

He followed the two lads out and stormed over to the car. He knew the Irish were big drinkers, but he expected better of them on the job. He slid behind the steering wheel and waited for them to climb in. "Did you find anything out?"

"He waited for a man in a trilby hat, who's definitely pulling all the strings," Liam said. "Rita's nephew, who by the way is called Martin, wasn't happy. It's like he's being forced to help this man."

"They are leaving the scrapyard for now because of the gypsy presence. Instead, they are going after the docks," Sean said. "Paul, this sounded personal. This man wants to crush you."

***

Paul slowed when he neared the traveller site. It had taken ages to get here—talk about no-man's land. This place was in the back of beyond. After he opened the gate and pulled through, he closed it and crawled along, checking out the trailers, although the chrome ones all looked the same to him. He stopped when he spotted Duke's Transit. He was greeted by Duke who seemed to appear from nowhere.

"Paul," Duke said.

"Duke, where's Millie?" He couldn't help the urgency in his voice. He had missed her.

"Follow me." Duke turned and walked to the trailer. "Millie, we have a visitor."

Paul stepped in behind Duke and was met with two arms flung around his neck.

"Paul," Millie screeched.

His lips found hers, and all his problems melted away. He moved back when Duke coughed.

"Connie, come on, let's give them some privacy," Duke told her.

Paul waited for the door to close and then smashed his lips against hers once again.

"Paul," she mumbled.

Without thinking, he unzipped his trousers, picked her up and, easing her underwear aside, he slipped inside her. He was in heaven. The faster he thrust, the more his heart rate soared. Minutes later, he let out a moan, and Millie threw her head back. He gasped for breath as Millie trembled.

"That was too quick," he complained.

"Considering we just did that in Connie and Duke's trailer, I think it had to be." She laughed. "It's going to be embarrassing facing them."

"You've gone red." Paul smiled. "I haven't made you blush for some time." An awkward silence followed. He studied her for signs of illness.

"Why are you here, Paul?" Millie asked. "Is it to bring me home?"

"No, babe. But it won't be much longer. What's going on with the doctor?"

"I feel fine, reckon it was just a bug. The tests were just a precaution."

"Are you sure?" He smiled when Millie nodded. "It's about time we had some good news… I've got a couple of photos I want you to look at." He reached into his jacket pocket and pulled out two. "Is this the woman from the funeral?"

Millie took the photo and shook her head. "No. The woman from the funeral was slim, to the point of appearing ill."

"How about this one? Is this the bloke from the scrapyard?" He handed her the photo.

Her face changed.

"I think it is…yes," she confirmed.

"Good, I'm making progress, Mil. Do you remember when you went through all Ronnie's paperwork? Was there anything about a brother?"

"A brother?" Millie shook her head slowly, as though she was thinking. "Do you know where Ronnie was born?"

"Islington as far as I know, why?" Paul frowned.

"You could check births, deaths, and marriages. If you know roughly when he was born. It will take patience, though, but if he had a brother there will be a record."

"You are a genius, babe." Paul smiled. "One last thing, the bloke from the scrapyard. Conor and Liam followed him into a pub. He was talking to this Ronnie Taylor double. They reckon he was being forced to help him."

"While you get a couple of boys to check through birth records, why don't you pay him a visit? If he is being forced, I'm sure he would be grateful for a way out," she concurred. "I would be, and even if not you could threaten him; you are scary when you're angry," she added.

"Are you scared of me?" Paul asked.

Was she?

CHAPTER 32

Millie tossed and turned all night. Seeing Paul just reminded her of how much she'd missed him. The time went too quick, and within the hour, he had left to return home. Without her.

Millie's thoughts turned to Finn. She needed someone to check on him.

Maggie?

She would phone the brothel and speak to her. She was one of the few people she could trust. Her help setting up the managers at the docks so she could get the lease papers signed had been proof of that.

She also needed to contact Rosie. She hadn't heard from her since she had left that day after the hospital visit. The anger and accusing tone of her voice still upset her.

She climbed out of bed and reached for her bag. After riffling through, she found her little address book. Scott's number would be in there.

"What's going on?" Duke called from the other end of the trailer.

"I've got cramp, I was just walking it off," Millie lied. This place was worse than Colditz.

"Do you want a cup of tea?" he asked.

Why is he being so nice?

"If you're making one."

Millie grabbed the new dressing gown Connie had bought her and wrapped it tightly around herself. She still had a bruise on the crook of her arm from the blood test. It ached a little when pressed. Rubbing it gently, she padded through to the other end of the trailer while Duke lit the gas.

"How come it's still warm in here?" Millie asked.

"I filled the fire up with coal. I didn't want you getting cold again." He placed the kettle on the gas and motioned to the bunk. "Take a seat."

Am I in for a lecture?

Millie sat and stared up at him. "What have I done now?"

"Nothing. I just want to make sure you're okay," he replied. "I know it's hard for you, Millie, being in a small space like this. You must miss your big house."

"No. I miss Paul." She glanced around the trailer. It was spotless. There wasn't so much as a fingerprint on the cut-glass mirrors, and the display cabinets proudly held the Crown Derby china that was perfectly arranged. Despite being a small space, everything had its place.

"Duke, it's nice in here, I can see why you like it, although I guess it's not much fun having me here."

"I love having you here, so does Connie. Look, why don't we go to the market tomorrow. You can get yourself some new clothes and we could go to a café for lunch."

"Do they have markets here, or cafés?" she asked flatly.

"They have markets and cafés everywhere, Millie. You need to travel a bit more." Duke laughed.

"I need to make some phone calls." She looked at him as he spun around to face her. "They are important, Duke."

"I presume that's why you're not sleeping... Okay, but first I want to know what's going on."

***

Paul returned to Martin's home after dropping the Irish off at the town hall. He had given them strict instructions on how to search for the mysterious Ronnie Taylor lookalike. He had even written down the names of Ronnie's parents and the rough date of his birth. If he couldn't get the answers from this prick, then he hoped the boys would come up trumps.

Paul slowed, making sure Martin's car was on the drive. Satisfied, he pulled up a couple of houses away. He slipped his knuckle-duster into his pocket and marched to the front door, knocking loudly.

The door opened, shock on the man's face. Before he had a chance to shut the door, Paul shoulder-barged his way in.

"Think we need to talk, Martin."

The man held both hands up in a sign of surrender. "You d-don't understand," he stammered, his face draining of colour.

"I think I understand perfectly." Paul slipped the knuckle-duster on and clenched his fist in front of Martin's face. "Your first mistake was to involve my wife."

"Whoa. That wasn't my idea; in fact, none of this is." Martin backed away, colliding with the banister rail.

"Maybe you'd like to tell me whose idea it was then, and fast, before I lose the remaining bit of patience I've got." Paul took a step closer.

"I can't, he'll kill my family."

"If you don't, *I'll* kill your fucking family and make you watch. Now start talking," Paul spat.

Martin's shoulders slumped.

Paul smirked. This was easier than he had anticipated. "I'm waiting."

With a loud sigh, Martin began. "After Ronnie died, a man came to see me. He reckoned he was my uncle, Ronnie's brother. Although there was a resemblance, and he seemed to know everything about Ronnie, I didn't believe him. Ronnie had never mentioned him, so when he left, I went and asked Rita. She was tight-lipped, told me not to have anything to do with this man and that he was an imposter, but it was too late."

"What did he want?" Paul snapped.

"He wanted everything that was Ronnie's, starting with the scrapyard. Ya see, he thought I would inherit it from Ronnie. He was going to force me to sign it over to him, but it had already been left to you. I didn't know that. I thought it had gone to Rita." Martin shook his head slowly. "I thought that would be the end of it, but no, he wanted me to contest the will. I refused. That's when he threatened my family."

"Why were you at the scrapyard?"

"He wanted me there to see how many men you had, what the setup was. I saw your wife staring at me, so I left. He wasn't happy about that either." Martin sighed.

"Why did you meet at the pub? What's his next step?" Paul pressed.

"Now there's a load of gypsies running the scrapyard, he wants to go after the docks to cause you problems. He's hoping you'll move your sights there and leave the yard open for attack."

Paul's jaw tensed. "What's his name?"

"I don't know. He never uses a name." Martin shrugged.

Paul blew out slowly, his forehead creased. "Where does he live?"

"I don't know. I wait for him to contact me, that's how it works."

"For fuck's sake!" Paul clenched his fists. "Right, you. You work for me now. If you value your life, you will do everything I say. Understand?"

Martin shook his head. "I can't, he—"

"You fucking can and you will. I will be leaving a couple of men here to make sure. I want to know when he contacts you and what he wants." Paul handed Martin a business card. "There will be someone on the other end of that phone day and night. Whatever time this prick rings, you let me know. Do as I say, and you will live." He yanked open the front door and turned to Martin with a sneer, his voice emotionless. "And if you don't, you won't."

CHAPTER 33

Millie lay on the bed, staring at the ceiling. Her brothers were outside on guard duty. Connie and Duke had nipped to the shops to buy groceries before they would all head off to the market. She wasn't sure whether she wanted to go, but Duke had insisted.

"I kept my end of the deal, now you keep yours," he had told her.

At the time it had seemed like a fair trade. Two phone calls for a trip to the market. At least she had spoken to Rosie, although after the conversation she was left with a sinking feeling. Her friend had sounded so down, so lost, so lonely. What a shit friend Millie had turned out to be. She should be there with her, helping her through the breakup, just like Rosie had helped her when she was recovering from the car crash and the death of her first husband.

Millie sighed. It seemed a lifetime ago she was married to Levi, the abuse she had suffered at his and his mother's hands now a distant memory. A lump formed in her throat. She swallowed it down. Then there was Elijah, her ex-father-in-law, whom she had murdered.

It was an accident, he did try to rape you.

The image of his twisted body, as it lay crumpled at the bottom of the stairs, slipped into her mind. Closing her eyes tight only amplified it.

Millie sat up and gazed out of the window. Winter was here. The heatwave also a distant memory. A loud bang boomed, and she jumped up and ran to the other end of the trailer. Her gaze rested on John Jo Ward. He was a good-looking man. Tall, muscular, and broad. At the end of his truck, a pile of logs lay in a heap. That explained the bang. He held an axe. His trailer door opened, and Gypsy's face popped out. She smiled. Maybe the marriage wasn't a sham after all. Millie shook her head. As if you could win a wife in a poker game, honestly. No, she seemed happy with her husband.

Husband.

Her mind turned to Paul. Was he any closer to catching the person responsible for her abdication? She wanted her own bed, with Paul in it. A small smile played on her lips.

Finn?

The smile dropped, and her mind flicked to Maggie. Unlike Rosie, Maggie had been so pleased to hear from her, promising to go and check on Finn. All Millie had to do was phone back tomorrow for an update.

It would normally be Rosie she asked for help. How times had changed. Her best friend was becoming a stranger.

Millie's head whipped around as the door opened. In walked Connie with Duke following, holding two large bags of shopping.

"Where are you gonna put all that?" Millie asked, her eyes wide.

"It won't last long. Not with your brothers' appetites. Pair of pigs, the both of 'em," Duke called over his shoulder.

"I hope you don't talk about me like that when I'm not around," Millie replied indignantly.

"You, my beautiful daughter, don't eat enough to keep a sparrow alive," he told her. "Now get your coat and wrap up warm," he added.

Daughter. Beautiful.

Millie half-smiled, and a strange feeling swept over her. She felt…warm inside. Were they bonding as father and daughter? Were they becoming a family?

You grew up in a children's home. Remember.

She grabbed her coat.

It wasn't their fault.

She buttoned it quickly.

Take the walls down then and let them in.

She trudged out to the Transit.

What if they decide they don't want me?

Duke held the door open and stood back. "Your chariot awaits, princess."

Millie hesitated. "If you decide you don't want me anymore, you will tell me," she asked him.

Duke stood deadly still, his expression a mixture of shock and hurt.

See what you've done? You just couldn't keep your big gob shut.

Millie stared at the ground, she couldn't face him. His hands rested on her shoulders.

"Look at me." His tone was soft.

But Millie knew it was an order.

"You." Duke squeezed her shoulders gently. "Are my daughter. I will always want you, Millie. Until the day I die, and even that won't be long enough. I'm your dad. This." He pointed between the two of them. "Is forever."

Millie sniffed back the threatening tears, then before she could take a breath, Duke had wrapped his arms around her and drew her into a tight hug.

"I love you. I loved you before I knew you and I'll always love you." He kissed the top of her head, adding, "Even though you can be moody."

Millie pulled away. "I am not." She huffed.

"I rest my case, Your Honour." Duke laughed. "Now get in the motor or you'll catch a chill. Connie, hurry up."

Millie smiled.

Forever.

***

It was still drizzling when they reached the market. Duke parked up and jumped out, marching around to the passenger side to help Connie and then Millie out.

"Right, you two lead and I will follow," he told them.

Millie headed off through the bustling market. It was a welcomed sensory overload. The sounds, colours, and smells reminded her there was life outside the four walls of the trailer. It had become her prison without her knowing it. She breathed in the crisp, cold air and closed her eyes. Was that sausages and burgers she could smell? Her tummy rumbled, and she was glad the noise of the crowd muffled it.

Connie stopped at a stall and riffled through a pile of tea towels. Maybe she needed to get out more! Millie ducked under a canopy, out of the rain, and inspected the clothes that were laid out.

"See anything you like?" Duke's voice travelled over her shoulder.

"No, just looking," Millie replied.

"Well, if it isn't Duke Lee," a loud voice called out in the distance.

"Well, as I live and breathe," Duke hollered back. "How's it going?"

The two men shook hands and strode off back in the direction they had come. Millie glanced at Connie who now looked at gold chains. Millie guessed it was a bit more exciting than tea towels.

She continued walking along the aisle of stalls, inspecting the goods along the way. The market was bigger than she had first thought, and before she knew it she was at the other end. Millie glanced around; she couldn't see Connie or Duke.

Shit.

Her heart raced. Every aisle appeared the same. She rushed one way and then the other. A man caught her attention; he was staring right at her. Turning, she rushed off down another aisle, abruptly coming to a dead end. She spun around. There he was again.

Fuck.

She ducked under the awning and out the other side of the stall. It had vans and trucks parked along the roadway. Millie did a quick scan of the stalls behind her. She needed to get to the other side, but further up. Half walking and half running, she quickly made it to the other end with her heart thumping. Now she needed to nip back in before the weirdo followed her.

She scanned around. There was no one there. Was she being paranoid? After a few deep breaths, her pulse slowed. She then dipped back through a brick-a-brac stall and emerged into the bustling market.

Where are they?

Millie checked around. There were people everywhere. She needed to climb up so she could get a good look. Her attention was drawn to a fruit and veg stall, the man shouting his wares to the watching crowd.

"Get your fresh veg 'ere, cheapest around. Roll up, ladies and gentlemen," the stallholder called. "Reckon you know a bargain, darling," he said to Millie as he stepped nearer.

She spotted the same man standing beside him, eyes on her. She stumbled back, and a strong pair of arms caught her. She turned to see a not-so-happy Duke staring back at her.

"Don't you think you should've waited for us?" he mumbled.

"You were too busy walking off," Millie replied. "Or did you expect me to run after you?"

"We panicked when we couldn't find you," Connie added, more than likely before an argument broke out.

"I'm sorry... I think I was being followed, this—"

Duke grabbed Millie's arm and pulled her behind him. "Can you see him?"

"Over there, next to the man selling the veg. Green jacket."
Millie pointed and then watched in horror as Duke bounded over and grabbed the man by the throat.

CHAPTER 34

Millie slipped her coat on and walked out to the motor. Duke hadn't said much to her after the market incident. She wasn't sure if he was angry with her or the market inspector.

"I'm sorry, Duke."

"So you've said a hundred times. Put your seat belt on." He didn't even look at her.

"You're still angry with me." Millie sighed.

"I'm angry, yes. But not with you… I should've kept you with me." He turned the key, and the Transit rattled to life.

"At least the market inspector's not going to press charges." Millie shrugged. "His face, though, when you accused him of following me." A giggle escaped her mouth.

She glanced at Duke who was now smiling.

"I don't suppose he gets accused of being a pervert every day." He laughed.

Millie waved to Connie who stood on the step. Why wasn't she coming to the doctor's with them? "Duke?"

"Hmm?"

"Why's Connie not coming?" Millie twisted her hands in her lap. Was something going on?

"I wanted to speak with you, clear the air. After the doctor's, we'll go to a café. We didn't get the chance yesterday, what with me nearly being arrested."

***

"Sit fucking still," Paul barked, wrapping Conor's finger in a tea towel. "How the fuck did you manage to slice through your finger?"

"Knife slipped. Think I need stitches." Conor winced.

"Jaysus, he's gone as white as a sheet." Aiden pointed. "He definitely needs a hospital."

Paul rolled his eyes. This lot had been more trouble than they were worth. Grabbing his keys, he motioned to his motor. "Don't get blood on the seats or you'll have more to worry about than just your finger."

He waited for Aiden to climb in next to Conor before setting off for the hospital. He headed down Stepney High Street, taking a double look at the Artichoke.

"Why are you stopping?" Conor asked, his voice croaky.

"Wait here, I'll only be a minute." Paul slipped out of the motor and crossed the road. He eyed the man who was putting up a For Sale sign. "What d'ya think ya doing?"

"What does it look like?" the man replied dryly.

Paul took a step closer and towered over him. "I asked a fucking question, so cut the smart comments."

"The pub's up for sale. I've been told to stick the sign up. If you wanna know anything else you will have to see the estate agent." The man picked up his tools and made a hasty retreat while Paul was left scratching his head.

Finn would never sell this place, it's his life.

He took hold of the For Sale sign and repeatedly smashed his foot into it until it came apart in his hands.

Storming back to the motor, he jotted down the number from the board and then wedged it into the boot. He would ring the estate agent from the hospital and then see Finn.

***

Millie sat across from Duke, her attention on her tea as she stirred it around and around and around, only stopping when Duke broke through her thoughts.

"You're gonna wear a hole in the bottom of that cup."

Millie placed the spoon down. She had to keep it together. "Sorry."

"Will you stop saying sorry? You have nothing to be sorry about. Now, what did the doctor say?"

Duke's eyes burned into her.

"It was just a bug." She hated lying to him. She hated lying to anyone. But she needed to tell Paul first, and this wasn't the sort of thing you told your husband over the phone. "Can we order, I'm hungry?"

She watched the smile spread on Duke's lips. He was placated for now.

"Good, that's good news, Millie, and you've got your appetite back." Duke grabbed the menu and handed it to her. "What would you like?"

Millie bit her bottom lip.

Shit. Shouldn't it be something healthy?

"Fry-up with bread and butter and another cup of tea, this one's gone cold… Please." She sat back and cursed. That wasn't a healthy choice, but she was starving now.

Duke was right. That was good.

What would Paul say? Would he be happy? It was pretty lousy timing with everything that was going on at the moment. She would phone him after lunch, ask if she could see him. Without thinking, she rested her hand against her tummy. A baby, she was going to have a baby.

***

Paul slammed the phone down and took a deep breath. He should have listened to Millie. "Fuck."

He made his way back to Accident and Emergency just in time to see Conor pass out. "What's happened?" he asked Aiden, who was busy grinning at the nurse.

"What?" Aiden asked, turning.

Paul motioned to Conor.

"He don't like the sight of blood, and apparently he don't like the sight of being sewn up." Aiden laughed.

"Stay with him. I'll meet you at the entrance when I've finished." Paul spun around and headed off to find Finn.

***

Millie placed the phone down, disappointment flooding her body. She knew it was a slim chance that Paul would be home, but even still, she had built her hopes up. She tried the club next. No answer.

Where the fuck is everyone?

"Are you done?" Duke called after tapping on the glass of the phone box.

"One more call," Millie mouthed, holding the receiver up and giving it a little wave. She waited for Duke to get back in the Transit and then phoned the brothel.

"Hello?"

"Gladys, it's Millie. Can I talk to Maggie, please?" She was met with silence.

What the fuck is going on?

"Hello. Gladys?"

"Oh, Millie, sorry. Umm, Maggie is out at the moment."

Millie waited for an explanation. Maggie was more likely to be in bed than out. Didn't she work until early hours of the morning? "Are you sure? She told me to phone her."

"Got to go, someone's here." The line went dead.

What the fuck was that about? Gladys didn't want me speaking to Maggie, but why?

CHAPTER 35

Paul peeked through the open door into Finn's room. Deciding the coast was clear, he sneaked in, pushing the door to behind him. He kept his attention on Finn. He looked pale, his eyes shut. Was he asleep or dead?

"Christ." Paul rubbed the back of his neck.

"Excuse me, what are you doing?"

Paul turned. A nurse stood at the door.

"I promised my wife I would check on Finn. How is he?"

"Are you Millie's husband?"

"Yes," Paul answered with a firm nod. This was promising. If she knew Millie, she might just let on what was going on.

"I remember seeing you with her before… You need to go. No one is allowed in here."

"And what do I tell my wife?" he pleaded.

The nurse looked around. Was she checking to make sure they were alone? "Millie was right, there's something off about Finn's daughter, Shannon. Finn was well on the way to recovery, but now…he may not make it."

"That doesn't prove this Shannon has anything to do with it. You'll need evidence," Paul advised.

"She's the only one who's visited. She made sure of that when she had Millie and Rosie thrown out. It was after that Finn started to go downhill… The doctor's taken bloods, he thinks he may have been poisoned."

"Poisoned?"

"Finn became disorientated, hallucinating. Things that you don't get with smoke inhalation. Hopefully the blood tests will show up whatever he has taken, and we can treat it, if it's not too late."

"When was the last time you saw Shannon?" Paul quizzed.

"The day Finn deteriorated. She said she would check on him later, but I haven't seen her since."

Paul nodded and left the room. He now had another job for Aiden and Conor.

He marched to the stairs and descended them two at a time. The smell of disinfectant was nauseating. It was one of those smells he would never get used to. It smelt like someone had got a bucket and doused every inch of the corridor with it.

He spotted them as he proceeded to the exit.

"Paulie, you look a little green around the gills," Conor called.

Paul ignored him and marched past, towards the door. He yanked it open and took a giant lungful of fresh air, cleansing his nose of the bloody awful stench. The sound of Conor sniggering followed.

"You can wipe that fucking smile off ya face, didn't you pass out at the sight of a needle?" Paul laughed. "Anyway, I've got a new job for you two. Now listen."

***

Millie sat peeling potatoes. Connie was making Duke's favourite meal. Boiled bacon, carrots, swede, onion, cabbage, and potatoes, all in one giant saucepan. Apparently it was a favourite amongst the Romani community. She guessed it saved on washing up, too. She had offered to help; it was best to keep busy, especially when there were so many unanswered questions.

"That's the potatoes done. I'm going outside for some fresh air." Millie slid on her coat while Connie stood in front of her.

"What's wrong, you've been quiet all afternoon?" Connie asked, concern lacing her voice.

"Just tired. I won't be long," Millie lied. She slipped out of the door and trudged along the camp. She could feel eyes on her from the men standing around the campfire. No doubt they would report back to Duke once he was home. Gypsy was unpacking shopping from a motor. She glanced at Millie but didn't speak.

Unsociable cow.

She continued along the camp, her head filled with worrying thoughts of Finn. Had something happened? She stopped and looked up at the brightly coloured wagon. This was where she would start. After all, the old girl had known she was pregnant before she did.

Millie walked towards the wooden steps, stopping abruptly, her vision falling on two dead rabbits that hung from a hook at the side of the wagon. "What the fuck!"

She took a shaky breath as one of the rabbits seemed to stare at her.

Did she kill them?

Millie gulped. This old woman was full of surprises, and evidently, not all of them nice. She raised her fist ready to knock, but the door opened before she reached it.

"I've been expecting you, girl," the old gypsy told her. "You'd better come in."

Millie was surprised to find a steaming hot cup of tea handed to her as she sat down. "Thank you."

"I know why you're here." Patience sat next to her, hoisting her skirt up. "But I must warn you, not everything in the leaves are good."

"I know you saw something last time. I wanted to know what it was," Millie replied, but in the back of her mind, a voice asked if she really wanted to know. All through her life bad things had happened. Would knowing have made her choices any different? There was an uncertainty there.

"Very well. Drink." The old woman eyed her.

Her eyes were set deep in there sockets. They looked like black bottomless pools. It was something Millie hadn't noticed last time, and it sent a small shiver down her spine.

"Have you always lived in a wagon?" Millie asked, trying to avert her gaze from the old woman's face.

"I was born in a wagon, girl. Used to be five of us. Mother, Father, two brothers, and me. I was the youngest…" The old woman trailed off and sighed. "I'm the only one left."

"Have you no family?" Millie felt a kinship, and a loneliness at the question. That was once her, no parents or siblings, just the other abandoned souls in the children's home.

"I'm a traveller, we are all related in some way or another." She fumbled with a set of beads, then hung them from the little curtain pole. "I sense a sadness in you, girl, a deep sadness from your past. You cannot change what has happened, and the past is not a good place to dwell."

"I didn't realise I was." Millie shrugged.

"I think you do, now drink up. Duke will be back soon. He wasn't too happy that you had been in here last time."

"I'll go where, and talk to, whoever I like. He hasn't been around long enough to dictate to me." Millie swallowed the last of the tea, spitting out the tea leaves.

"See what I mean, thinking about the past?" Patience chuckled. "Let it go, girl. He will be a good father to you." She took the cup and turned it over on the saucer, then spun it around three times. When she lifted it, she studied the leaves.

Millie glanced in the cup and then up at the old girl's wrinkled face. "Well, what do they say?"

CHAPTER 36

Paul slammed the phone down. He was tempted to rip the fucking thing out of the wall and smash it. It had been four days since the Ronnie lookalike had been seen at the pub. No contact. No sightings. Nothing.

"Everything all right, Paulie?" Aiden asked while poking his head out of the lounge door.

"No, it fucking isn't, and stop calling me Paulie. It's Paul. P. A. U. L. Paul," he spat.

Aiden held his hands up in surrender. "Okay… Paul."

"I need to go and see Millie. You wait here, just in case Sean calls, and remember, he's to follow him and find out where he lives. Do not make contact and certainly don't get seen." Paul rubbed the back of his neck. This bloke had disappeared into thin air.

Has Martin tipped him off?

"Don't worry, he knows what to do," Aiden replied. "I'll be going up the hospital soon to take over from Conor."

"Another one on the fucking missing list. Shannon's got to be staying somewhere... Right, where's my keys?" He patted his empty pockets before marching to the kitchen. "And get this place tidied up, I've seen cleaner fucking coal scuttles."

***

Millie caught the rumble of the motor pulling up and drew the curtain back. She knew it was Duke before she saw him. The Transit had a noise all of its own. She sat back quickly and turned to the door just as it opened.

"All right, Con?" Duke asked, slipping his arm around her waist and planting a quick kiss on her lips.

"Everything okay at home?" she replied.

Wait. What? Home?

"You've been back to Stepney?" Millie's stomach dropped. Why hadn't he told her where he was going? She could have seen Paul. Given him the good, or maybe not so good, news.

"Millie, I had to check on me parents, make sure everything was cushty at—"

Millie had heard enough. "Oh. You. Had to check on your parents. I have a husband I'd like to check on." She took a deep breath; the tears were coming. If she had learnt to drive like she had wanted to, she could've taken a motor and driven back instead of relying on bloody men.

"Millie." Duke took a step towards her.

"Don't. Just don't." Grabbing her coat, she threw open the door and stormed out.

Behind her, Connie told Duke to give her some space.

Space, ha. No such bloody thing as space here.

Millie marched to the only place she had felt any comfort on the traveller site. Gypsy Patience's wagon. The old woman was at least honest with her, even if she was a little strange.

Without knocking, Millie opened the door and climbed in. "Do you mind if I sit here for a while?"

"Do I have a choice?" The old woman cackled.

"Everyone has a choice," Millie replied.

"You remember that, girl. Everyone has a choice." Patience stirred a bubbling pot of what looked like chicken stew. "Have you eaten?"

"No. I'm not hungry…" Millie trailed off. She wasn't sure what she was. All she knew was that she needed to see Paul.

"You're eating for two now, a nice bit of rabbit stew will do you and the chavvie good." Patience reached for a bowl.

"No. I can't eat, and I certainly can't eat rabbit." Millie gasped.

"Why? You eat beef, pork, chicken. Rabbit's no different." Ignoring Millie, she handed her a bowl of stew.

"Rabbits are cute and furry," Millie mumbled.

"And they taste good," Patience added with another cackle.

***

Paul knocked on the trailer door, then stood back waiting for it to be answered.

"Paul. To what do we owe the pleasure?" Duke asked.

"I need to see Millie." He knew there was an urgency to his voice. He didn't care. He needed to see her despite not looking forward to the conversation that had to be had.

"I'll go get her," Duke replied.

"What do you mean, go get her? Where the fuck is she?" Paul growled.

"Calm down. She found out I'd been home and stormed out because I didn't take her with me. Wait in here." Duke jumped out of the trailer and landed with a crunch on the gravel.

"I'll come with you. Fucking hell, Duke, it's pitch-black. Don't you think you should have stopped her?" Paul panicked. He peered around the site. A group of men stood at the bonfire. "If anything's happened to her…" He left the threat hanging in the air.

Duke stopped and spun around. "You'll do what, Paul?"

"Paul!"

Millie's voice was like an angel's, washing over his senses. "Mil, where have you been?"

"With a friend. I am allowed friends, I take it?" she snapped.

Don't upset her, you prick.

"Of course you are, babe. Listen, we need to talk… Inside," Paul added. Her arm slipped though his, and he was grateful for the contact. "I've missed you so much."

"I've missed you, too. Can I come home now?" she asked.

It killed Paul listening to the hope in her voice, but it wasn't safe. "Not yet, Mil, but I'm close. Come on, let's get in the warm and talk."

CHAPTER 37

Millie held on to Paul while Connie poured the tea. His arm was around her waist, and he pulled her closer to him. She felt safe. Not that she didn't particularly feel safe with Duke, but Paul was her husband.

Duke's your dad. Shouldn't a dad make you feel safer?

Millie shook the thought away. She had to tell Paul about the pregnancy. And what about the reading, should she tell him about gypsy Patience's warning? No. He wouldn't believe in that mumbo-jumbo.

"Here's your tea." Connie placed the two cups on the table then headed out of the door.

"So what's happening with Rita's nephew?" Millie asked, staring at Paul. He seemed thinner. Was he eating properly?

"It's under control, Mil, it won't be long until you're back home." He paused. "I wanted to talk to you about Finn."

"What's happened, is he okay?" Panic rose in her voice, and she had to swallow down her fear. This was not going to be good. Paul had told her to not worry about Finn, and yet here he was, coming here especially to talk about him. She watched him sigh, and her heart sank a little deeper. "Paul?"

"You were right about Shannon, she's up to something," he finally admitted.

"Is Finn dead?" Her hands trembled slightly.

Paul must have noticed because he grabbed them. "No! He's not dead, babe. He has taken a turn for the worse, though. Finn was making a good recovery, and then suddenly he's gone downhill. I spoke to a nurse, umm, Susan I think her name was. Anyway, she said he went downhill after Shannon got you kicked out—"

"I knew it!" Millie jumped up and paced the floor. "I'll have to come home, Paul, I can't leave Finn there at her mercy."

"You're not coming home—" He began.

"But—" She started until she was cut off by an annoyed Paul.

"You are not coming home until the other business has been taken care of… Look, Mil, I've got the boys watching the hospital in case she shows her face again. We'll find out where she lives and then deal with her. Finn's safe for now. They are running tests to determine if he was poisoned."

"Poisoned?" Millie threw her hands up in the air and then pointed an accusing finger at him. "If you had listened to me in the first place, we wouldn't be having this conversation."

Paul grabbed her hand and pulled her towards him. "You don't know that for sure, and besides, you would still be here, where you're safe."

She shrugged him off. If she had known Finn was in that much danger there was no way she would have allowed them to bring her here.

"I could've kept this from you, babe, but I didn't, I've been honest," he reasoned. "And now I'm sorting it out."

Am I being too hard on him? Probably.

"Fine. But I want to be kept up to date with Finn's progress, and if he goes downhill you are to come and get me. Understand?"

Another sigh from Paul, great.

"Okay…now I can't stay long, so can we not argue?" he pleaded.

A small nod from Millie put the smile back on Paul's lip's. She forced one in return, her head still in turmoil.

What about the baby?

"Paul, I've something to tell you, too." She stopped. How could she tell him now? If he knew about the baby he wouldn't let her return home, even if Finn was on his deathbed.

No. You can't tell now.

"I love you," she blurted out. Whilst it wasn't a lie, it wasn't what she really wanted to tell him either. She closed her eyes as his lips touched hers.

It's for the best, the little voice in her head reassured her, but was it?

***

Millie sat watching Aron. He slurped the stew up like a hoover. The noise was grating on her.

"Where's Duke?" she called over to Connie who packed away clean washing.

"Around the bonfire, I expect," Connie replied.

"I'm going outside." She jumped up and headed towards the door after grabbing her coat. She stood for a minute. At least it had stopped raining. There were different smells in the air tonight. The campfire smoke wafted towards her mixed with boiled veg. Someone was having a roast.

She trudged over towards the group of men. Women never seemed to be seen around the fire, but she wasn't one of them. She was different.

You are half Romani.

"Oh, shut up."

"Who are ya talking to, girl?" one man asked her. He was built like a mountain, his hands the size of dinner plates.

Does he think I was talking to him?

Duke stiffened; obviously no one was allowed to speak to his daughter.

Millie rolled her eyes. "Myself, if that's all right?"

Duke flung his arm around her shoulders. "My Millie can talk to whoever the fuck she wants. Anyone got a problem with that, they can see me."

"I only came out for some fresh air, maybe I should go back," she offered. She didn't want Duke getting into a fight on her behalf.

"Oh no you don't, you can stay out here and chew the fat with ya old man." Duke pulled her closer. He stank of beer.

Millie held her hands towards the flames, her eyes transfixed on them as they licked the night sky. "It's peaceful here, a little too peaceful. Gives a person too much time to think."

"Think about what?" Duke asked. He even sounded interested.

She shrugged. "Just stuff."

"Anything you'd like to share with me?" He dropped his arm and took her hand. "Come on, let's take a walk." He led her towards the end of the camp, where he leant against a fence, placing one foot on the bottom rung. "What's bothering you, Millie?"

Her eyes watered. Did she want to share her thoughts with this man?

He's your dad.

"I had something important to tell Paul, but because I was angry about Finn, I didn't tell him." She glanced down at the ground, her shoes once again covered in mud.

"So, tell him the next time you see him," Duke reasoned. "I'm sure he'll be back here in a couple of days."

"Theres something else..." Millie trailed off.

"Go on, I'm listening." Duke turned his head towards her.

"When the old girl read my tea leaves—" She stopped as Duke abruptly cut in.

"I told you to stay away from her for this very reason. You can't believe everything she tells you."

His voice was angry, but Millie was sure there was a hint of uncertainty there also.

"Okay. I'm gonna head back in." She pushed herself away from the fence.

Duke's hand grabbed her arm.

"What did she say?" he urged.

Millie swallowed. "She said there was betrayal in my leaves. Someone close is going to betray me." She left out the part about someone dying. That was a burden she would carry herself.

CHAPTER 38

Duke lay on the bunk, his head facing the bedroom. The sound of Millie twisting and turning all night had kept him vigilant. Why had he brought her here? There were a hundred sites he could have taken her, but no, he'd come to where the witch was staying. Damn Patience Lee and her warning. She had got under Millie's skin, and now his daughter was worried about something she had no control over. Hadn't he warned her not to go there?

Pushing the blankets back, he stood. He reached for a log and placed it in the burner. At least the trailer was nice and warm for her. That was one thing he was capable of, keeping her warm.

He should've made it clearer to the witch what would happen if she upset his daughter. With a loud sigh, he reached for his trousers and slipped them on along with a jumper and then his jacket. He grabbed his dealer boots and pulled them on, making sure not to step on the cream carpet. As he stood on the doormat, he took one last look in the bedroom. All seemed quiet.

Duke stepped outside and took a deep lungful of the cold damp air. Being a Romani, he loved all the seasons. Even the shitty rain. The trees had recovered from the drought of 1976, but now they were almost bare of their leaves. Autum had turned to winter.

The glow of embers were all that remained from the campfire, and everyone had settled down for a peaceful night's sleep. Not him, though. How could he sleep knowing his daughter was worried? It was etched into her face. He would do anything to see her smile, not that he could do that. There was a barrier there. He didn't know why. Why she wouldn't let him in. Connie said it would take time, but he was impatient. He wanted her to call him Dad again. His heart hurt a little every time she called him Duke. He couldn't let that show, though, he was a tough travelling man, a fighter. He'd had many fights over the years and since the age of twenty-two he had never lost. This fight, however, was one you couldn't train for and one he didn't know how to win. It seemed, to him, Millie had the upper hand.

When he looked up he found himself standing outside the witch's wagon.

The door opened, and the old woman motioned for him to come in. Duke obliged and took a seat. They sat in silence as the kettle boiled. Patience poured the tea and handed Duke a cup.

"I'll not be having my leaves read, old woman," he told her while taking it.

"Then why are you here if not for answers?" she replied with an eyebrow raised. "You know you can't fool me, Duke Lee. I can see what you want."

"And what do I want?" Duke snapped, his temper wearing thin.

"You want the love of your daughter. You want her to need you just like those boys, but Millie isn't like them. Her life has been hard. Harder than you realise." She motioned to Duke's cup. "Drink."

"And just how do you know all this?" Duke huffed. He was close to storming out, but he needed to know if this witch *did* know what his daughter thought of him.

"It's in her eyes, boy, you need to look closer... I know why you won't ask her about her past." She reached over and stoked the small fire. "You're scared of what she'll tell you, but you need to remember, you didn't know she existed. It's not your fault."

"That's not what Millie thinks. She blames me and..." Duke stopped. Millie was right to blame him, he was her dad. He should've known, Connie should've told him.

"She doesn't blame you. Not now." She stood, taking Duke's cup. "It's late, get yourself to bed and, Duke, remember, she's the child, you need to let her come to you, when she's ready."

Duke gave a curt nod and left the warmth of the wagon. Standing his collar up against the cold night wind, he trudged back to his trailer, surprised a soft glow emitted from the end window. Someone was up.

He reached for the door handle, and the noise of the kettle whistling caught his attention. Someone was making tea. He pulled open the door, and there stood Millie, with her back to him.

"You couldn't sleep either?"

She turned, panic in her eyes. Had he scared her? "I'm sorry, I thought you had gone out. I'll go back to bed."

"No, you're all right, I'll have a cuppa, too, as you're making one." Duke slipped off his dealer boots and headed to the bunk. He rolled up his blankets and perched on the edge. Resting his elbows on his knees, he placed his head in his hands. The old woman's words whizzed around his head.

"You know you can't fool me, Duke Lee. I can see what you want. You want the love of your daughter. You want her to need you just like those boys, but Millie isn't like them. Her life has been hard. Harder than you realise. It's in her eyes, boy, you need to look closer. I know why you won't ask her about her past. You're scared of what she'll tell you, but you need to remember, you didn't know she existed. It's not your fault."

Millie handed him his tea and sat, her face showing how weary she was. She seemed pale—was that the worry? For a second they made eye contact, Millie being the first to turn away. The witch was right, she had a haunted look in her eyes. Duke's heart broke a little bit more.

"So you couldn't sleep either?" Duke asked again.

Stupid question, Duke. Well done for stating the fucking obvious.

"No. I thought I'd have a hot drink, see if it helps settle me." Millie had a sadness to her voice that wasn't lost on Duke.

"Is there anything you'd like to talk about, maybe something I can help with?" Duke took a large sip of his tea, immediately regretting it, and spat it back into the cup.

Fuck, that's hot.

"Are you okay?" Millie's eyes went wide.

"Tea's hot, and I'm more interested to know if you're okay." He placed his cup on the side then turned towards her. "Tell me about your past."

"What?" she said, her voice a mixture of disbelief and panic. "Why do you want to know about my past?"

"Because I want to know you, and to do that I need to know your past... I've been telling you about Romani traditions and our way of life, but not once have I asked you about yours. So tell me." He leant back against the bunk, eyes trained on hers.

"What version would you like? The good one or the honest one?" Millie asked. Her eyes watered. Was she going to cry?

"The honest one. I want to know everything, and then you can ask me whatever you want. Do we have a deal?" Duke spat on his hand and held it out, waiting for Millie to do the same.

When she continued to stare, Duke informed her that's how Romanies made a deal. He laughed when she did the same and then grimaced as she wiped her hand on the blanket behind her.

Millie's shoulders slumped. "Okay, Duke. You may not like everything you hear, so be prepared."

CHAPTER 39

Millie closed her eyes and thought back to the earliest point she could remember. She could almost smell it.

"It was Christmas time, I must have been five years old. I had started school in the autumn. I can remember being taken up to my bedroom and tucked into bed. I can still feel the excitement. Father Christmas was coming, and I had to go to sleep or he wouldn't leave me a present. That's what Mrs Green had told me, along with, 'Stay in your bed, Father Christmas doesn't like naughty children.'" Millie sighed. "She scared me more than the bogeyman." She took a deep a breath before continuing.

"I remember lying there in the darkness. The noises of the night scaring me. A loud scream coming from outside. I pulled the covers over my head. There was no one to call, no one to comfort me. I could hear the sound of my heart beating wildly in my ears. Tears fell, making the pillow damp. My body trembled. I closed my eyes tightly. It was at that point I knew what I wanted for Christmas. A mum and a dad, just like the other children had at school."

Millie looked up. Duke rubbed his face. He was getting upset.

"That wish became the same wish every year. Sometimes a child would get taken to a new home because they were good. 'Only the good ones get chosen, Millie,' Mrs Green had reminded me."

Wasn't I good enough?

"I had asked myself that same question every day of my life. Wasn't I good enough? It wasn't until I met Finn, and he took me in and gave me a job, that I started to believe I was. He had single-handedly given me hope. He supported me."

I digress. Back to the past, Millie, concentrate.

She smiled when the image of Scott, Rosie, and herself sat on the steps of the children's home eating ice creams. The sunshine warming their faces and making the ice cream melt. It dripped down their arms, and they tried so eagerly to lick it so as not to waste any.

"School had been okay. I had never got into trouble. There were the bullies, though, who called me and Rosie names. The care home scum. 'Nobody wants you, not even your own mum and dad,' had been a favourite taunt, but by then I was used to it."

Had I really got used to it?

"My life had picked up when I met Levi. He was the most handsome man I had ever seen. He paid me compliment after compliment, and I soon fell in love with him. Before I knew it, I was in a registry office, saying, 'I do.' And that was when my life really took a turn for the worse. Between him and his mother, Flo, I had entered the world of living nightmares. It started with the verbal abuse but soon turned physical. I had become Levi's property. I was taunted, ridiculed, and abused by the man I loved. The first physical beating took place in my mother-in-law's kitchen."

She curled up in a ball on the floor and tried desperately to protect herself from the punches Levi was raining down on her. She let out a scream as she felt her wrist crack...

"That was the first fracture... And then there was the great Flo Cooper."

She wouldn't tell Duke everything. That part of her life had gone, and she had worked too hard to leave it in the past. She wouldn't have it all dragged up now. "I stood in Flo's front room. She had called me down from the bedroom. I soon found out why."

Millie stood in Flo's front room.

The coalman stood in the doorway, smiling at Flo. "One bag of coal for a look, or two for a look and a feel."

Flo nodded and turned to Millie. "Take ya top off, girl, and hurry up," Flo demanded.

Millie stood her ground and shook her head.

"Don't make me fucking angry, or I'll tell Levi you've been out flirting. Now what's it to be?" Flo grinned.

Millie knew Levi would give her a good hiding if he thought she had been out, so there was no choice. She pulled her top over her head and stood there while the coalman enjoyed himself.

"They say the first time's the worst, but that's a lie, every time is the worst..." Millie took a deep breath.

Duke jumped up. "I need some air."

She watched as he lunged for his boots and left. He didn't even look at her. Was he disgusted?

You shouldn't have told him.

She turned to the window.

But he asked.

She peered out. Where had he gone?

He's left because he's ashamed.

Lights shone in other trailers now. Was he telling people about his daughter's dirty, disgusting secret?

But he asked.

Millie sniffed back the tears. "I am not ashamed and I'm not gonna cry."

It's your own fault, you can't trust anyone. Remember the warning. Betrayal.

Millie jumped when the door opened. Duke stood on the mat. She couldn't make out his expression. Was it anger or pity? Christ, she didn't need this man's pity.

"I'm sorry, I shouldn't have left like that." He sat back next to her and grabbed her hand, his eyes red. Had he been crying?

"Am I a disappointment to you?" Millie asked. "I know it's a lot for you to deal with. Maybe I should've kept my big mouth shut."

"You are not a disappointment, Millie. You know men say I'm the bravest man they have ever met. I'll fight anyone, in or out of the ring, at the drop of a hat. The fight you've had, at the hands of those bastards, all alone." He swallowed loudly, and his voice trembled. "I don't come close to you for bravery. If he were still alive I would kill him with my bare hands." His temper was building. Was the red mist descending?

"Duke?" Millie whispered with no reply. "Du... Dad?"

The word Dad seemed to snap him back to reality. "What... Sorry, Millie, I want you to continue."

"I don't want to go into detail with everything. I was abused right up until the car accident. Violently by Levi and rented out to pay her debts by Flo. The car accident was the turning point of my life — it more than likely saved my life — although I didn't realise it at the time." She glanced up at Duke. "You need to let it go, I have."

Duke nodded without taking his eyes off her.

"Okay. The last bad bit, the time I killed Levi's dad. I had been to get my belongings from Flo's house while they were at Levi's funeral. I knew if I had gone back when Flo was there, she wouldn't have allowed me to leave, instead becoming her meal ticket."

The front door slammed, followed by footsteps coming up the stairs. Millie placed her bunny into her bag and stood behind the bedroom door. The footsteps got closer, and she closed her eyes. Swallowed down the fear that was overtaking her body.

"Hello. Who's there?" Elijah called.

Millie yelped as the door pushed her back into the wall, unable to move. The door was pulled away from her, and Elijah's face came into view. He was shocked, but that was soon replaced with anger. He grabbed her by the arm and dragged her onto the landing. Millie struggled against his grip, but it was too firm.

"Why, you little bitch. Thinking of robbing us, are ya, while my son's being buried? Time someone taught you a lesson."

"He was going to rape me. He deserved what was to follow."

Elijah scrambled to his feet. He had been caught out by Rosie. He was flustered. Panic-ridden. He stood there with his trousers around his ankles.

While Elijah was focused on Rosie, Millie took her chance and kicked out. He was knocked off balance. He swayed at the top of the stairs. She brought her legs back one more time and kicked out harder, sending him backwards down the stairs. Millie stood, pulling her trousers back up. Her gaze rested on Elijah.

"He's not moving... I've killed him."

"That did take a while to get over. Okay, so he deserved it for what he was about to do, but taking someone's life changes a person. Whether intentional or accidental, it still hits you inside. You can see it in a person's eyes. They are different," Millie concluded.

"Anyway, on to the day my life started to improve, which, funnily enough, was the same day I had killed Elijah. The day I met Paul Kelly."

Millie was running into the hospital when she collided with a man.

"Watch it!" he bellowed.

Millie's eyes went wide as she shrank back against the wall. He was built like a mountain. "I'm sorry," she said quietly. "I didn't see you."

She watched him. He looked at her clothes, and a grin spread across his face.

"Did you get dressed in the dark?" he asked.

Millie ignored the comment and turned to Rosie. "I'll get changed; you find a wheelchair."

She reached the toilets and peeked back at the stranger to find he was still staring at her. She threw him a dirty look before she entered the safety of the women's loos.

"Was it love at first sight? No... Yes... Maybe. There was something there, a small flutter in my tummy, but the fact that I had just committed murder made my emotions unreliable. Do you know, I had never admitted it to anyone, but I had thought about Paul after that day. Often, in fact. He was as annoying as he was handsome, and he always had to have the last word."

Millie sat in the wheelchair and grimaced. He continued to stare at her. She put her head down and avoided eye contact until he spoke again.

"You been out on day release then?" He grinned.

"Don't think that's any of your business, do you?" Millie snapped.
"Rosie."

"What, Mil?"

"Someone's watching me."

"Yeah. His name is Paul Kelly," Rosie replied.

Millie swiped at her eyes. A lone tear trickled down her cheek. Duke stared. Was he crying again?

"Look, things picked up after that. As I got to know Paul, I also started searching for my parents… You and Connie. That's it. You know the rest. That's my life story so far."

"I'm so sorry, Millie." Duke spoke softly, like he was ashamed.

"You have nothing to be sorry about, Duke. You didn't know I existed, and I didn't know you. It's time we both look to the future and forget the past." She reached for her tea. "I'll make us another cup, it's gone cold."

"Wait." Duke's hand rested on her arm. "I will make it up to you. I'll find a way."

Millie nodded. "Okay. You could start by teaching me to drive."

CHAPTER 40

Paul entered the estate agent's. It was a dowdy little office. The windows let in barely any light due to the pictures of houses stuck to the windows, making it appear smaller than what it probably was. And it was busy, too fucking busy. All he wanted to do was throw a few threats around, get Shannon's contact details along with an address, and get them to take the pub off the market.

"Someone will be with you in a moment, sir," a pompous prick sitting behind a large desk told Paul.

He didn't reply. Instead, he walked back towards the door and studied the street. People were busy going about their day, rushing in and out of shops and trying to avoid the rain.

What was Millie doing now? Was she in the warm? He missed her more and more each day. That was mainly why he had decided to come here. Force the ginger tart's hand. Finn was stable. Now

Paul would concentrate on finding the culprit. As for the other business, any day now that bastard would show himself.

"Good morning, sir, how may I help you?"

Paul did a double-take. Some spotty kid was asking how he could help him. Had he even finished school? Paul stiffened.

"I'm here about a property you have for sale," Paul replied bluntly.

"I can certainly help you, please take a seat." The young man pointed to a desk.

Paul grabbed the chair and sat. "It's the pub at Stepney Green. The Old Artichoke."

"We've had a lot of interest in that property. Let me just take some details... Name?"

"None of your fucking business. I want to know who is selling it." Paul leaned forward, placing both hands on the desk. "You do know it's illegal to sell a property without the proprietor's permission." He glanced around at the other customers who all stared back at him. "Ladies and gentleman, I would suggest you get any property you look at here checked by the police, just to make sure the sale is legal."

"Sir, I can quite assure you we have full permission—"

"The geezer who owns it is in hospital, so tell me, before I involve the Old Bill, how did he authorise you to sell his livelihood from a hospital bed, especially when he's unconscious?" Paul watched the young man stutter, his face becoming the colour of a tomato. "Now I suggest you take it off the market, and I want the contact details of the perpetrator."

"We can't give out personal details, sir, it's—"

"Fine." Paul held his hand up. "I'll come back with the police. You can tell them, and then they can look into all your other dodgy dealings." He turned towards the door.

"Wait!" This time it was the pompous prick who replied. "If you give us a minute to clear the shop, I will assist you in any way that I can."

Paul folded his arms, a scowl in place. He would show them he meant business.

***

Millie climbed in behind the steering wheel. She was more than a little excited. She waited for Duke to get in next to her and then reached for the key.

"Whoa. Not so fast, flash. Now preparing to drive is like preparing to get in the ring for a fight. You need to do your checks first," he advised her.

"Like what?" she asked, wide-eyed. Paul never did checks, he just got in, started the engine, and went.

"Like adjusting your seat. Can you reach the pedals comfortably?" He bent down. What was he doing? "You need to move the seat closer, Millie."

She sat and stared at him. How the fuck was she supposed to do that? Duke must have realised because he leant across, grabbed a lever, and slid the seat forward. Millie let out a scream in surprise.

"Does that feel comfortable?" he asked.

"Yes." Maybe this was going to be harder than she thought. "Now what?"

"Check your mirrors. Can you see out of them?" He yawned.

"Sorry, am I boring you?" She sighed loudly. "I can always ask someone else to teach me."

"I haven't had any sleep, and there's no need to get snotty. Now if you can see okay, make sure the motor's in neutral." Duke grabbed the gearstick and a gave it a wobble. "Now you can start the engine."

With one flick of the key, the motor roared to life. Millie smiled and placed one hand on the wheel. She followed Duke's instructions and rammed the gearstick into first.

The crunching noise had him grabbing her hand. "Christ, there goes the clutch. Make sure your foot's—"

She lifted her foot, and the motor lunged forward in a succession of bunny hops.

"The brake. Put your foot on the brake." He placed both hands on the dashboard, preparing himself for the impact as the motor headed towards the Transit. *"Brake!"*

The bang was loud enough to bring people out of their trailers. All standing staring. Some even laughing.

"I need a drink," Duke mumbled. The colour had drained from his face.

Heat flushed Millie's cheeks. Would she ever live this down? "Let's forget it."

She jumped out of the motor and slammed the door, the headlight falling off with the impact. The glass smashed, and another loud bellow of laughter came from somewhere behind. She glanced at the Transit that now had a big dent in the side. Storming to the trailer, she kicked her shoes off in temper.

"My motor's damaged, and you throw a tantrum?" Duke called while chasing after her.

Connie appeared, worry evident. "Are you hurt? Let me look at you."

"I'm fine." Millie huffed.

"Duke, calm down, please," Connie warned. "It's only a motor."

"This is calm," he replied before turning to Millie. "What the fuck was that about?"

"You didn't want to teach me, I could see it in your face. You should have been honest, and then this wouldn't have happened." Millie sat on the bunk and folded her arms.

"You crash me motor, and now it's my fault?" Duke's voice rang with disbelief. "Really?"

"I've been nothing but a problem to you since you found out about me, so do us both a favour and take me home." Millie turned towards the window. She wouldn't let him see her cry.

"You can't go home, Millie. You know that." Duke's voice had softened.

The bunk moved. Millie knew he had sat next to her. She still didn't look up. "You never asked for a daughter, Duke, and let's face it, you're not really dad material, are you?"

Silence followed. Had she hurt him, or was he silently agreeing with her?

"No, I never asked for a daughter, Millie, but I'm glad that I've got one, even if I'm not dad material." Another silence followed his reply. His hand touched her chin, gently pulling her face around.

Their eyes met.

"Truth is, I don't know how to be your dad. I'm scared of messing it up. I'm not perfect, I know that, but I love you, and I told you this is forever. You need to give me a chance, forgive my mistakes and let me learn to be your dad. And just for the record, I do want to teach you to drive, and I won't allow anyone else to do it. It's my job as your dad. Next time, though, maybe we should go somewhere more private, where there's less chance of you crashing." Duke laughed. "Jesus, you only moved five foot and managed to damage two motors in the process."

Millie let out a nervous giggle. "Is the damage bad?"

"Nah, nothing that can't be fixed… So d'ya think you can give ya old man a second chance?" He wiped a tear from her cheek.

Millie nodded. "I'm sorry."

"You've nothing to be sorry for. Come here." Duke's arms wrapped around her and brought her into a warm hug.

She was mistaken, he *was* dad material.

CHAPTER 41

Waiting for the last couple to leave the estate agent's, Paul sipped the steaming cup of tea the spotty lad had made him. The smarmy prick had taken a deposit from them which had put a big smile on his face. It showed his yellowing teeth. Paul had taken an instant dislike to the man. He wore a cheap polyester suit with wide lapels and the most enormous flared bottoms he had ever seen. It was made all the more hideous by the psychedelic shirt he had matched with a striped tie.

Jesus, I think my eyeballs are melting.

"Sorry for keeping you waiting, sir," the prick apologised, holding his hand out. "We have been exceptionally busy today."

Paul glanced at his hand; his fingers were stained with nicotine. There was no way he would be shaking that. "Can we get down to business? I want to know who you are dealing with regarding the Artichoke."

"Sir, we can't gi—"

"I'm sorry, you seem to think you have a choice. You don't. Now let me make this clear. I want the contact details of the person selling the boozer—let me add, illegally." Paul folded his arms and sat back.

"We only have the Artichoke address for correspondence, and we have been told to deal with the daughter. I have a number for her." The estate agent riffled through his desk. "It's here somewhere…ahh, here it is. That's all we have, I'm afraid."

Paul grabbed the number and studied it. "Okay. So here's what you're gonna do. I want you to tell her you've received an offer, but you need her to come in and sign some paperwork before the deal can go ahead."

"But what happens when she comes in and there's no paperwork to sign?" the spotty lad asked.

"You ain't gonna be here, I'll take over once she's through the door. Do you think you can do that?" He waited for a nod of confirmation from both men before he continued. "I want the pub taken off the market immediately, and you forget all about this conversation, cos I don't want to have to come back for any more problems. Understood?"

***

Connie sat staring at Millie. It was starting to make her feel uncomfortable.

"Is something wrong?"

"No… You know, sometimes I feel like I'm in a dream, you being here."

More like a nightmare.

Millie smiled. "It's been nice spending time with you."

"But?" Connie pressed.

"But…" Millie sighed. "I miss Paul. If I stay much longer I'd have spent more time sleeping in your bed than I will have my own."

"You know Paul will be doing everything in his power to sort things. Is there anything I can do to help?" Connie asked.

"Actually, there may be. I need to visit my friend, Rosie, even if only for an hour. I need to make sure she's okay."

"I can't make that happen, Millie, you know that. Duke won't be influenced by me. You, on the other hand..." Connie raised an eyebrow.

"Me?" Millie laughed. "You have got to be kidding."

"No, I'm not. You're his little girl, and little girls have a way of wrapping their dads around their little fingers." Connie wiggled her pinkie finger.

Could she sweet talk him? "Where is Duke?"

"Scrapyard, trying to get a light so he can fix the pickup. Said he needs to get it fixed before your next driving lesson."

"I'm surprised he still wants to teach me." The sound of the headlight smashing filled her head. Heat warmed her cheeks again, and she dipped her eyes to look at the floor. Next time she would do better, she was sure of it.

Connie grabbed a large bag and dropped it by the door. "Are you sure you don't want to come to the launderette?"

"No thanks. I'll stay here and wait for Duke." She watched Connie lift the heavy bag, passing it to Jess who placed it into the back of a motor. Whose, she didn't know.

Fuck spending hours up the launderette.

That was definitely the down side of travelling. Actually, there were many down sides. No shower or bath. No indoor toilet. No privacy. No cupboard space for clothes, so you only had a few. Millie shook her head. No, this life was not for her, and yet, she loved the freedom, the great outdoors, the closeness of the community. She loved the people. Maybe it wasn't so bad after all.

She stood and walked towards the glass cupboard. Inside it, an array of crystal bowls and vases. Connie certainly had a lot of stuff. The Royal Crown Derby was placed in the top cupboards that ran around the trailer, and all the crystal was in the central cupboard. It was carefully set out so you could see it all. There were a couple of photos; Millie assumed they were of her brothers. They looked almost identical as babies, not so much now, although some people had trouble telling them apart.

At the bottom of the cupboard stood a model of a gypsy wagon. It had one horse pulling it. The wagon was brightly coloured, just like Patience's.

"Where's Con?" Duke's voice interrupted Millie's thoughts; she almost jumped.

"Launderette," she replied without looking.

Girls have a habit of wrapping their dads around their little fingers.

"Can I ask a favour?" She turned to face him.

Duke stared at her with a suspicious frown. "What?"

"I need to visit my friend, Rosie, to make sure she's okay… Please, Dad."

Surprise widened his eyes. Was that delight or shock?

"You know you can't go back there, Millie, not yet anyway."

"Rosie didn't sound good on the phone. I'm really worried… We could go really early in the morning and be back before you know it," Millie pleaded.

"You could be going home any day now," he reasoned.

"And what if any day is too late?" she asked.

The sigh that left Duke's lips sounded almost theatrical.

That's a no then.

CHAPTER 42

Paul stood back while his men dug up a fix-by-five-foot part of the floor in his warehouse. He'd had this idea in bed last night while he was lying awake and missing Millie.

"Swap over, lads. You other two start loading up the truck." Content that it would be finished in a few hours, he strolled outside. The grey sky matched his mood perfectly.

"I need to get back to the dock. Any problems, you can reach me there." He climbed into his Range Rover and glanced at the empty passenger seat. That's where Millie should be, not in the back of beyond.

Fuck.

He knew she was where she had to be, but it didn't make it any easier. Did she miss him as much as he missed her?

You know she does.

Starting the car, he headed off to the docks.

***

Duke parked outside Scott's flat. "Wait here while I make sure the coast is clear."

"Are you serious?" Millie sighed.

He was acting like an MI5 agent. He had driven around the flat twice, making sure they hadn't been followed. If she wasn't so desperate to see Rosie she would have laughed. But this wasn't a laughing matter. Due to the shitty weather, there was hardly anyone about. Everywhere looked grey and miserable.

"Okay, follow me." Duke grabbed Millie's arm and helped her out.

"Can I take these sunglasses off now?" she asked as she tripped up the kerb. "I can't see a sodding thing."

"We had a deal. They stay on, unless you want to go back," he snapped.

"Fine," she mumbled while rubbing her toes. She slipped her shoe back on and followed Duke up the path. "I've never been here before."

"Stepney's a big place." He reached the communal door and gave it a hefty shove.

"I meant Scott's flat, not this part of Stepney… I went to school up the road," she replied with a roll of the eyes.

"Is this the same school where you were called names?" Duke's voice hardened.

"Yes, but it was only a couple of kids who did that, most were okay." Millie looked at the staircase. "Up here, number…three."

"I'll wait outside. You've got an hour," he warned.

"I know, I know." Millie reached the door and spun around to face Duke. "Thank you for bringing me here. I do appreciate it… Dad." That was a little sweetener, in case she needed more time.

He smiled. "Ya know I feel like a king when you call me Dad. I'd imagine your mother would feel good if you called her Mum."

She gave a small nod and refocused on the door. With a clenched fist, she knocked three times. Nothing.

"Someone's in, I can hear the television." Millie knocked again. This time she shouted through the letter box, too. "Rosie!"

"Let me see." Duke crouched and spied through the slit. "I can see an arm. She's not moving."

"Show me." She pushed Duke out of the way. Her gaze fell on Rosie's hand. It was open. It looked like she was laying on a sofa, although she couldn't see properly though the letter box. The lounge door was partially in the way. "What's that stuff on the floor?" She moved aside so Duke could see.

"I think it's pills. Fuck. We need to get in, now." He stood and shoulder-barged the door. "Move back." He then kicked out.

Millie glanced at the neighbour's door when it opened.

A worried-looking woman poked her head out. "What's going on?"

"Call an ambulance," Duke ordered. He continued to kick out at the door.

Millie stood back. Time stopped. People shouted. Another man joined Duke and kicked the door with him. Rosie was in trouble.

Someone's going to die.

Were they too late?

The door gave way, and Duke rushed in. Millie stood glued to the spot. Her legs wouldn't work. Why?

"*Millie!*"

"What?" She glanced up.

Duke grabbed her arm. "She's still breathing."

She crumpled into his arms, loud sobs echoing around the landing.

"Shh, it's okay. The ambulance is on it's way." He stroked her hair. "We need to go, Millie."

"No!" She listened to the sound of the siren, it was getting louder.

"We can't stay here," Duke reasoned. "She's going to hospital, she'll be safe there."

"I need to go with her. Please." Millie knelt next to Rosie. Her eyes widened when she saw her gaunt face. Her once tanned skin had taken a grey tinge, and her dreads that had always danced on her shoulders appeared limp and lifeless. Just like her. "Are you sure she's still alive?"

"I found a pulse. It's weak, but she's still breathing." He caught Millie's arm, pulling her back. "We can't go to the hospital, Mil, it's not safe."

"But you'll keep me safe," she begged. "You said you wanted to be my dad, now's your chance."

***

Paul hid in the back of the estate agent's. He had men in cars at the front and another three at the back. Once Shannon was in, there would be no escape.

"She'll be here soon," Spotty called through the doorway.

"Once I come out, you leave, and not a word to anyone," Paul reminded him.

The warning tone to his voice did just the job. Spotty nodded so hard, Paul thought his head would fall off.

The door pinged. *Here we go.* Her voice grated on Paul immediately. Demanding the sale go through as quickly as possible. She needed to get back to Ireland for business. What fucking business? Did she have more family members to rip off?

"Take a seat, and I'll grab the paperwork," Spotty told her.

He passed Paul and gave a sharp nod. "She's all yours," he whispered.

The two estate agents let themselves out at the back while Paul sauntered through to the shopfront. Shannon sat with a man. He had long hair and a big nose, just like Rosie had said. Shannon was the first to spot him. She went to stand, but Paul placed his hand on her shoulder, pushing her back in the seat.

"Think we need a little chat, don't you?" He smiled and then signalled to his men at the front.

"What is the meaning of this?" she asked.

"The meaning?" Paul rubbed his chin. "I think it means you're both pretty much fucked."

CHAPTER 43

The hospital brought back nothing but bad memories for Millie. The car crash. Paul's fight. Finn's fire, and now Rosie. If she never set foot inside one again it would be too soon.

Duke sat next to her and hugged her close to him. Was this to comfort or protect? Probably a bit of both, she decided. She wasn't complaining, he was bringing her comfort. After phoning the brothel and reaching Scott, they had been sitting here for the last twenty minutes.

"Hey," Scott said as he was led into the waiting room. "What's happened?"

"She took an overdose. They are pumping her stomach now. Once she's stable you'll be able to see her," she replied, standing and throwing her arms around him.

"Thank God you found her, Mil. I had no idea she was that low. You warned me, and I didn't listen…" Scott closed his eyes. Did he blame himself?

"She's in the best place now, she'll get help." Did she really believe that?

"You shouldn't be here, Mil. Paul will do his fucking nut if he finds you here." He stood back and motioned to the door. "You need to go."

"No. I'm not going until I know she's okay, and you or Paul can't make me." She spun around and motioned to Duke. "I'm with my dad. I'm safe with him."

"You don't understand, Gladys was gonna phone him, he's more than likely on his way here."

"Mrs Kelly?" the nurse called. "The doctor will be with you in a moment."

"Thank you. This is Rosie's brother, Scott," she informed her. "Her next of kin."

***

"What is it with fucking women and doing as they are told?" Paul slammed the motor into gear and pulled away from the traffic lights. "And Duke. He had one fucking job. Keep Millie safe… I should've know the pikey bastard couldn't do that."

Paul glanced at Tony who looked out of the passenger window.

Paul breathed out slowly. "Fucking women. Do yaself a favour, Tone, and stay single."

"Do you wish you had?" Tony asked.

Paul was momentarily stunned. Did he? He shook his head. "No… I'd be lost without her. I love her. I love her, and she deserves better."

"Why? You've given her everything," Tony reasoned.

"I let her down." Paul sighed.

"What did you let her down with? Making her partner of the club, the house, the docks, or the scrapyard? I think you're being too hard on yourself."

"I did something I shouldn't've." Paul stopped the motor and turned off the ignition.

"Are you going to tell me?" Tony asked.

"No... I'm a fucking idiot, though," Paul conceded.

"So whatever this is, don't tell her. Does anyone else know?"

"No. Just me, and that's the way it's gonna stay." Paul grabbed the door handle, momentarily stopped by Tony's reply.

"Just remember, secrets have a way of coming out, Paul."

***

Millie saw Paul approach from the corner of her eye. He looked angry.

Shit.

"Is it to much to ask that you do as you're told?" he roared from the doorway.

"Do not shout at my daughter like that, she's upset enough," Duke intervened.

"Do not tell me how to speak to my wife." He squared up to Duke.

"Stop!" Millie sobbed. "Please. Just stop." Her hands trembled. This couldn't be happening, not here, not in hospital. Her best friend was lying at death's door, and he comes in shouting. She stared at Paul and shook her head. "This isn't the time or place for arguing. You and I will discuss this in private another time. So if you have a problem with me being here, you need to suck it up or leave, because I'm not going anywhere until I know Rosie is okay."

She wrapped her arms around herself and rocked backwards and forwards. She had done this all through her life. First at the children's home, then when she'd married Levi. It soothed her slightly in times of trouble.

"Sorry, Mil." Paul sat next to her.

She refused to look at him.

"Which bit are you sorry for, Paul? Gaining a scrapyard that's forced me into hiding, not believing me when I've warned you people are not who you think, or shouting like a madman in the middle of the hospital?" She stood and walked to the door. "To be perfectly honest, I'm getting more than a little fed up with being told what to do or what's best for me. I'm an adult. I get to have a say on my life." She stopped. There was more she could say, like because of his greed she had been forced away and now her friend might die because she hadn't been around.

Was that unfair? Maybe.

"Do you think I like you being away from me? It kills me a little more every day, but this is something we both have to do, and I'm not going to apologise for wanting to keep my wife safe."

"Well, it's lucky for you I'm looking forward to going back with my parents." Millie sat across from Paul and glared at him. That comment had hit the mark.

"Am I interrupting?" the doctor asked. He stood in the doorway seeming extremely awkward.

"How is she?" Scott and Millie said in unison.

"She's over the worst of it. We managed to clear out her stomach, however, some of the pills have managed to get into her system. We will monitor her, and once she makes a recovery she will be moved to a psychiatric hospital for evaluation."

"An asylum?" Scott shook his head. "No. No way. She is not going into a nut hospital, people don't come out of those places."

"When will you expect to move her?" Millie asked.

"Millie!" Scott's eyes widened. Did he really think she would allow that?

"A couple of weeks at least," the doctor cut in. "I must get on, other patients to see."

She waited for him to leave then turned to Scott. "She is not going into a psychiatric hospital. Now listen to me closely. Two weeks minimum, he said, so we keep an eye on her. Once she seems okay to move, we take her."

"You can't just snatch someone from a hospital, Mil—"

Cutting Paul off, she continued. "She will be brought to me, and I don't care how you do it, Paul Kelly, but if you value your marriage, you will."

CHAPTER 44

Paul stood outside the hospital entrance. He was still in shock. Millie had blamed him. Not only with her words but also he could see it in her eyes. Was she right? He rubbed his neck.

"She's upset, Paul, I wouldn't take what she said too seriously."

He turned to Duke. "So you think you know my wife better than me?"

"No." Duke plunged his hands into his pockets.

"You shouldn't have brought her here." Paul sighed. Did he really believe that?

"And if I hadn't and Rosie had died, then what? Who do you think she would blame, me?" Duke turned towards Paul. "No, she would still blame you, only I don't think she would forgive you. At least you've got a chance to put things right."

Paul spotted Millie walking towards the exit. She looked drained.

He grabbed the door, opening it for her. "Can we talk?"

"I thought you wanted me to leave?" Her voice had a coldness to it.

He sighed and stared at the ground. "Of course I don't want you to leave, Mil. I want you with me, it's where you belong."

"Funny, I don't feel I belong anywhere." She motioned to Duke. "Can you give us a minute?"

Duke nodded and walked away.

Paul was grateful, she was going to hear him out. "I'm sorry."

"So you've said."

He reached for her hand, pleased that she didn't pull away. "I shouldn't have shouted like that. I was just so scared when I saw you..."

"I know."

"I don't want you to go like this, Mil. Can't we make up?" he pleaded.

"We normally have sex to make up, Paul. I don't fancy having a shag at the hospital entrance."

Paul stiffened. "Fucking hell, Mil, we don't shag, we make love." Throwing his arm around her waist, he brought her closer. His lips met hers. Why couldn't she see how much he loved her?

She relaxed into the kiss. Paul's heart raced. Had she forgiven him?

"That was nice."

Millie smiled. "I need to go. Duke's waiting, and Connie will be worried. I didn't think we would be here for so long."

"Okay. I'll see you in a couple of days." Paul kissed her one last time then watched as she walked away.

Time to force the mystery man's hand before I lose my wife.

***

Millie sat with her head against the window of the motor. Duke had put a Dean Martin cassette in, and some song about trailers for sale or rent blasted out. What was it with these travellers and their country music?

"Can you turn it down a bit, please, I've got a headache." She could feel Duke studying her. She really didn't have time for this.

The music quietened, and Millie closed her eyes. She needed peace. Peace to process the day's events. The doctors had asked why Rosie had tried to kill herself. Millie knew the answer to that. Having grown up in a children's home, finding love and a place to fit was something they all aimed for. Rosie had been settled with Bobby. She loved him. He was her life. Now he'd betrayed her, she felt she was left with nothing. That wasn't reason to take your own life, and Millie would never condone that, but she did understand.

"Finn looks a lot better." Duke's voice broke into her thoughts.

It annoyed her.

"Yes." She kept her eyes closed. Didn't he realise she just wanted to get her own mind in order?

"I bet Connie's still up when we get home," Duke continued.

Please shut up.

"I'll borrow a motor tomorrow, and we can continue your driving lessons."

She opened her eyes and turned towards Duke. "I know what you're trying to do."

"And what's that?"

Christ, does he really think I'm that stupid?

"Take my mind away from my problems. The trouble is, though, at some point you have to face them."

"True, but not while everything is so fresh... You gave Paul a hard time," Duke added.

"I know." Millie turned back to the window, her mind a jumble of emotions she couldn't straighten out. Had Paul deserved that? He was the one shouting. He also wouldn't allow her to see Rosie.

Everyone has a choice

The words of the old woman, Patience, flashed through her mind. It wasn't Paul she was angry at. It was herself.

CHAPTER 45

The light was on when they returned to the traveller camp. Connie's face appeared at the window. Next, the door flew open. Jess jumped out followed by Aron. Millie glanced at Duke. He switched the motor off and got out. She sat there. The calm before the storm.

"Dad, Mum's been worried," Jess called.

"Not now, boy." Duke opened Millie's door.

She didn't want to get out. She wanted to be left alone. She kept her gaze forward.

"Go inside, boys. Millie?" Duke motioned to the trailer.

"I need a minute." She relaxed when the door closed, Duke's retreating footsteps a welcome noise. She waited for the trailer door to shut and then got out. Slowly, she headed towards the gypsy wagon, unsure why she was going there. Shouldn't she have wanted to be with her family?

Patience is your family, we are all related.

Millie climbed the steps. This time a pheasant hung from the hook, its neck hanging limp. Lifeless. That was how she felt. The door opened, and the old woman smiled.

"Come in, girl."

Millie sat on the bunk. Silence followed. This old woman got her. She knew what she needed. Tea was made and handed to her. She sipped quietly while her mind emptied.

"How come you never married?" Millie asked, surprising herself. "Sorry, it's none of my business."

"It's okay, girl. My mother said I was a beautiful baby, proper handsome." Patience cackled. "But as I grew they realised I was born with the gift. I told them things before they happened, good and bad."

"Why would that stop you from marrying?" Millie placed her cup down and turned to the old woman.

"Everyone was scared of me. My predictions, my warnings. I hadn't had a chance to learn, you see. Control is very important with seeing the future. Some things are better not known," Patience replied.

"But what about when you had, couldn't you have met someone then?" Millie pressed.

"Would you be with a woman if you knew she could see what the future holds, or all the bad that would happen? No, girl. My ability to see was a gift, and the price I paid was solitude."

"Don't sound like much of a gift," Millie said.

"Maybe not, but we don't get to choose these things. Now go, get yourself to bed." Patience ushered Millie out. "You need to look after yourself, girl, you have a chavvie to think about now. That's what you must concentrate on."

Millie headed towards the trailer. Duke sat on the step. Waiting.

"Sorry. I needed a minute on my own." She forced a smile.

He stood and opened the door. "Ladies first."

She gave a nod in return and kicked off her shoes then wiggled her toes. Connie's arms seemed to come from nowhere. Wrapped in a hug, Millie rested her head on Connie's shoulder. Jess and Aron watched, their faces creased with concern.

"I'm okay," Millie assured them.

Was she, though? How much shit could one person take before they broke?

***

Millie woke to the smell of bacon. Her stomach rumbled loudly. Had she eaten yesterday? No.

She climbed out of bed and reached for her dressing gown. She felt grubby. She was tired of having strip washes every morning; it was like being back in the summer heatwave. No fucking water. She internally screamed.

"Millie? Is that you." Connie's voice travelled through the closed door.

"I'll be out in a minute," she called back.

Opening the door, she was surprised to see the table set. Her brothers, Jess and Aron, along with Duke, sat waiting for breakfast. Connie flitted about, dishing up the fry-up.

"Take a seat, Millie. Here, take that." Connie handed the plate to her.

Millie sat next to Duke. He was busy talking to the boys about his upcoming fight. They both listened intently. Connie sat opposite after handing out the plates. They all carried on as though everything were normal. Chatting and laughing. Like a real family.

"I've borrowed a motor, Mil. We can go out after breakfast." Duke rammed a large forkful of sausage and egg into his mouth.

He reminded Millie of the hamster they had in the children's home with his bulging cheeks.

"You'll need to apply for your provisional licence, too," he mumbled through the mouthful of food.

A nod was all she could manage. The fry-up was welcome. She even surprised herself at the amount she had eaten. Touching her tummy, she wondered if the small bump was the food or the baby. Surely she would start showing soon. Then what? She had to tell Paul, before he found out from other sources.

***

Paul turned off the shower and reached for the towel. What he wouldn't give to be washing Millie's back right now. Pushing the thought away, he dried and dressed quickly — there was no time to bang one out. Today was going to be the day he caught that bastard. How? He wasn't sure. Sorting Shannon had been easier than he'd expected, so now it was time to turn his attention to the mystery man. Why hadn't he followed him out of the pub? He was a fucking idiot. It could have all been over by now with everything back to normal.

A crash from below had Paul gritting his teeth. Those fucking Irish were turning out to be a right pain in his arse. Descending the stairs two at a time, he marched to the kitchen. "What the fuck was that noise?"

"Sorry, Paul, I pulled too hard on the knife drawer." Conor at least had the decency to look ashamed.

"Pick it up and be quick, we've work to do—" Paul stopped when the phone rang. Was this the lead he needed?

Snatching it up, he smiled. Millie's gentle voice drifted into his ear. "Mil, everything okay?" His face fell. She needed to see him. It was urgent.

Fuck

"Okay, I'll come now." Paul replaced the receiver, then stared at it for several minutes. Was she ill? Had she had enough of him? Did she want to stay with Connie and Duke for good?

There's only one way to find out, you prick.

Grabbing his keys, he slammed the door behind him. Maybe today wasn't going to be so great after all.

CHAPTER 46

Millie lay on the bed, tired after the driving lesson. At least she hadn't crashed this time. Duke seemed pleased with her performance, too. That was once she had stopped muddling up the accelerator and brake. They had stopped off at a post office and picked up a provisional licence application. She would fill that in later, after the conversation with Paul. What would he say? The timing wasn't ideal, but he did tell her he wanted kids.

Well, it's too damn late now. The baby's in there and it's gotta come out.

Pulling her top up, she studied her stomach. It definitely wasn't flat anymore.

Rosie always said I needed to put a bit of weight on.

Millie could imagine Rosie's reaction. Her eyes would light up, and she'd scream while jumping up and down and most likely applaud, too.

Would have done.

Not now.

How was Rosie doing today? Had she had a good night?

Millie sat up. Was that a car? Sliding off the bed, she walked to the other end of the trailer. Paul's car was parked outside. There was no going back now.

"Mil?" Paul called as the door opened.

"Paul. Come in." She motioned to the bunk.

"Where is everyone?" he asked. He sounded nervous.

"I asked for some privacy, you don't get much around here."

"Look, Mil—" Paul stopped when she placed a finger against his lips.

"Shh," she began. "I have something to tell you."

"Whatever it is we can fix it. I can fix it. Mil, I'll do whatever it takes…"

"Do you think you would be a good dad?" Millie asked with a smile.

"What? I'd try to be." Paul sounded confused. "What's going on?"

"I'm pregnant, you're going to be a dad." Millie's smile fell when Paul simply sat there, staring. Had he not heard her? "Paul, I said—"

"I heard."

***

Paul sat in the warehouse and glared at Martin. He had nabbed him and brought him here for questioning. Questioning and punishment. "So you are trying to tell me you haven't heard anything from him?"

It didn't sit right with Paul. Why would this lookalike prick disappear into thin air? He had to have been warned.

"I haven't heard a thing. I swear." Martin's voice had a tremble to it.

He was scared. Good. But what the fuck was Paul supposed to do now? Pull the gyppos out of the scrapyard and wait to see if he struck? No. It seemed this mystery man knew all of Ronnie's businesses, but did he know Paul's? The girls were okay at the brothel. That was one business that was secret, but what about the club? Anyone could look it up and find out who the owner was. Fuck it, he needed to make sure Martin was telling the truth. This whole debacle was costing him too much money. The gyppos alone were making a fortune off his back.

"I'm going to ask you some questions. For each lie you tell me, I'm going to chop a finger off." Paul grinned when all the colour drained from Martin's face.

"But I've told you everything. Please."

"Get the toolkit out, Tone."

Paul waited for the instruments to be unrolled, then reached for the secateurs. He squeezed them shut a few times, making sure Martin watched.

"Hold him down." Paul liked to see them struggle. It gave him a small thrill, not that he'd admit it. "Right, Martin, question number one. When was the last time you heard from that prick?"

"The pub, you know, you were there." Martin gulped.

"Hold his hand steady." Paul placed the secateurs against Martin's little finger. "Last chance. When was the last time you heard from him?"

"I've already told you, argh." Martin passed out before his finger was off.

"Fucking hell, we've got a soft one here, Tone." Paul stared down in disgust. He squeezed harder, and the finger dropped to the floor. "Throw some water over him, that should bring him round."

Martin gasped as the water hit. "What…?"

"I did warn you. Now, Martin, you have nine fingers left. After that I will take your toes. If by then I'm still not satisfied, I will take your life. Understand?"

"Yes." Martin nodded. The colour had completely drained from his face now, and his gaze darted around the warehouse in terror.

Paul thought he looked a bit green to be honest. "Next question. Two. Have you warned this prick that I'm onto him?"

Martin didn't reply; in fact, he looked like he was thinking.

Paul glanced at Tony. "Next finger."

"No, wait. He phoned when your man was there. The Irish one. I didn't warn him, I swear."

"Then what did you do, Martin, because it sounds to me like you most certainly did?" Paul grabbed another finger and snapped it back. He then walked away while Martin was left screaming. "Shut him up, Tone."

Tony shoved a rag into Martin's mouth. It didn't stop the noise completely, but it did muffle it.

"I think we will skip the next step and go straight in for the kill." Paul knelt next to Martin. "I told you what would happen if you fucked me over. Once I've finished with you, I'll be going after your family."

If that didn't get the rat speaking, nothing would.

"Take the rag out." Paul gestured.

Martin looked like he had gone ten rounds in the ring.

Paul laughed. "Any last words before I chop you up into little pieces and feed you to the fish?"

"I didn't tell him, I swear. He heard the Irishman speaking in the background. He then said it was a setup and slammed the phone down." Martin struggled to hold his head up. "That's the truth," he replied before finally slumping forward.

Paul walked outside, he needed some fresh air. He hated it when they shit themselves. The stench was worse than rotting flesh. Didn't they have any self-respect?

Tony followed. "Where the fuck do we go from here?"

"What about his mum? She may know something. It's worth a try anyway. We'll leave him here for now, go see her, and then decide what to do with him," Paul answered.

"Do you want him put in the ground?" Tony asked.

"Nah, he can stay right where he is. Lock up and we'll get going."

CHAPTER 47

Paul knocked on the door then stood back. He plastered a smile on, although he didn't feel like smiling. What had started with a week or two max had now turned into week five. This was his last card to play. Martin's mother. If the old bag didn't speak, she would go the same way as her son.

"Hello, can I help you?" the woman asked.

"I certainly hope so," Paul replied, pushing his way past her. "We need a little chat. It's about your son and a mystery man."

The woman followed Paul into the lounge. Her eyes had gone wide, and she hobbled with a walking stick.

"We alone?" he asked.

"Can you tell me what this is about, young man?"

Jesus, she was polite. That unnerved Paul. She reminded him of his dear old gran. "Your son has been helping some man plot against me. Now I'm not to worried about myself, but they have included my wife in their little scam, and she is pregnant."

"Congratulations." She smiled.

"Thanks." Paul rubbed the back of his neck. He hadn't expected that. "I need to protect my wife and unborn child, and to do that I need to know who this man is." He did a quick glance around the house. It was in disrepair. Paper hung off the walls in places, and a damp patch riddled the corner. Some son Martin was, leaving his mother to live in a shit-hole like this.

"I see." She hobbled to a chair and sat. Even that was threadbare. "Please, take a seat," she offered.

"You seem very calm considering you have a strange man in your home," Paul said as he sat on the sofa, which was equally threadbare.

"Your kind don't scare me. You need to remember my sister was married to a thug. Ghastly man. Never told the truth for as long as I knew him." She pulled a tissue from her sleeve and coughed into it. It was a raspy cough.

Was she ill?

"I knew Ronnie well, or I thought I did." Paul studied the woman. Was she as old as she looked?

"I remember seeing you at the funeral and at my sister's."

"I'm sorry for your loss." He wasn't, but wasn't that what you were supposed to say?

She waved her hand in the air as if swatting away a gnat. "Wrong 'uns, the pair of um."

"So you didn't get on with Rita either?" This was turning out to be interesting. Paul sat forward.

"She was always a schemer. Went after what she wanted, no matter who it hurt, and, might I add, she always succeeded."

"Sounds like she hurt you in the process." Paul couldn't believe what he was hearing. This was too good to be true.

"She took the man I loved. We were to be married. What hurt the most is that she only wanted him because he was mine. Once she had him, she moved on to the next one. I had never forgiven her, but I had to play nice for my parents' sake. Anyway, I digress. What did you want to know?"

"Do you know who this man is, a name, address, anything that might help?" Paul studied the old woman. What was she thinking?

"Does he dress like Ronnie?"

"Yes, he wears a trilby, and funnily enough, he has Ronnie's mannerisms. At first I thought it was a brother," Paul said.

"No. Ronnie never had a brother. This man is, or was, Rita's last love interest."

"What? She was playing away from home?" Paul stifled the laugh building in his throat. This was gold. Rita had cheated on Ron. He'd bet Ron never knew that.

"She had a lot of men, but Ronnie also had a lot of women. I slept with him, not because I liked him but purely for revenge against my sister." The old woman smiled.

Paul sat there with his mouth open. What a fucked-up family. "So have you got a name for this man, address, anything that might help find him?" he repeated.

***

"You coming to watch your old man fight?" Duke asked Millie, opening a can of beer.

Millie watched as he knocked it back. "Jesus, you're fighting, shouldn't you prepare?"

"What do ya think I'm doing?" Duke said with a belch.

"That's disgusting." Millie shook her head. "Does everyone go to these things?"

"Con and the boys will be there. I don't want you staying here on ya own."

"I can sit with Patience," Millie offered.

Straight away, Duke frowned. She didn't know why he disliked the old girl. So what if she had the gift. She was honest, and in Millie's book that meant more than anything.

"No," was all Duke said. A big flat no. He disappeared into the bedroom and shut the door.

Millie, deciding to press for a bit more, stood outside the door and listened to the sounds of Duke moving around. He must have been getting changed.

"What is your problem with her?"

"Leave it, Millie."

"Why won't you tell me?" she asked.

"*I said leave it, I'm preparing for a fight,*" Duke shouted through the door.

"Fine. Let's leave everything, *Duke.*" If that didn't hit the spot, nothing would. She stepped back.

Silence.

Millie turned as the door opened. Duke stood there. Had she hurt him?

"I just wanted to know. Why?"

The sigh was probably the loudest she had ever heard. His shoulders slumped. Duke walked past her, as though she wasn't there. Had she touched a nerve? Maybe the old girl had given him bad news and he couldn't forgive her. She followed him to the cupboard where he pulled out another beer.

"Okay. I get it, it's private. I shouldn't have asked." Millie slumped down onto the bunk. The plastic covering annoying her more now she was in a bad mood.

"It's not private," Duke said.

"Then what is it?" Millie glanced at the floor; she could feel Duke's eyes on her. "Why do you hate her so much?"

"I don't hate her. She scares me, more than getting in the ring with a ten-foot giant." He laughed and then sighed. "We camped in Kent. Connie and me, she was pregnant with the boys. Patience was on the site. I'd known her all me life, she's like a great-aunt. Anyway, I had a reading. I wanted to know if it was a boy or a girl, healthy, all the usual stuff. She told me it was twins. Twin boys nonetheless. I was happy."

Millie sat there, confused. He'd admitted he was happy.

"So what changed?"

"She told me I also had a daughter…"

CHAPTER 48

Finn sat forward while the pillows were plumped behind him. He wanted to tell the nurse to piss off, but he was too weak to argue.

"There ya go, Finn, sit back and relax. The tea trolley should be round shortly."

He replied with a grunt then nestled back into the pillows and closed his eyes. Things were still hazy. He could recall the fire, but very little else since. He had questions. Like how long he had been in this bloody bed?

"Finn?"

He opened one eye. There, standing at the side of the bed, was Paul Kelly. "Paul. About time I had a different face to look at," he grumbled. "Poxy nurses keep bossing me about."

"Glad to see you're keeping ya spirits up." Paul laughed.

THE STEPNEY ALLIANCE

The tea trolly trundled in, cups rattling. "Tea, Finn?" the woman asked.

He gave a sharp nod. "I'll have one for my friend, too." He waited for her to leave and then focused on Paul. "Where's Millie? Why hasn't she been to see me?"

Paul rubbed a hand over his face.

Finn, even though not on top form, could tell something was wrong. "Is she all right?"

"Yeah, she's okay. That's another story for another time... Look, I wanted to talk to you about Shannon," Paul started.

"She was here. She found me." How had he forgotten his own daughter?

"She's not who you think she is, Finn, she—"

"What the feck is that supposed to mean?" He wouldn't have anyone telling him about his own daughter. Least of all Paul fecking Kelly.

Paul held his hands up as if in submission. "Whoa. You need to hear me out."

"I don't need to do anything. I think it's best you leave. *Nurse!*"

***

Paul stepped out of the hospital entrance, annoyed with himself for fucking up. Millie had warned him to keep his mouth shut for now. It would have to come from her. Finn trusted Millie like she was his own flesh and blood. He had taken her in and given her a chance when she'd been at her most vulnerable. They had a close bond.

Unlocking his car, he drove back to Aiden and Sean, who staked out Rita's lover. Mr Jeremy fucking Armitage. The name itself pissed Paul off. This shitbag thought he could have one over on him with a fucking name like that. The fucking liberty.

He parked behind the Irish lads, then sat there for a minute or two and savoured the silence before joining them.

"Any movement?" he asked as he slid in the back seat.

"No. He's still in there. What do you want to do, go in and grab him, or wait and see where he goes?" Sean asked.

Paul wanted to grab the bastard, but would that be wise? What if this piece of shit was working with someone? He couldn't risk that, and now he knew who, and more importantly, where he was, he could afford to wait it out a day, two at max.

"We'll wait twenty-four hours, then pounce."

***

Millie pulled her coat tightly around her. The weather was gruesome. Who in their right mind would arrange a boxing match in a cold barn? The wind whistled through the cracks in the door, and the tin sides shook. Would the bloody thing blow away?

Millie glanced at Connie who appeared equally as cold. "I feel like I'm in Kansas, about to get blown away to meet Scarecrow, Tin Man, and Lion."

Connie laughed. "If you get too cold we can sit in the motor, although Duke will be disappointed. I think he's looking forward to fighting in front of his daughter."

"Really?"

Duke obviously didn't know her at all. She hated fighting. Hated seeing the people she loved fight. Did she love Duke? He was her dad, but until that moment she hadn't thought about it.

"Come on, it's starting." Connie grabbed her arm and led her towards the corner of the imaginary ring.

"Don't you worry about him fighting?" Millie asked. Didn't her mother care?

"I did at first, but I had to get used to it. Travellers love boxing, it goes hand in hand with betting." Connie smiled.

Millie followed her eyeline. She was smiling at Duke, and he was smiling back.

Millie shook her head when she spotted the can of beer in Duke's hand. "He shouldn't be drinking."

"Your father has his own rules. He reckons it unsettles his opponents." Connie pointed towards the building crowd. "He makes a lot of money from fighting."

"Well, I guess it's worth having ya brains knocked out then." Rolling her eyes, Millie turned her thoughts to Paul. Had he seen Finn? How had Finn taken the news? This was a whole other shitshow about to happen, and she wished she could have been there. If only to give Finn comfort. It was what he deserved for all he had done for her. Giving her a home and a job. Supporting all her stupid decisions and for forgiving her for all her selfish ones.

"Ladies and gentlemen."

Millie peeped over to Duke and his opponent. "That man's bigger than him."

"Don't let size fool you," Connie assured her.

Just how could she be so calm? Her husband, the man she loved, was about to get hammered into the floor by a seven-foot monster. A bell clanged, and all carnage let loose. Shouting and jeering roared from the crowd. Millie stumbled as the rowdy travellers surged forward. This was not at all civilised. She glanced at Duke. He pounded the monster in the face. Millie turned to Connie; she had to get out. She felt herself shunted to the side and staggered to get her footing. What type of parents brought their daughter to this? Their pregnant daughter.

Fuck. They don't know.

"I need to get out." She pushed her way through the crowd, only stopping when she reached the barn door. Leaning against the tin wall, she placed her hands on her knees. Eyes closed. She breathed deep, taking in lungfuls of air.

"Millie?" Connie's gentle voice was laced with concern.

Maybe she should have been concerned before bringing her here. Millie opened her eyes and straightened. "I need to get out of here. It's not safe."

"Would you rather sit in the motor?" Connie placed her hand on Millie's arm. "I don't think this is going to last much longer."

Millie climbed onto an old tyre rim and peeked over the crowd. Duke had blood dripping from a cut to his eye. "I don't like seeing him hurt."

"No. Neither do I. Come on, we'll wait in the motor."

"No. You go back and watch him," Millie urged. "I'll stay here for a bit." She watched her mother dive through the crowd, pleased to be alone at last. Closing her eyes, she once again wished for her bed.

"Are you okay?"

Millie opened her eyes and stared at the woman. "I'm fine, thanks."

"My name's Gypsy. I've seen you at the camp."

"Yeah, I've seen you, too, and your husband." Millie glanced at the floor awkwardly. "You're not Irish then?"

"No, but I married an Irish traveller. I'm a Romani," Gypsy replied.

"Isn't that the same thing?" Millie asked, glancing up.

"No, Irish travellers are a different breed. I'm like your dad, Romani." She laughed.

"Paul's family are Irish, just regular Irish, I guess… So do you live here all the time?" Millie was never good at small talk, and to be fair, she didn't give a shit where this girl lived, but talking about the weather didn't seem fitting.

"No, we're here because of you."

"What?" Millie's pulse quickened. "Why?"

"John Jo was hired by Duke to watch you. I thought you knew. So were a couple of the others."

Saved by the bell. "Looks like the fight's over. It was nice meeting you, Gypsy, I need to find Connie." She walked to the edge of the crowd. Everything made sense now. She had noticed the men watching her whenever she left the trailer, and now she knew why.

CHAPTER 49

The rain had finally stopped, and the moon made an appearance between the clouds. Paul glanced at his watch.

The lights had long gone out in Jeremy's windows, the house now plunged into darkness. Paul rubbed his eyes. He would sleep for a week once this was over. A smile played on his lips. A week in bed with Millie. It had seemed an eternity since they had shared a bed together. That's why he had decided to grab Jeremy tonight. Once he had him, she could come home.

They had an announcement to make, a nursery to decorate, and some serious celebrating to do. He still felt dazed from her words.

You're going to be a dad.

Him, a dad. That was his life complete. Everything was on the up, apart from the fucking gyppos at the end of the garden. Although they proved useful, he still would never trust them. If it wasn't for Duke being Millie's dad, he wouldn't have a bar of any of them. Was he being unfair? Probably, but he couldn't help the way he felt. And now they would be connected through the baby, it would have both their blood running through its veins.

Paul sighed. There was nothing he could do about that. Instead, he focused back on the mission.

"Yous ready?" He turned to look at the three nodding faces behind him then glanced at the car beyond them. "I'll let Tony know. Sean, once me and Tone are in, pull the car out front and get ready to open the boot. Conor, you stay with him in case there's any trouble. Come on, Liam."

Paul gave Tony a nod and waited for him and Aiden. "Are the boys in place?"

"Yeah, in place, tooled up and ready to go," Tony replied.

"Ready?" Paul whispered.

"Ready," Tone affirmed, holding up a crowbar. "Shouldn't have any problems getting in with this."

Paul felt his pocket for the tape and cable ties. "I've got everything else. You two." Pointing at Liam and Aiden, he motioned to the back of the house. "Wait at the gate, out of sight. If you hear anything, come in... I've got a bad feeling."

"You think there's gonna be trouble?" Aiden asked.

"What's the first thing you would do if you thought someone was onto you?" Paul continued without waiting for an answer. "You'd get protection."

He held the handle of the gate and pushed gently. "The fucking gate's padlocked." Finding a bin, he climbed up and over the fence at the side of the house, dropping to the other side with a loud thud. "Shit." He took a quick gander at the back of the house, making sure he hadn't disturbed the arsehole.

Tony appeared a second later. "I've ripped me fucking bottoms," he mumbled. "Caught 'em on a nail."

Paul sniggered. Tony had a large rip right in the groin of his jogging bottoms. "Lucky you didn't rip your cock off," he whispered. "Jimmy the window while I keep watch."

Paul scanned the garden. Jeremy would've placed men out here if he thought he might be under attack. Maybe he wasn't as clever as Paul had thought.

"I'm in," Tony whispered.

Paul pushed the door open and stepped inside. This was too fucking easy. Placing his finger to his mouth, he motioned for Tony to go first. Tony stopped in front of him and pointed to a cupboard under the stairs. Paul gave him a nod. It was possible that someone was in there. A noise from outside stopped him in his tracks. He spun around and peered out into the garden. Three large men headed towards the house.

Bingo.

Paul kept his eyes on them until his own men snuck up from behind. Turning to Tony, he motioned for him to wait at the cupboard. If there was someone in there, Tone could sort them out while Paul continued up the stairs.

He tiptoed up, as lightly as he could. The fifth step creaked. He held his breath. Reaching down into his sock, he pulled out the gun he had carefully hidden. A low squeak came from below him. The cupboard door was opening. A loud crack followed, with a groan and a thud. Tony had taken care of that one. Paul turned as Tony joined him. They continued up the stairs and hit the landing. Tony gestured to the first door. He slipped in front of Paul and reached for the handle. Paul looked at the remaining two doors. With a quick nod to Tony, he kicked in the first and then the second.

"Empty," Tony called, exiting the small bedroom.

"So are these. Fuck." Paul looked around the empty bedroom. "He knew we were coming."

"Do you think the old girl told him?"

"Nah. She couldn't fucking stand him." Paul sighed. "This was a setup, though."

He walked to the landing and stared down at the body on the floor below. Claret coated the carpet. "Jesus, Tone, how hard did you clobber him?"

"Hard enough so he didn't get up." Tony laughed. "What we gonna do with 'em all?"

"Tie them up and put them in separate rooms. One of the fuckers is gonna talk." Paul descended the stairs and headed towards the door. He would go and see Rita's sister first thing in the morning, but first, he had some punishment to dish out.

CHAPTER 50

Duke staggered into the trailer. Millie stood back for fear of him collapsing on her.

"How much have you had to drink?" She didn't need to ask, he stank of beer and cigarettes.

Duke waved her away and fell on the bunk. The blood on his eye was now dried. Millie boiled the kettle and poured the hot water into a bowl with a generous amount of salt.

She grabbed a washcloth and knelt next to him. "This might sting a bit."

"Ouch." Duke held her hand. "I'll wash it off in the morning, I need sleep."

"Millie," Connie called from the bedroom. "Leave him. He'll have the hangover from hell in the morning, he can sort himself out."

Millie stood and backed away from him. He was already snoring. What a fucking sight, lying there, beat up with blood on his face. Glancing at his hands, she realised they weren't much better. His knuckles were split. "Fine."

"You disapprove?" Connie asked.

"It's nothing to do with me how you lot live." Millie opened the door and threw the water out. All she wanted to do was go home. To be with her husband.

Duke let out a loud snort, almost waking himself up.

"Don't think we're gonna get much sleep tonight. Not with that fucking racket."

"Come to bed, Millie, I'll roll Duke onto his side."

She climbed into bed, pulling the blankets over her ears. She could still hear him, though. This, she decided, would be a perfect torture method.

The bed moved. Connie had climbed in.

"Does he always do this after a fight?" Millie asked.

"Mostly. If it's a planned fight. He makes a lot of money fighting, and gambling." Connie twisted around and faced Millie. "I heard, you know. The other night when Duke asked you about your life…" She trailed off, her voice showing her discomfort.

"We all have a past," Millie replied. "That was mine. I'm tired, do you mind if I get some sleep?"

"Of course not. Goodnight."

Millie turned away. She didn't think for one minute she would sleep, not while Duke was chugging away like a steam engine. She placed her hand on her belly. Hopefully, the little one was getting some rest in there. Was it even a baby yet? It was hard to imagine. There was a very slight bulge to her stomach. They would have to announce it soon before she could no longer hide it. Not that she wanted to hide it, that was Paul's idea. He wanted to tell his family, before everyone else knew. Millie had agreed, family should know first. But shouldn't that include hers?

***

Paul stood at the front door and waited for Rita's sister to open it. On the third attempt, he started to think something was wrong. Had she had a fall? He looked at the side entrance; maybe the back door was open. He slid around to the back, checking no one was around. The door opened. As Paul went to close it... Blood on the handle caught his attention. His heart beat a little faster. Her legs came into view first, lying sprawled on the front room floor. He peeked over the chair. The old girl's eyes stared back at him, her face bloodied.

Shit.

He knew she was dead. Tortured? Because of him? Most definitely. "I'm sorry." Paul turned and left the house. Had Jeremy been watching him? More to the point, was he still watching? He climbed into his motor. "She's dead."

"He's been one step ahead every time," Tony replied. "But he's gotta fuck up sooner or later."

"We haven't got time to wait, we need to push his hand." Paul rubbed his face. "I want my fucking wife back."

"You miss her?" Tony yawned.

"Of course I fucking miss her. She's my wife... I've got something to tell ya, it's a secret so you can't tell anyone. Millie's pregnant." Paul's smile grew.

"Congratulations, mate. That's brilliant news." Tony slapped him on the back. "I'm pleased for ya."

"Thanks, you're the first to know, so whatever you do, don't let anyone, including Millie, know that I've told ya."

"Your secret's safe with me." Tony grinned.

Paul's smile grew even more. It felt good to tell someone. "Let's go and work on his men again, show them what we're really capable of."

Tony started the motor. "D'ya reckon they've got them all out?"

"Yeah. They should be on their way to the warehouse. I gave strict instructions to drive around for a while in case they're followed. But to be honest, I think he's here somewhere, watching me. I can feel him."

"Let's hope he falls for it then." Tony smiled. "Ready?"

***

"Will you keep the fucking noise down?" Duke moaned.

"We're not making any noise, unlike you last night." Millie banged the kettle down and smiled when Duke held his head.

"Here." Connie handed him a couple of aspirin and a glass of water. "I'll do you some breakfast, might help soak some of that beer up."

"Where's me fags?" Duke felt his pocket then pulled out a squashed pack of Number 6. "Shit, must've slept on 'em."

"Can you smoke that outside. Please?" It came out as demand rather than a request.

"Oh, I'm sorry, princess, I thought I owned this place."

"The smoke makes me feel sick." Millie grabbed her coat. "It's okay, I'll go."

"No. I'll go. The fresh air might do me good." Duke stood, swayed, and crashed back down. "I'll have one later," he mumbled.

"Here, drink this." Connie handed him a mug of tea. "You need to get some fluids, other than beer, into you."

"Are you both ganging up on me?" He rubbed his forehead. It even hurt when he spoke.

"Maybe we don't like seeing you like this." Millie sat next to him. "I mean, if you feel as bad as you look, then…"

"Thanks," Duke snapped.

"Dad," Aron shouted as he crashed through the door. "Jess has gone."

"What d'ya mean, gone?" Connie pulled her son in and held on to his jumper. "Well?"

Aron glanced between his mum and dad. "He's run off — with Sherry."

CHAPTER 51

Millie lay on the bed listening to all the excited chatter. Duke was over the moon, whilst Connie was a little more reserved. The boys had just turned seventeen. Wasn't that too young? Millie herself had married young, and look how that had turned out. Would it have been different if she had met Paul back then? Maybe.

"You gonna come out, Mil, and join us?" Connie stood in the doorway staring down at Millie. "Have you been crying?"

Millie swiped at her eyes. "No." She had, but she didn't want to talk about it. She was tired of repeating herself. "I'll be out in a minute." She watched Connie retreat back along the trailer. Swinging her legs around and off the bed, she sat. She would be twenty-five in a couple of weeks' time. Would she be home by then? Dragging herself off the bed, she joined the rest of them, sitting on the bunk with her body turned towards the window.

"Reckon this time next year we'll be grandparents." Duke beamed. "That'll keep ya busy, Con. I'll have to get home and have another base done for their trailer, might have two. Won't be long before Aron's off."

"When do we leave?" Millie asked, the comment about grandparents having got to her. If only he knew.

"Not we. Me. You know you can't go back until it's safe," Duke replied. "What is wrong with you? You've had the hump all morning."

She sighed. "I'm just tired. I might go and get some fresh air." As she stood, Duke's hand touched her arm.

He gave it a little squeeze. "If something was wrong, you would tell me, or Connie?"

Millie nodded, pleased when Duke dropped his hand. "Everything's fine. You should be celebrating the new family member. A daughter-in-law, someone for you to hang out with, Connie." She smiled. Did she feel jealous?

Marching along the camp, she ignored the staring faces. There was only one person she wanted to talk to. Patience. She needed the peace and quiet that only the old woman could offer. Peace and quiet so she could think. Millie had been miserable when Duke and Connie had moved onto the land behind her house, but then finding out they were her parents, she'd kind of liked it. Now, though, it sounded like it was gonna be a gypsy site, and she wasn't sure how she felt about that. Did she want them to herself? No. She had never been selfish. So why was she struggling? Was it because of the baby? Shouldn't her parents know so they could be happy for her?

"Hey, wait up."

Millie rolled her eyes. "What do you want, Duke?"

"Thought I'd have a stroll with ya." He pulled his cigarettes out of his pocket and lit one.

Millie waved the smoke away. "That's a filthy habit."

"I know."

They walked along in silence until she couldn't stand it any longer. "Stop." She glanced at Duke who studied her. "What are you really doing out here?"

Duke dropped his fag and ground it out with his boot. "I know something's wrong. I want to know what it is."

***

Paul kept his eyes on the wing mirror. He was sure someone was following. They headed out towards an old abandoned airfield. It was quiet. No through traffic. It was the perfect place for an ambush. "Just up here, Tone. Pull in after the wooden shed."

They had driven three miles down this lane and hadn't seen a soul.

"Do ya think he's gonna fall for it?" Tony asked. He yanked the handbrake up and turned off the ignition.

"I'd bet my life on it. Come on, let's get out and see." Paul opened the door. The distant noise of a motor disturbed the peace. "We'll make our way back through the trees, pop the boot, and leave it open. He'll think we're up to something."

The pair headed for the trees and jogged back parallel to the lane. They reached their destination and ducked down, watching and waiting.

"Well, what have we got here?"

The car slowed as it manoeuvred over potholes, the engine revving loudly.

"Fucking hell, he's gonna blow the bloody thing up."

"Come on, let's get back to the road." Paul knew there was no way out, other than the way they had come. If this was Jeremy, then he was a sitting duck. He waved at Aiden who was driving the first car.

"I'll get in here, Tone, you get in the next one."

Indicating to the passenger's seat, Paul waited for Aiden to get in the back. He wasn't leaving anything to chance. They drove away and headed back to where he had left the car. There in front of him was a blue Ford Cortina. He couldn't make out how many men were in there, at least four, he guessed.

"Reckon we might have us a shootout." He grabbed the gun from the glove compartment and checked it was loaded.

The Cortina sped up.

"Look out, they've clocked us. Speed up, I'll tell you when to slow down." Paul knew the lane stopped abruptly. Thanks to him and his men, they had blocked it off with a large tree trunk. There was no way around it, and it was difficult to spot as it was on a bend. "And remember, I want that prick alive. Slow down."

Paul smiled when he heard the bang. "I bet that was a fucking shock." He climbed out of the car and stood behind a tree. He could see four men. Which one was Jeremy?

There he is, in that ridiculous fucking trilby.

Paul held his gun out, finger ready on the trigger. "I've counted four, but stay vigilant… Everyone in place?" He waited for a nod from Tony. "Let's get the bastard."

CHAPTER 52

It had been three days since Jess had run off. Duke had bought a nice trailer for him and had pulled it next to his. Connie had been out and bought some bedding and towels. It had become the main topic of conversation.

Millie knocked on Patience's door. She needed to escape this madness.

"Come in, Millie," the old woman called through the closed door.

How did she do that?

"Hello. How did you know it was me?" Millie asked, sitting opposite the fire.

"Lucky guess." She cackled. "Tea?"

"Yes, please." Millie sat back against a cushion. "It's peaceful in here." She sat forward and peeked out of the little window.

Duke reversed Aron's trailer out.

Where the fuck is he going with that?

"Is that why you're here, for peace?" Patience asked. "Because you won't find peace wherever you go if you are troubled inside."

This old girl knew everything; her wisdom showed in her words.

"You still not told 'em?"

Millie sighed. "No. No one knows, only you, me, and Paul. I promised I would wait so we could tell everyone together."

"You sure about that?" Patience snapped.

"Sure about what, who knows?" Millie took the cup she was offered and sat back. "I think I know who I've told."

"But do you know who he's told, girl? Men are funny things, they make the rules and then they're the first to break them." She sighed. "They are your parents, and if you don't like your brother getting all the attention, you should tell 'em."

"I wanted to tell them, the other night at the fight I was close, but a promise is a promise, and now I don't want to spoil Jess's moment. It must be exciting for him. Starting out in life with the woman he loves. Actually being able to sleep in the same bed. I'd give anything to sleep in my bed with Paul."

"You need to put yourself first. You're 'aving a chavvie, that trumps everything in my book." Patience opened the fire and shoved another log on. "Bleeding weather, it's getting colder by the hour."

Millie laughed. "I'm surprised you've noticed, it's like one hundred degrees in here. I reckon this wagon is warmer that India."

"It's just how I like it. Now you get off into your trailer, it will be dark soon." Patience motioned to the door. "Girl, make sure you say goodbye before you leave."

Millie stepped outside. The wind was bitter. She pulled her coat around her tightly and walked back to the trailer. Connie dished up a beef stew. The aroma hit Millie before she saw it. There was a plate of crusty bread on the table.

"Smells delicious. Is there anything I can do?"

"It's all done, take a seat." Connie motioned.

Duke walked in behind her and slid onto the bunk. "Smells cushty, Con."

"I've got something I want to tell you." Millie smiled when they both looked up. "I'm—"

"Jess is back," Duke called over her. He slid out from the table and headed towards the door. "You better make two more plates, Con." He called over his shoulder.

Millie stood back. Connie rushed out to great her son and his new wife.

Wife? But they ain't married.

"Come on in. Yous hungry? Here, take a seat." Connie ushered Sherry into a seat behind the table. She placed a plate in front of her. "Eat up. Jess, here." Grabbing another plate, she placed it in front of Duke. "Millie, sit down."

Millie, sit down. Just who the fuck does she think she's talking to?

"I'm all right standing, thanks, Connie." Millie glanced at Jess. He stared back at her. "Congratulations, both of you." She smiled.

"What did you want to tell us?" Connie asked. She even sounded interested, but it was too late.

Millie wasn't going to tell them about the baby. She was now grateful Duke had cut her off. It showed what sort of a father he was. What was important to him. He was trying to be a father to her, not because he wanted to be, but because he had to be. That was the difference between her and her brothers. They were wanted.

Millie lifted her chin defiantly. "I'm going home tomorrow, and none of you can stop me."

***

Paul lay on the table at the brothel while the doctor prodded and poked his wound. The bullet had caught him on his left side, near the rib cage, narrowly avoiding his lung.

"The bullet's grazed you. An inch to the right and it would have been a different matter." The doctor grabbed a sterile cloth and dabbed at the wound. "A few stitches and you'll be right as rain. Just don't overexert yourself, and no driving for a week."

Paul gritted his teeth; the stinging sensation was subsiding. "A week?"

"Yes. A week. You need the wound to heal. Driving is more likely to pull the stitches. You have lost quite a bit of blood, so I suggest you put your feet up for forty-eight hours." Picking up his needle, he began to sew Paul up.

He took a sharp breath as the needle broke through his skin. It hurt, although not as much as the thought of not being able to bring Millie home. Wasn't that the end goal? Tony could drive him, but then would seeing him with a bullet wound upset her, upset the baby? No, he couldn't chance it. He would have to leave it a week. The whole fucking thing had turned into a shitshow.

***

Millie stood with her hands on her hips. While Duke ranted, at her, for being stubborn and selfish. The others all sat open-mouthed, watching the floor show.

"I think we should discuss this in the morning," Connie intervened.

He waved her away. "No. We will discuss this now. She is not going anywhere."

"Who's she?" Millie poked him in the chest. "I have a fucking name, Duke."

Jess banged his fist on the table. "This is a night to celebrate, and you have to go and spoil it. D'ya know, with the way you carry on, Millie, it makes me wonder if you deserved Levi."

How the fuck did he know?

The trailer fell silent.

Millie wiped the first tear from her cheek.

His tone then softened. "Millie, I—"

"No, Jess. I want you to tell me what bit of Levi I deserved." Millie pulled her jumper over her head then held her arm out and pointed to the scar. "Was it when he held a cigarette to my skin?" She held her wrist up. "Or was it one of the times he fractured my wrist?" She wiped at her eyes. "Or was it one of the many other injuries that now can't be seen?" She sniffed loudly. "So tell me, Jess, which bit did I deserve?"

CHAPTER 53

Duke rolled over on the bunk. Connie had kicked him out, and he was sleeping in the tourer with Aron. Only he wasn't sleeping. He couldn't. Would Millie forgive him for telling the boys about Levi? He doubted it. Her face had crumpled as soon as Jess had mentioned Levi. It broke his heart to see her cry. He was responsible for that. Not Jess. Him. Not that he would forgive Jess either. He should have kept his big gob shut. Now his daughter wouldn't talk to either of them.

Sitting up, he reached for his watch. It was five a.m. He dressed and pulled on his dealer boots. A walk might clear his head. He glanced at Aron. He was sleeping soundly. Was Millie?

He headed across the field in the darkness. Stumbled over the first fence. The air was cold. Too cold to snow, but it had been forecast.

You are a fucking dinlow.

How did you make something better that was broken beyond repair? He didn't know but he had to at least try. She was his little girl. Why couldn't she see that? Why did she have to fight him at every twist and turn?

Stop blaming her. You're the parent.

"I'm not blaming her," he whispered. "I'm blaming myself."

How could he make her see he was sorry? Flowers always worked with Connie. They wouldn't work with Millie. It had to be something big. A car? Duke smiled. He would teach her to drive and buy her a car.

He turned and made his way back across the field, almost running. He jumped the gate and headed for the trailer. It was still in darkness, but he would go in and wait. Connie would be up soon. He opened the door and peered in. All was quiet. Slipping off his dealer boots, he climbed in.

"Millie?" Connie called, her voice raspy from sleep.

"It's me. Where's Millie?" Duke hurried to the bedroom.

Connie sat, tapping the bed. "She's not here."

***

Millie's pace slowed. She had been walking for a good forty minutes and had only just reached the outskirts of the village. Halstead was rural. Few shops, no train station, but they did have buses. She walked on along the high street, stopping when she reached a bus stop. A welcome rest, out of the wind. Millie dumped her case onto the seat and then studied the timetable. She could barely make out the print in the darkness. Dawn was yet to break. She sat hunched in a corner. No one would see her here while she waited for daylight.

***

"Have you checked the toilets?" Duke asked, pacing the floor.

"She's not in there," Connie replied, her voice laden with worry. "If anything's happened…"

"I'll go and see the witch. See what she knows." Duke didn't wait for a reply. He leapt from the trailer and ran towards the wagon. He wasn't surprised to see the soft glow of light coming from the window. Patience barely slept, just adding to Duke's assumption that she was indeed a witch. He grabbed the door and yanked it open. "Where's my daughter?"

"Duke. It's customary to knock."

"Millie's gone. What do you know, old woman?" he growled.

Patience seemed to study him for a minute, as though she was choosing her words. "She's troubled… I know she comes across as a strong, confident young woman, but deep down she's still a scared little girl, looking for a place to belong."

Had he not given her a place to belong?

"She needs love, Duke, and lots of it," Patience continued. "She'll be heading home, to where she feels she can get it."

Duke turned, the old woman's voice drifting over his shoulder. "She needs your love."

He marched back to the trailer. Connie stood waiting at the door.

"What did she say?" she asked, pulling the door closed behind him.

"She'll be going home." Duke turned to the door as it opened.

"Dad, what's going on?" Aron asked while stepping in.

Jess and Sherry followed.

"Your sister's gone missing." Connie clutched her chest. "You can go and find her." She pointed to Duke. "This is all your fault."

"We'll go, too," Jess offered.

Duke's temper bubbled. "No, you and your big mouth can stay here. Aron, you take the pickup, I'll take the Transit. Con, you wait here in case she comes back." He grabbed his keys. "She'll head for town."

Jess stood in the doorway. "What do you want me to do?" He looked down at his feet.

Duke felt the urge to throttle him, but there was no time for that. "Stay away, Jess, you've done enough damage. Come on, Aron." Duke jumped out of the trailer and headed to the Transit.

This girl would be the fucking death of him. He knew he deserved it. Was she punishing him, or did she feel like she didn't belong? Probably a bit of both, he conceded. The Transit roared to life. Duke slammed it into gear and sped away. Dawn was breaking over the horizon. It would make her easier to spot. He headed towards the village. How far could she get? He slowed when he reached the high street. If she was going to be anywhere it would be here. He crawled past the bus stop, catching sight of her in the wing mirror. He stopped the motor. Now he had to put everything right.

Millie heard the Transit before she saw it. Her stomach dropped when it stopped. Why couldn't he leave her alone? She knew what he thought of her now. There was no going back.

The wind whistled through a hole in the side. She shivered. Duke's footsteps got louder. She wrapped her arms around herself and kept her attention on the ground. The seat moved. He had sat next to her.

Silence.

Was this a game? Was he waiting for her to speak, to tell him to fuck off, that she hated him? Did she? That was the question. No. She didn't hate him, just the opposite, which was why his words had cut so deeply. Her eyes stung with unshed tears.

"I'm sorry."

Was that it? Was that all he had to say?

Ignore him and he'll go away.

"Millie, look at me."

"Why?" She kept her eyes down.

"Because I want you to see that I mean it." He sounded so sincere, but was he?

"I take it Connie made you come." She held no emotion in her voice. She wouldn't give him the satisfaction.

"No, she didn't. I'm here to take my daughter home and apologise. I thought telling the boys about Levi would help. What Jess said was a stupid off-the-cuff remark."

"Well, just for your information, that stupid off-the-cuff remark broke me. Again. Just like they did." Millie glanced at Duke. "Not the kind of thing you'd expect from someone who claims to love you, although I should've known, Levi always did stuff like that. It wasn't always physical. Sometimes the mental abuse seemed worse. You could recover from a black eye or a fag burn, but what's in here…" Millie tapped her head. "The hurtful, vile words never leave you, you just learn to live with it."

"I'm sorry."

"So you said… You should get back to your family, the ones you actually love." Millie sniffed.

Do not cry. You've lived through worse and survived.

"I do love you, so does your mother. More than you'll ever know... I want a chance to make it up to you." A loud sigh gusted between Duke's lips. "Come home, Millie, give me a chance. It's cold, and you've got hours before a bus will turn up. Please."

"I am going home. Stepney," Millie replied bluntly.

"Okay, give me twenty-four hours. If you still wanna go then, I'll drive you."

Millie looked him directly in the eye. "I don't want you to drive me, Duke, I don't want to be anywhere near any of you. We're done."

CHAPTER 54

Paul sat behind the desk at the scrapyard. He stared at the photo in his hand. Him and Millie on their wedding day. They both had the biggest smiles. It was only back in the summer but seemed a lifetime ago. He missed her.

"Tone, I need you to drive, I'm going to get Millie." He stood. "Fuck waiting a week."

"Okay, but should we feed the animals first?" Tony replied. "It's gonna be a long day."

"We'll do it on the way, and not a word about them in front of Millie. She might not understand." Paul grimaced as he moved. The stitches seemed to be getting tighter.

"You all right?" Tony asked.

"Yeah, I'll see the doc tomorrow. Get these fucking stitches out." Paul headed towards the car, locking the Portakabin behind him.

He couldn't help smiling. Tonight he would be in the arms of the woman he loved.

***

Connie ran from the trailer, her face dropping when she spotted the empty seat next to Duke. "Where is she?"

"She doesn't want a bar of me, Con. I tried me hardest…" Duke trailed off.

"So she's gone?" Connie whispered, grasping her chest over her heart.

"No. She's with Aron. I'll be sleeping in the tourer with him, she'll stay with you. That was the deal." Duke turned at the sound of the pickup. "She's here. I'll make meself scarce." He headed towards the end of the site.

"All right, boy?"

Duke glanced over to his dad's brother, Henry. He waved a greeting and carried on. He didn't want to make small talk. His mind was still firmly on Millie and the look she had given him. If his words had hurt her half as much as that look had hurt him, then he finally knew how she felt. He shoved his hands in his pockets and stood at the fence, his heart plunging further when Henry stood next to him.

"You look like you've got the weight of the world on ya shoulders," Henry said.

That's an understatement.

"What's wrong, boy?"

"I've fucked up, Henry. Upset me daughter, and now she's finished with me. Won't even sit in the same motor." Duke kicked out at a stone and watched it fly through the air.

"So what you doing here? Get over there and sort it."

"Didn't you hear what I just said? She doesn't want a bar of me." Duke sighed.

"If it were my daughter, I wouldn't give up. I'd move heaven and earth just to make things right. We all fuck up, us men, but what's important is how we deal with it." Henry slapped Duke on the back. "Now go, before your face sours the camp."

***

Paul left the warehouse and took a deep lungful of air. "Jesus, they stink." He leant back on the car and waited for the obnoxious odour to vacate his nostrils.

"It's only gonna get worse," Tony added. "The longer you leave them there."

"I can't worry about that now. Today is all about Millie. Come on, let's get going." Paul slid into the passenger seat. Once Millie was with him they would ride in the back.

"When do your cousins return to Ireland?" Tony asked.

"They want a few days here to let their hair down before heading home, plus I want Millie to meet them before I take her over there, so I agreed." Paul shook his head. "I didn't expect to get shot by one of 'em." He laughed. "Fucking liability, that lot."

"They won't slip up in front of Millie, will they?"

Paul glanced at Tony. Good question. "I'll warn them that if they do, I'll cut their fucking tongues out."

***

Millie slid onto the bunk, Aron next to her. He was sweet. Of them all, she felt closer to him. They had shared secrets and bonded. Jess, on the other hand, hadn't been around as much, and now she knew why. Sherry. Had he discussed Millie's past with her? The smirk on her face would say definitely.

Shit-stirring little bitch.

She rubbed her hands together; they were stinging from the change in temperature. She hadn't realised how cold she was. Her hands had turned a bluey-purple colour.

Connie clucked around like a mother hen, the jangle of cups and the whistling kettle music to Millie's ears. She hadn't had a drink since the night before.

The door opened, and Duke appeared. Millie stiffened. She should have known he wouldn't keep his word. She glanced at him. He looked defeated. His slumped shoulders and miserable face almost made Millie feel sorry for him. Connie placed a peck on his cheek. Duke smiled. Millie knew it was forced. When Duke smiled his eyes shone, just like hers. People often said her smile could light up a room. Duke's was the same.

That's because he's your dad.

He stared straight at Millie. Apologetically. "I've just come in for a cuppa. I'll drink it outside."

Oh God, now I feel like the bad one.

"This is your home, Duke. You should drink your tea in here, in the warm," Millie replied.

"No. I promised to keep out of your way, and that's what I'll do." Duke picked up his cup. "Thanks, Con." Another peck on the cheek, and he left.

Millie sighed. Why did she feel bad?

"Do you think you'll ever forgive him?" Aron asked.

Could I?

"I don't know… It's pretty raw at the moment." *How do you explain to someone who hasn't lived your life how you feel?* "He betrayed me." Just like Patience had said.

Aron lowered his voice. "He is sorry, Mil… I heard him crying last night."

"Is that supposed to make me feel guilty?" She snapped.

"No. Course not. I've just never seen him cry before," Aron added.

Millie slid out of the seat and grabbed her coat and then her cup.

"I didn't mean to upset you, Mil," Aron called as she left the trailer.

"No. None of you do." She marched to the end of the camp.

Duke stood speaking to some old man. He stopped when he spotted her.

"Can we talk?" Millie asked as she approached. Not that he would say no.

"I'll see you later, Henry." He waved off the old man and turned back to Millie. "We can do whatever you want."

"Firstly, you're trying too hard. I just want loyalty, nothing else." Millie leant back against the fence. "Secondly, I don't expect you to spend all your time outside. It's too cold for that."

"Okay." Duke nodded. "So what did you want to talk about?"

"Why did you tell them?" She gulped down her emotions. "That was private, what I told you."

"It was a shock, finding out I had a daughter. The boys felt the same. None of us knew how to behave, so in my infinite wisdom I thought if they knew your past they would better understand you. Look out for you."

"You did shout at me, in front of them, and then Jess joined in, only he went one step further, and you…" Millie never finished the sentence. What was she supposed to say? You betrayed me?

"I thought Jess and Sherry might have bought us all closer together, something to celebrate. I was wrong. You felt pushed out before you was even in." Duke took a large mouthful of his tea. "You're looking for somewhere to belong, Millie."

"And you think I belong here?" She motioned with her head.

"No… You belong here." Duke pointed to his heart. "You always will."

His words hit her. No one had ever said anything so meaningful. They stood in silence for what seemed like ages until Millie spoke.

"I know I've been moody. There is a good reason for that." She pushed away from the fence and tipped the last of her tea out.

"And that is?" Duke asked.

"I need to speak to you and Connie." She turned and strolled back to the trailer.

Duke appeared at her side. He opened the door for her.

"Aron, you need to give us a minute." Duke pointed to the door.

"He can stay. Lock the door, please." Millie waited till all three were sitting. She took a shaky breath. "This is a secret, so please don't tell anyone, not even Paul… I know I've been a bit moody lately. When I went to the doctor's—"

Connie jumped up first. "You're ill. I knew I should've come with you."

"No. I'm not ill. Can you let me finish?" Millie smiled. "Paul and I are having a baby."

CHAPTER 55

Paul rubbed his forehead, it was damp. "Turn the heater down," he mumbled. His side was giving him gyp, the pain getting worse by the hour. "Fucking traffic." He loosened his tie.

"Should be there soon. You okay, you look a bit grey?" Tony turned the heater off. "Do you wanna stop and get a drink?"

"No." Paul rested his head back and closed his eyes. The journey seemed to be taking forever. It would be worth it, once Millie was in his arms.

"Where now?" Tony slowed the motor and veered into a bus stop. "Fucking hell, this is the middle of nowhere."

"Keep going straight. Just after the next bend there's a track on the right. It's at the end of that." Paul flopped back. He had a weird taste in his mouth. He huffed as the motor hit a dip in the lane. Why couldn't they live at the end of a fucking road, like normal people?

"We're here. Where shall I park?"

"There, where that Transit is. Pull in front of it." Paul waited for the motor to stop before grabbing the handle. Pain shot up his arm. "Help us out, Tone."

The trailer door caught his eye as it swung open. Millie's face appeared. She smiled.

"Paul!" She ran towards him and stood waiting for him to get out. "What's wrong?"

"He got shot, I think it might be infected," Tony replied before Paul could.

"I'm fine," he mumbled.

"Get him inside, quick." Millie took off running down the camp.

"Millie?" Paul called, his voice weak. His legs were heavy. He stumbled up the step and into the trailer.

Millie's face came into view. She led him to the bunk and pushed him down.

"Where's the wound?" She pulled at his jacket. She undid his tie and unbuttoned his shirt. "We need to take the bandage off. Patience is gonna take a look at it." She worked quickly.

An old woman stepped forward and studied the gash. "It's infected. I'll need boiling water and clean towels." She rolled up her sleeves. Was this Patience? Paul had never seen anyone so old.

He turned his attention to Millie who helped Connie get the towels. Duke filled a bowl with water. Millie finally knelt at his side.

"I've missed you," he said.

"Shh. Don't talk, save your energy," Millie warned. "Christ, Paul, what the fuck happened?"

"It was an accident." Paul rolled onto his side so Patience could pull out the stitches.

"Whoever done this was a butcher." The old woman moaned. "Where's the towels?"

Millie passed her the towels then laid one underneath Paul. "It looks bad, Paul. Why didn't you go to hospital?"

"And explain it how, exactly?" He coughed. "Jesus, woman, do you have to be so rough?"

Patience cackled. "Be thankful, boy, I'm only helping because I like the girl."

Paul released his breath when the last stitch was pulled. He glanced at the old woman. What was she holding? A potion?

"What's that?" He winced when the liquid was tipped over the wound. "Fuck."

"I've got most of the poison out, the potion should take care of the rest. You can re-bandage him now, Millie." The old woman stood to take her leave.

Paul refocused on Millie. She seemed to get more beautiful every time he saw her. "You ready to go home?" he asked as she wound the bandage around his chest. "Not too tight, I still wanna be able to breathe."

"If you're gonna keep moaning, I think I'll stay here." Millie smiled.

He grinned. There was no way he would allow that. "I might have to kidnap you then. Make you my prisoner."

Her smile dropped. Hadn't she just been a prisoner for the last six weeks?

"How's Rosie and Finn, are they both getting better?" Millie had changed the subject.

Paul sighed. "Finn should be out in the next few days, and Rosie is still being evaluated."

"Okay, you're done." Millie stood and took the bowl of dirty water to the door. She disappeared and then reappeared a few seconds later. "You'll need to get that checked out by a doctor, and not the butcher who did that to you."

"Yes, boss." Paul liked it when she looked after him. "We will need to make tracks, Mil. Get your stuff."

Millie emptied the cupboard of her clothes and packed the suitcase again. She then packed up her toiletries. Tonight she would be having a proper shower. That thought alone filled her with joy. She looked up at the doorway. Duke stood, filling the space.

"You okay?" he asked. "Must have been a bit of a shock seeing that."

"I'm fine. I don't think anything he could do would shock me." she sighed. "I guess you'll be staying here for a while, with Jess and Sherry."

He shook his head. "No. But it's a bit late to pack up now. We'll leave early morning. There's no way I'm staying away from my daughter, especially now she's talking to me again." He bent down and whispered in her ear, "Granny out there will be chomping at the bit to buy stuff for our grandchild."

Millie laughed. "Shh. Remember what I said, it's a secret."

"You nearly ready, Mil?" Paul called from the other end of the trailer.

"Nearly," she called back. She turned to Duke. "Thanks for looking after me."

"That's what family is for, and remember, you belong here." Duke pointed to his heart.

She handed him her case and returned to Paul. "Okay, I've just gotta say goodbye to someone. I'll only be a minute." Millie flew out of the door and ran to Patience's. Without knocking, she opened the door and stepped inside.

"You come to say goodbye?" the old woman croaked.

"Yes, we're about to leave. Will I see you again?" Millie asked with a hopefulness she didn't realise she felt.

"No, girl. This is the end of our journey together." Patience reached for her beads that hung over the little window. "Here, take these, they will keep you safe."

Millie reached out and took them. "But what will keep *you* safe?"

"I don't need them where I'm going. God bless, girl."

CHAPTER 56

Millie let the water run over her body. She stood motionless. Eyes closed. Heaven.

"*Millie. Open the fucking door,*" Paul bellowed.

"No. You can't get your bandage wet," she shouted then blew out slowly. The door rattled, followed by another loud bang. "If you bang on that door one more time you will be sleeping on your own tonight."

Silence followed. She turned the water off and stepped out of the shower. Whatever muck was in that potion had certainly picked him up. The journey back had been nice. Paul had wrapped his arms around her. Enveloped in the feeling of love and safety, she had slept. What were Duke and Connie doing now? Connie said she would start packing tonight so they could hit the road early. Would

Jess and Sherry come back with them? Millie would have to prepare Paul for that one.

"How much longer are you gonna be?" Paul whined through the locked door.

"I'm just drying."

"Mil, you can do that out here."

She slipped her dressing gown on and unlocked the door. Paul stood there with a face like thunder.

"I needed a shower."

"I could 'ave washed ya back," he moaned.

"There will be none of that tonight, not until you've seen the doctor. You might need more stitches." Millie brushed past him. "Do you fancy a cuppa?"

"No. I fancy you." He grabbed her arm, tugging her back.

His lips smashed into hers. The kiss passionate. Heat built inside her.

She pushed him back. "Do you ever take no for an answer?"

"Not where my wife is concerned." Paul threw an arm around Millie's waist. She was pulled against him.

***

Millie lay with her head on Paul's arm, annoyed with herself for giving in. "You asleep?"

"Yes."

She lifted her head and studied his face. He opened one eye.

"You haven't told me what happened with Shannon and the Ronnie lookalike."

"Can't we talk about it in the morning?" Paul closed his eye. "I'm feeling weak after you having your wicked way with me."

"Well, I don't know why, considering I did most of the work." Millie teased.

"Ouch." Paul rolled onto his side. "That was a bit harsh."

"Maybe. Anyway, now I've got your attention. Shannon and Ronnie lookalike?"

"They are taken care of, that's all you need to know. Just concentrate on Finn and Rosie, babe." That indicated the end of the conversation.

She stared at the ceiling. Why wouldn't he tell her? She'd had to tell him everything about Ronnie Taylor when she'd taken him out. With the help of Duke.

She slipped out of bed and wrapped her robe around her. Paul gently snored. She needed a cuppa. She crept out onto the landing. The Irish lot were all in bed, thank God. She continued down the stairs and into the kitchen. She busied herself making the tea.

A pile of brown envelopes caught her eye. Riffling through them, she spotted one for herself. She tore it open and pulled out her provisional licence. Shoving it into her pocket, she grabbed the kettle and filled the pot.

Millie rubbed her eyes. She was tired, and yet sleep would not take her. She knew why. It was the fear of seeing Rosie. She knew Rosie wouldn't be her old self. It would be a long road to recovery. Scott had been there every day, ready to nab her when the doctor said she would be moved. And then there was Finn. Would he forgive them for Shannon? Should she tell him even? Of course she should. He deserved to know the truth. Didn't he?

***

Millie sat at the window, waiting for Tony to arrive. He was their chauffeur again today.

Poor bloke must be sick of driving. Still, I'll be driving soon enough.

Millie smiled.

"What you smiling for?" Paul asked. He pulled her up and sat in her seat, then drew her back down onto him.

"It's good to be home." She pecked him on the lips. "What time do that lot get up?" She motioned to the ceiling.

"They didn't get in till late, you heard them. Like a bunch of fucking elephants. I'll be pleased to have the place back to ourselves." Paul moaned. "Come on, Tone's here."

They headed out to the car in silence. Millie held Paul's hand. More for comfort than anything. She slid into the back seat, and Paul got in next to her.

"I'm nervous," she admitted.

"Don't be. I'm with you, babe," Paul reassured her. He squeezed her hand.

Millie turned and stared out of the window. Nothing had changed in the last six weeks. Had she really expected it to?

"I want us to go and see my parents later, give them the good news," Paul told her.

Millie clocked Tony in the rearview mirror. He was smiling. He knew. "Who else have you told apart from Tony?" Her voice sounded accusing.

"What?" Paul's cheeks went a slight pink colour.

"Don't lie to me. I can see it in both your faces." Millie continued to stare out of the passenger window. She felt vindicated for telling her parents.

"Look, it sort of came out. I was worried about you and the baby..." Paul sighed. "Sorry. I was excited. No one else knows. I promise."

Millie ignored him. She didn't have the right to be angry. Hadn't she done the same? Patience's words rang true.

Men make the rules, but they're the first to break them.

What was Patience doing now? Probably sticking another log on her fire. Millie laughed inwardly. What a character she was. She hoped she would see her again, although if Patience said she wouldn't then she knew deep down it wasn't going to be.

"You all right, Mil?" Paul asked.

Millie faced him and smiled. "Yeah."

"Pull up out front, Tone." Paul squeezed her hand again. "Ready, babe?"

"As ready as I'll ever be." She waited for Paul to get out and then slid along the seat to join him.

He took her hand and helped her out. Just looking at the front of the hospital made her feel sick. The memories flashed back again. Herself, Paul, Finn, and Rosie. This was the last place she wanted to be.

They walked up the stairs towards Finn's floor. Millie spotted the matron just as they exited the stairwell. Was she gonna shout at her again?

"Quick, before the battleaxe sees us." Millie ducked into Finn's room. She was pleasantly surprised to see him sitting up in bed. "Finn?"

"Well, ain't you a sight for sore eyes." Finn beamed. "Come here." He held his arms out.

Millie was only too pleased to crumple into them.

"How are you?" she asked, standing back. "You look so much better than the last time I saw you."

"Now I've seen you, I'm feeling just fine." Finn nodded to Paul. There seemed to be a bit of friction between them.

"Do you know when you can go home yet?" Millie pressed. She didn't want a row to break out.

"In a few days, they hope. My bloods are back to normal, and I'm allowed out of bed. Wasn't great using a fecking bedpan, I missed more than once."

Millie giggled. "Paul, can you give us a minute?" She waited for Paul to leave before continuing. "Do you know what happened?"

"They say I was poisoned. Paul seems to think it was Shannon. Why would my own daughter track me down to kill me? Fecking lies."

Millie shook her head slowly. "It's not lies, Finn. She poisoned you then put the pub up for sale. Paul caught the estate agent putting the sign up. When he went in there, they said you had phoned and told them to put it up for sale and that they were to deal with Shannon."

Finn's face contorted. "I don't believe you."

"Why would I lie?" She knew it was a lot to take in; he would need time to process it.

"I think you should go, Millie." Finn turned away from her.

"Okay, I'll go. I just want you to remember this. I love you." Millie stepped towards the door then paused. She faced him. "Also, I wanted you to be one of the first to know. Paul and I are having a baby."

Still no reply. She left the room.

Paul grabbed her as she approached him. "I guess he didn't take the news well?"

"There's nothing more we can do. I'll come back in a few days' time. He may have thought it through by then. What's he going to say when he finds out she's gone?" She rubbed her forehead.

Paul reached for her hand. "We don't tell him."

CHAPTER 57

Rosie was pale, her eyes dull. She had a drip in her arm. Millie assumed it was for fluids. She hadn't reacted when Millie had sat next to her, her eyes unblinking, staring into space.

"Hey, Rosie." Millie spoke softly and, grabbing her hand, she gave a gentle squeeze.

No reaction.

"You're looking a bit better. How are you feeling now?" *What a stupid question.*

No reaction.

Millie sighed. This was harder than she'd imagined. "I've been staying with Duke and Connie. It's been quite an eye-opener into their way of life... Do you remember when we started looking for them?" She kept her eyes on Rosie, waiting, or was that wishing, for a response. "It seems a lifetime ago, and yet it's not even a year. So much has happened."

No reaction.

Millie stood and leaned over so she could stare down at Rosie. "I'm sorry I wasn't there for you. I will never forgive myself."

"Not everything's about you," Rosie mumbled. She turned to face the wall. "I just want to be left alone."

"I wish I had stopped you... from going," Millie added. "I should've—"

"My life is not your responsibility. Do you know what I wish? I wish you hadn't found me. Now please leave." Rosie pulled the cover up around her head.

"Okay, I'll go for now, but I will be back, and one more thing before I go. I'm having a baby, you're gonna be an aunty." Millie stood rooted to the spot. No reply. "This baby is going to need Aunty Rosie just as much as its mummy does."

Her heart sank as she left the room, cursing herself with each step. Why in God's name did she think Rosie would be pleased to hear that when she was lying in a hospital bed, narrowly avoiding death? Death that she'd wanted. Death that Millie had stopped. She had made things worse.

Millie strolled out into the cold winter's air. It was only a week until her birthday. She wasn't interested in celebrating. Not after spending the last forty minutes with Rosie. Did she really wish Millie hadn't found her? If that were true, then she would need specialist help. Making a mental note to let Scott know, she scanned the car park.

Paul's car was a couple of rows away. She headed towards it. As she approached, mumbled voices came from inside. What were they saying?

"We can't keep them at the warehouse indefinitely, Paul. You need to make up your mind what to do with them." Tony's voice drifted through a small gap in the window.

Millie tapped on the side of the car. Both men jumped.

"What's up with you two?"

Paul got out of the motor and opened the back door. "How long you been standing there?"

"I've just got here. Why?" Millie glanced at Paul. He was hiding something.

She climbed in. Paul slid next to her and placed his arm around her shoulders.

"Was worried about you getting cold, babe." He smiled.

Fucking liar.

So now she knew he was up to something. What had Tony said? *We can't keep them at the warehouse indefinitely, Paul. You need to make up your mind what to do with them.* Them? Millie smiled at Paul then turned away. She would find out one way or another.

***

When Millie returned home, Connie and Duke were back. The trailer was parked up in the corner of the field, and the door was open. Connie was obviously cleaning. Millie's heart sank when she spotted Jess and Sherry, manoeuvring there trailer into place. It was right near her fence.

"What are you looking at?" Paul asked. He walked to the bedroom window. "You have got to be fucking kidding me."

"Paul, calm down. It's their land, they can do what they want." Millie sighed. "But this is our land, we can also do what we want, and I want an eight-foot fence put up."

"I'll go and phone the boys." Paul grinned. "Get ready, we'll head to my parents' about five and then go for something to eat."

"You can't get Tony to sit and wait for us while we eat." Millie laughed. "That's a bit of a piss-take."

"Relax. I'm driving." Paul pecked Millie on the lips then left the bedroom.

She continued to stand at the window, fuming. Why would they park a fucking trailer right alongside her fence? What an eyesore. She threw her bag down, turned, and ran down the stairs. Paul looked up as she hit the bottom.

"Babe?"

She ignored him and marched out of the door and along the path. When she reached the end of the garden, she peeked over the fence. "*Dad!*"

Duke appeared a minute later holding a steaming cup of tea. "Millie." He smiled. "Do you fancy a cuppa?"

"No thanks. Look, does that trailer have to go there? It's all I can see from the house." Millie pointed. "I know it's tidy, but I like seeing the trees at the back, and I don't want them spying on me."

"Spying on you?" Duke laughed. "I'm sure they wouldn't spy, Mil."

"Well, you betrayed me, so I reckon he would, too. I tell you what, don't you worry, Duke, I'll sort the problem myself." Millie turned and walked away, Duke calling her. He could go and do one.

Millie marched into the kitchen.

Paul was waiting. "What was that all about?"

"That was about asking my dad if he would get that fucking thing moved because it's upsetting me." Millie reached for the kettle. "I can't trust that lot, bunch of Judases."

"Mil, calm down." Paul grabbed the kettle before she had a chance to launch it at him. "Christ, Mil, think of the baby."

"I am thinking of the baby." She sat on the chair and placed her head in her hands. "I want that fence up tomorrow, and in front of it I want trees. Fucking great big ones. Let them deal with that."

***

Paul sat on the sofa next to Millie. He kept glancing at her to make sure she didn't have another meltdown.

"It's grand to see you both," Bridie, Paul's mum, told them.

"It's lovely to be here, with family," Millie replied.

Paul squeezed her hand. "Actually, Mum, we've got some news. He took a deep breath. "We're having a baby."

"Oh, joy be to God. Congratulations, both of you." Bridie stood and hugged her son. "This will be my first grandchild." She beamed.

Paul sat and threw his arm around Millie. "Hopefully the first of many." He didn't bother looking at Millie this time; he could feel her eyes burning into the side of him.

CHAPTER 58

Duke watched the fence being removed. He scratched his head. What the fuck was Paul planning now?

"What's going on, Dad?" Jess asked.

"I reckon Paul's putting a taller fence up." Duke marched back to the trailer. Jess followed, going by the sound of footsteps.

"But that will block the light out," Jess moaned. "Can't you go and 'ave a word with Millie?"

"Millie doesn't want the trailer there, that's why I asked you yesterday to move it. Can't you do as you're told, boy? I own this fucking land," Duke spat.

"And Millie gets what Millie wants." Jess sneered. "Well, just so you know, I have a wife, and she comes first."

"Millie is my daughter, Sherry isn't. So Millie will come before her every fucking time, you dinlow. Now get out." Duke opened

THE STEPNEY ALLIANCE

the fridge and pulled out a can of beer. He cracked it open and took a large mouthful.

"Duke, what's going on? Jess said he's leaving?" Connie asked, her face strained.

"That's up to him." Duke slammed the can down. "I'm going to see Millie."

He walked past Jess as he was winding the draw bar up. *Fucking children*, Duke fumed. Things were okay when they were little. Now everything was a fight.

Duke marched past Paul's men, ignoring them when they asked what he wanted. He stood at the kitchen door and knocked loudly. Millie's face appeared. She still looked pissed off.

"Can I come in?"

She nodded then stood back. Duke kicked his boots off. They had picked up a ton of mud walking through where the men were working. "I asked Jess to move the trailer yesterday. Like you asked. I assumed he would do it today. Anyway, he's leaving, so you don't need to worry about your spoilt view or him spying on you." He turned. As far as he was concerned, he had said what needed to be said. If she wanted to know him she would, and if she didn't, then at least she would hopefully talk to Connie.

"Wait," Millie called. "Would you like a drink?"

Duke smiled. "I'd love to have a drink with my daughter."

Millie poured Duke a scotch. It looked expensive. She poured herself a lemonade.

"I can't drink, one of the many joys of being pregnant." She held the glass up. "Cheers."

Duke clinked the glass and took a sip of the amber liquid. He wasn't quite prepared for the burn he got as it travelled down his throat. "Jesus. That's some serious stuff."

"Duke, I'm sorry for shouting yesterday. I saw the trailer there and lost it. I even tried to whack Paul with the kettle, so you got off lightly."

Duke's shoulders bobbed up and down. The vision of Millie hitting Paul was just too much. "Sorry, Mil, I would have paid good money to see you whack Paul with the kettle."

"He caught it, I've never seen him move so quick." She laughed.

Duke wiped at his eyes. "Well, that was worth coming over for."

"Look, what I said about being betrayed…"

Duke held his hand up. "You're right. I did betray your trust, but I promise you it will never happen again."

Millie sighed. She doubted he could keep that promise. She would be more guarded. Things that were private she would share only with Paul. "I don't like Sherry either. I don't know why, there's just something about her I don't trust, and over the years I've found my instincts to be right."

"It's funny you say that. I'm not keen on her either. She's got Jess wrapped around her little finger," Duke agreed. "You know it's hard trying to please everyone. Just wait until you have a few chavvies, you'll see what I mean."

"You sound like Paul. He told his mum this is the first of many."

"Well, it doesn't matter how many you have, me and Con are gonna love them all, just like we love you." He smiled. "Maybe you could have a gate put in the fence. Would save walking the long way round."

"Maybe... When you have time, could we continue the driving lessons? Unless you're too busy, of course."

Duke beamed. "Of course. Let's get you driving before this chavvie makes an appearance."

"That would be great. Can we start the day after tomorrow? I need to visit Finn and Rosie. And one more thing, don't tell Paul, I want to surprise him."

"If that's what you want." Duke agreed, but he had a nagging sensation that it wasn't the real reason she didn't want him to know.

***

Paul threw his keys on the side. He was glad to be home. He sniffed his jacket. Was that the rancid stench from the warehouse?

Don't let them spoil your evening.

With the Irish dropped off at the airport, he finally had the place to himself. And more importantly, Millie. Tonight he would unwind. "Babe?"

"In the kitchen," she called back.

"Place looks tidy. You been cleaning all day?" he asked, marching towards her. "Something smells good."

"I thought you'd like a home-cooked meal," she replied.

Paul slipped his arms around her waist and nuzzled into her neck. "I know what I would like."

"Paul. I'm cooking. Go and pour yourself a drink."

Millie stiffened. Had he done something wrong?

"Fine… How's the fence looking?" He opened the door and stood outside. He could just about make out the row of fence posts in the fading light. "Did they say when it would be finished?"

"They said the day after tomorrow. Cement needs to go off. Apparently it takes longer in the cold weather," Millie said through the open door.

Paul stepped back into the kitchen. "Why are two posts close together?"

"I've asked for a gate to be put in."

"I thought you'd had enough of them. Christ, Mil, it would be good if you could make up your mind."

Paul stomped to the lounge. He grabbed the scotch and poured a large measure. He drank it down in one go. He glanced at the doorway. Millie stood there, her tight skirt hugging her hips. Her blouse unbuttoned just enough to show her cleavage. Was she wearing stockings? Paul's pulse quickened.

"Isn't that a woman's prerogative?" she asked, wiping her hands on a tea towel. "You seem stressed, Paul. Is everything okay at work?"

He stepped towards her. "I've got a lot of catching up to do at the docks and scrapyard. That fucking bloke has cost us money. It's nothing to worry about. I'll make an early start in the morning and get things back on track." He grabbed the tea towel and flung it on the seat. "I also have a lot of catching up to do with my wife, and that, to me, is more important." He smiled.

CHAPTER 59

Millie was sick and tired of trotting up the hospital day after day, trying her best to put things right. No one appreciated her efforts, least of all Rosie. Today, Rosie was being moved to a secure hospital. Millie had wanted to nab her and take her somewhere safe, but after their last conversation, she realised she wasn't up to the task. Rose needed help from a professional. It was with a heavy heart Millie had said goodbye to her. Would she ever see her again? She had heard the stories of people going into mental hospitals and never coming back out.

Pushing the thoughts away, she briskly made her way to Finn. He was now in the main ward and continuously moaned about every Tom, Dick, and Harry who either snored too much, ate too loudly, or treated the nurses with disrespect. Millie had laughed because he did all three of those things himself.

"Morning, Finn." She planted a kiss on his cheek and sat next to him. "How are you feeling today?"

"Millie," he grumbled. "I'm fecking sick of this place. I want to go home."

"Paul's got the builders in, the pub should be liveable by the end of the week. If you're discharged before, you'll have to come stay with us." She braced herself for the onslaught, surprised when none came.

"You know, I find it strange Shannon hasn't been in to see me. Do you know anything about that?" Finn's eyes burned into Millie's.

"As you already know, Finn, I was away with my parents, but now you know what she did, do you really want to see her again?"

"She's my daughter, Millie. I…"

She could see why it was so hard for him. Who would want to admit that their own flesh and blood hated you enough to commit murder?

She reached over and rubbed his arm. "I know, Finn." He could never know her real fate.

***

Millie turned the key over, again and again, in her hand. She had taken it from Paul's pocket last night after he was asleep. Did she feel guilty? No. He was hiding something, and she was going to find out what that was.

She jumped at a knock at the kitchen door.

"Calm down," she whispered, heading to open it.

Duke stood there smiling, pickup truck keys in his hand.

"Ready?" he asked.

"Ready." She smiled. "I know where I want to go."

"What?" Duke stopped and stared at her. "I thought this was a driving lesson?"

"It is, but I have the perfect place to go and practice." Millie locked the door behind her. She followed Duke down the garden and stood at the passenger door.

Duke frowned. "Shouldn't you be driving, as this is a driving lesson?"

"I will when we get there." She climbed into the pickup while Duke walked to the other side.

He climbed in, shoving the key into the ignition. Millie waited for him to start the motor. Why was he just sitting there?

"Is something wrong?"

Duke turned in his seat to face her. "I don't know, Millie, why don't you tell me?"

She slumped into the seat. What was she supposed to say? Paul was up to something, acting cagey, being a fucking typical man? "I need to check something out."

"And what is that, exactly?" His tone sounded interrogating.

She didn't reply.

"Should I ask Paul?" He still kept eye contact.

Her face heated up.

Fuck.

"Paul's up to something. He won't discuss it." She turned and faced the passenger window. She could still feel his eyes penetrating the back of her head.

"You don't trust him?"

Millie spun around and glared at Duke. "This has got nothing to do with trust."

"Really? He's your husband, Millie. Maybe he's doing whatever for a good reason." He sighed. "Why don't you talk to him tonight? If you don't get any answers, I'll take you to this mystery place tomorrow."

"I need to go today," Millie snapped. She grabbed the handle of the motor. "Don't worry, I'll get a taxi."

Duke's hand clenched around her arm, stopping her dead.

"You aren't going anywhere on your own, not in your condition." He started the motor. "You can fill me in on the way."

***

Paul blew on his hands, then rubbed them together. He stood on the quayside watching his men unload the cargo. The Thames Estuary was choppier than usual. Probably because of the gusting wind. The boat bobbed up and down, the men swaying. He was half expecting one of them to fall in. The last straw was when a squall of wind pushed the boat into the dock, spraying him with water.

"Fuck this, Tone, I'm heading inside." He turned swiftly and marched back to the office, closing the door firmly behind him. The taste of the saltwater lined his mouth. It was nice here in the summer. With the smell of the salt air, if you closed your eyes, it was like being at the seaside. It reminded him of his childhood.

"They're nearly done," Tony called after poking his head in the doorway.

"Come in, I want to discuss the other business." Paul waited for Tony to shut the door before he continued. "We'll head to the warehouse from here and take care of the remaining loose ends."

"I think that's wise," Tony replied. "The longer you leave it, the more chance of something going wrong."

Paul nodded. "Agreed… Millie keeps asking questions." He leaned across the desk and grabbed the bottle of scotch that sat on the corner. "Fancy a nip?"

"Yeah, why not. Could do with warming up." Tony held up a cup while Paul filled it.

"Cheers." Knocking it back in one, Paul reclined. "Fucking needed that, it's proper taters outside."

"You were saying about Millie asking questions?" Tony reminded him.

"Yeah… I hate lying to her, but I don't want her involved in this, not with her being pregnant. We get rid of the loose ends, and everyone lives happily ever after. Well, not everyone." Paul's laughter was interrupted by the ring of the phone. He snatched it up in annoyance. "Hello." After a minute he slammed it down.

"What's up?" Tony asked when Paul jumped up.

"Millie's at the warehouse."

***

Millie glared at Paul's men. "You know who I am?"

"We still can't let you in, Mrs Kelly. We've had strict instructions from your husband. No one goes in or out." At least the prick had the decency to look embarrassed.

Breathing out loudly, she glanced at Duke. "I'm going in there one way or another."

Her eyes widened when he threw two punches at each man's head. They both slumped against the wall.

"Christ, they didn't put up much of a fight." Millie dipped her hand in her bag and felt for the key. Then she went for the door, but Duke blocked her way.

"Are you sure you want to go in there? If Paul's got men guarding it, it's serious, plus you don't know what your gonna find."

"I need to know what he's hiding. Like I said, I'm going in one way or another." She took a deep breath then placed the key in the lock. It was stiff. "A little help, please." She stood back so Duke could do the honours.

A click sounded as the key turned. Her stomach knotted. Was she doing the right thing?

Duke pulled the door open so Millie could step inside. The smell hit her first. She covered her mouth and nose, the urge to vomit strong.

"Millie, get out." Duke tugged her back. "Whatever's in here isn't pleasant."

She took a step back; she needed to rid herself of the rancid stench, to fill her lungs with sweet fresh air. She stumbled. Duke caught her.

"Will you tell me what you find?" she asked. Satisfied when he agreed, she stepped outside. Gulping in great big lungful's of air, she leant against the pickup.

Duke opened the door and helped her in. "Sit there. I'll see what I can find."

CHAPTER 60

Duke studied the warehouse, boxes piled around the edges. All neatly stacked. His gaze settled on boxes that were randomly dotted about, off-centre of the middle. They looked out of place. The nearer he walked to them, the stronger the smell became. He picked up the first box. Heavier than expected. He fumbled, then dropped it.

"Let's hope there's nothing valuable in there," he mumbled.

He slid it away. What was he doing? He couldn't believe how different his life had become with Millie in it. Killing and now investigating for her. He knew he couldn't leave her to do it. And she would, he was certain of that. She was stubborn, that was the first thing he'd noticed about her. Her stubbornness matched his own. Duke grinned. She was a lot like him. He wouldn't tell her that, though. She might not be as pleased as he was.

He paused. Did he hear something? Muffled voices. They were coming from below him. Pushing the last of the boxes away, he reached for a gap in the floor. Was this a trap door? Sticking his fingers in, he pulled the wooden floor up. It was heavy. He could've done with the boys' help. Groaning, he lifted the piece of wood up until it fell to the side. He stared down in shock.

Two pairs of eyes stared back at him.

***

"Jesus, Paul, can you slow down?" Tony whined.

"No, I fucking can't. I should've known she was up to something. All the fucking questions and suspicious glances." He bibbed as a truck darted out. He slammed his foot on the brake. "*You fucking prick!*" He pulled away and swerved around the truck, sticking his middle finger up in the process. "She can't find 'em, Tone, she's pregnant. Who knows what damage it might cause."

"She's made of strong stuff, Paul, stronger than most women I know."

"She shouldn't have to be strong, that's my job." Paul sped up as he neared the warehouse. "Look, there's Duke's pickup."

***

Duke studied the bodies, three in total. One on the floor, dead. That was the smell—he could tell a rotting corpse when he smelt one.

"Help me," the man begged, his voice raspy.

"You must've done something pretty bad to end up here. Who are you?" Duke asked.

"Jeremy... and I only wanted what's mine."

Duke tensed. "Why would I help you? You're the one who went after my daughter. If anything, I should kill you." He had to hand it to Paul. This punishment was perfect.

"I never went after your daughter, it was always Paul, he took what didn't belong to him."

"You left her a note saying: *I know what you did*. She was upset and worried—you caused that." Duke went to grab the wood and seal the opening.

"No. You're wrong. That was meant for Paul. As you are her father, how do feel knowing he cheated on her?"

Duke stood still. His anger rose. "Explain yourself."

"I know he slept with Rita just to keep the scrapyard. She told me."

Was that true? Duke clenched his fists. A noise from behind caught his attention. Turning, he came face to face with Paul. "I think you've got some explaining to do."

Paul sidestepped him. "Still spewing your lies, Jeremy? Millie knows what really happened." He faced Duke. "Do you really think I would sleep with some old hag and jeopardise my life with your daughter?" He returned his attention to Jeremy. "She tried to blackmail me, that's why I killed her. And now it's your turn."

He looked down at Shannon. She was slumped on the floor. "And as for you." He pointed. "Trying to con a man out of his livelihood. Tut, tut, tut. You and ya boyfriend should have stayed away. Now you both need to pay the price. Tone, cover them up while I speak to Millie."

"Wait. I haven't finished with you yet." Duke stood in front of Paul, blocking his way. "You seriously expect me to believe that drivel? The Paul Kelly I know would betray anyone or anything that got in his way, and that includes my daughter."

"Wasn't it you who betrayed Millie when you told your sons about her past?" Paul was pleased he had hit a nerve.

Duke's shoulders slouched briefly before he composed himself.

"Yeah, that's right, she told me how your son used it against her. I bet that was a proud dad moment for you."

"You're right, and I've held my hands up to my mistakes, something I've never seen you do," Duke replied. "And just for the record, Paul, I believe him. I could see it his eyes just as I can see it in your face, you slept with her. You may have fooled my daughter, but you haven't fooled me."

CHAPTER 61

Millie sat in the pickup. Duke was unusually quiet. It unnerved her. Should she make conversation? She glanced at him. His mouth was set in a straight line, his eyes narrowed. Something had gone down in that warehouse, and neither him nor Paul were letting on what.

She turned to the window and stared blankly at the passing houses, the sky grey. It seemed to match everyone's mood. She could barely comprehend what Paul had done. Holding three people prisoner in a hole in the floor seemed a bit excessive. Shouldn't he have just warned Shannon off? Wouldn't that have scared her enough to make her leave? The Ronnie lookalike was a different matter, which was personal, just like the real Ronnie. He had to be dealt with.

A loud sigh came from Duke.

She looked at him. Was he all right? "What happened, in the warehouse?"

"Nothing for you to worry about." He glanced at her, smiled, and then focused back on the road.

She bit her lip. Wasn't that what they always said to her? Nothing for you to worry about, don't you worry your pretty little head, and the one that pissed her off the most, it's men's business.

"You know whenever I hear those words I worry more."

"You've spoken to Paul, what did he have to say?" Duke pulled onto the side of the road and switched off the ignition. He stretched in the seat, raising his arms above his head, then faced her.

"He told me who was in there and what he had planned. I'm not happy with Paul, but I'll deal with him when he gets home. I want to hear what you've got to say. You came out of that place with a face like thunder and you've barely spoken two words since."

"We had a disagreement," Duke replied.

"About?" She pressed. This seemed serious. Neither men were talking.

"Are you happy being married to a man like Paul?"

"What's that supposed to mean, a man like Paul? I know what he's capable of. In case you forgot, we killed Ronnie, remember?" She rubbed her forehead. Just what she needed, a bloody headache.

"I killed Ronnie, not you. Let me ask you another question. Do you trust him?"

"He's my husband, of course I trust him," she snapped.

"When I spoke to Jeremy—"

"Who's Jeremy?" she interrupted.

Duke sighed. "The Ronnie lookalike." He paused. "He told me it was Paul he was after, not you. When I asked why, he said it was because Paul had slept with Rita."

"He didn't sleep with her, he told me what happened." Sickness washed over her at just the thought.

"So you believe him?" Duke grabbed her hand. "I know you're married and marriage is for life. You take the good with the bad, but if you need to escape, you come to me."

"You gonna hide me on another gypsy site?" She laughed. "In case it escaped your memory, I'm having Paul's child."

"I hadn't forgotten. You're my daughter, it's my job to protect you."

"So this is what you were arguing over." Millie pulled her hand away. "I don't want to keep reliving my past. Patience said I have to let it go, otherwise I'll never be happy."

"Patience," Duke mumbled. "What else did she have to say?"

"She said I should give my dad a chance, because he will be a good dad to me." Millie was pleased to see him smile. "I've learnt that lies have a way of resurfacing. If Paul did lie to me, I will find out eventually."

"And then what?"

"And then I would leave... Without trust there would be no marriage."

The motor roared to life. She had eased Duke's mind and in turn sent hers spiralling in turmoil. She had believed Paul when he'd told her he hadn't slept with Rita, but was she being naive? "Turn around."

"What?" Duke slowed the motor.

"I said turn around. I need to go back."

CHAPTER 62

Paul stood at the doorway of the warehouse while Tony revived the two men. He had to hand it to Duke, knocking them both out before they could react was no mean feat. The geezers were both handy with their fists.

"About fucking time." He spat. "Get the overalls on, we're shifting them."

"What about the corpse?" Tony asked. "That needs disposing of in case anyone comes snooping around. It fucking stinks."

"Wrap him up, we'll take him to the scrapyard after dark. The other two—" Paul stopped as the pickup approached. "Now what?" He gritted his teeth. He couldn't lose his temper in front of Millie. When the motor stopped, he marched towards it, halting at the passenger door.

"You need to go, Mil."

"I need to see Jeremy," she snapped.

Paul glanced at Duke. What had he told her? "I'm not letting you in there. It's not safe."

"Not safe for who, me or you?" she said while pushing the door open.

"It's not safe for the baby, and I don't want you witnessing this."

"I've witnessed worse. Now are you going to let me in there or are you scared?" She sidestepped Paul and stopped abruptly when he grabbed her arm.

"Firstly, I've nothing to be scared of, and secondly, there's a dead body in there, I don't want you seeing that."

Her cold glare hit him right between the eyes.

"Fine," he said. "Let the boys clean up a bit first."

Millie gave a short, curt nod and leant back against the pickup. Was she being unreasonable? She turned when the two men appeared from the warehouse carrying what she assumed was a body.

"Place it around the side, and make sure it's out of sight," Paul told them.

"Who is that?" She pointed.

"That was whoever Shannon was working with," he replied quickly.

So that was the smell. "Why did you kill him and leave him in there?" She faced him; she needed to see him, to see if he would tell the truth.

"I didn't. We turned up here a few days ago and he was dead."

"So how did he die?" she pressed.

"I don't know, and to be perfectly honest, I don't care. Why are you here, Millie?"

"I want to question Jeremy."

"Duke told you what he said." Paul sighed. "Has it occurred to you he's trying to cause trouble? Still. He wanted to take everything from me, and you are my everything. You and the baby."

"If you haven't done anything wrong then you've nothing to worry about." She glanced up at Tony as he walked towards them.

"Shall I throw her bag in with the corpse?" he asked.

Millie cut in before Paul answered. "Not yet. Have you been through it?"

Paul shook his head. "There was no need."

"Give." She held her hand out and grabbed the bag. Turning it upside down, she tipped the contents out onto the wet ground and riffled through it. "Look, her purse." She unzipped the back and pulled out a driving licence. "Who's Barbera?"

"What? Let me see." Paul took the licence and studied it. "Could be fake."

"No. She doesn't come across as a criminal mastermind, but she does come across as a greedy, money-grabbing cow. If she is Barbera then Shannon is still alive, and she knows where she is. We have to tell Finn." Millie smiled. "He could find her and have his daughter back in his life."

"Mil, this woman knew everything about Shannon. What if Shannon was working with her? You'd be setting Finn up to fuck knows what."

"Question her. Find out what she knows. Isn't that what you're good at after all?" Millie asked. "And I'll question Jeremy."

Paul's sigh seemed to fill the air.

She ignored him. "Shall we get this over with?"

She stood covering her nose. The smell of rotting flesh lingered in the air. Christ, that was surely punishment enough for anyone. No, she didn't believe that for one minute. Paul's men had tied Barbera and Jeremy to a chair each and gagged them. Plastic sheeting had been placed on the ground. Was that for the blood? Barbera's eyes were wide like a madwoman. They darted between Paul and herself. Millie smiled. She wanted her to pay for what she had done to Finn. The greedy, money-grabbing whore.

Pulling her gag down, Paul stepped back and glanced at Millie. She gave him a swift nod and returned her stare to the woman.

"What's your real name?" Paul asked. He waited for a few seconds. When she didn't reply, he motioned to Tony who stepped towards him with a knife. "Every time you don't answer me, or you tell a lie, I'm gonna cut a body part off. Now shall we start again? What is your real name?"

"Barbera."

Millie stepped forward eagerly. "Where's Shannon?"

"I don't know."

"You don't know and yet you know everything about her. Is she in on this with you?" Millie took the knife from Paul and waved it in her face. "Think I'll start with your nose."

"No. No, she has no idea. I met her while working in Cork. We spoke about our families, that's how I knew about Finn. He wasn't hard to find."

"Does Shannon know where he lives? Will she be coming after him next?" Millie continued.

Paul snatched the knife away and held it to Barbera's nose. "You'd better start talking."

"She has nothing to do with this. I don't even know if she's still in Cork. I swear."

"I think we're done here." Paul hoisted the gag back into place and walked to Millie. He leant down towards her. "Just remember, he wants to destroy my life," he whispered.

She nodded. A cold sweat covered her body. Did she really want to know the truth? With Paul on one side and Duke on her other, she should have been comforted by these two men, but she felt nothing but apprehension. A sick feeling filled her stomach. She swallowed it down.

"Jeremy, we meet at last."

His eyes had trouble focusing. Was he gonna drop dead before she had a chance to question him?

"He needs water," she told Paul.

"He's not gonna be alive long enough to need water," he replied and kicked him. "My wife is talking to you, fucking answer her."

Jeremy's head slumped forward. He slowly looked up. "Did you tell her what you've done?"

"I know he killed Rita, if that's what you're implying. To be perfectly honest, he saved me the job." Millie stepped closer. "Why did you put a note through my door?"

"Ask your dad."

"I'm asking you. Why?" she pressed.

"Your husband took what was mine…" Jeremy's head slumped again.

She would have to be quick, his voice was weak. Millie stepped forward and crouched in front of him. "What was yours?" She spoke softly. She didn't want Paul intervening.

"Rita," he croaked.

She raised her voice so Paul would hear. "He didn't sleep with her. She tried by blackmailing him, that's why he killed her."

The gun clicked behind her. Was Paul worried about what he would say? She stood slowly and leant towards Jeremy's face.

"I believe my husband," she whispered.

Jeremy pulled his head up. She looked into his eyes.

"He's lying," he whispered back.

She stepped away. Uncertain. Arms grabbed her; it was Duke. He guided her out of the warehouse. She stood in the cold winter air, dazed.

Was Paul lying?

The End

ABOUT THE AUTHOR

Carol Hellier was born in Oldchurch Hospital, Essex, in the mid-sixties. When she was in her mid-twenties she discovered her parents were, in fact, her grandparents, and her eldest sister was her mum.

She married a Romany and started her married life off living in a caravan/trailer. This has given her a useful insight into the Romany world which shows in her writing.

Now residing back in Essex, she spends her time working, writing and with family.

Previous title: Book One - The Stepney Feud

You can follow the author on :-

Instagram: author_cahellier

Facebook: https://www.facebook.com/carolhellier

TikTok: carolmc441

Printed in Great Britain
by Amazon